MW00612297

ALTER EGO

ALSO BY ALEX SEGURA

Secret Identity

Araña and Spider-Man 2099: Dark Tomorrow

The Pete Fernandez Mysteries

Star Wars Poe Dameron: Free Fall

Dark Space (with Rob Hart)

Encanto: Nightmares and Sueños

ALTER
EGO

a novel

Alex Segura

FLATIRON
BOOKS
NEW YORK

This is a work of fiction. All of the characters, organizations, and events portrayed in this novel are either products of the author's imagination or used fictitiously.

ALTER EGO. Copyright © 2024 by Alex Segura. Comic book sequence artwork by Sandy Jarrell, lettering by Jack Morelli. The Lynx, related characters, and artwork copyright © 2022, 2024 by Alex Segura. All rights reserved. Printed in the United States of America. For information, address Flatiron Books, 120 Broadway, New York, NY 10271.

www.flatironbooks.com

Designed by Michelle McMillian

All emojis designed by OpenMoji—the open-source emoji and icon project.
License: CC BY-SA 4.0

Library of Congress Cataloging-in-Publication Data

Names: Segura, Alex, 1980– author.
Title: Alter ego : a novel / Alex Segura.
Description: First edition. | New York : Flatiron Books, 2024
Identifiers: LCCN 2024022183 | ISBN 9781250801777 (hardcover) |
    ISBN 9781250801784 (ebook)
Subjects: LCGFT: Detective and mystery fiction. | Novels.
Classification: LCC PS3619.E4155 A78 2024 | DDC 813/.6—dc23/
    eng/20240513
LC record available at https://lccn.loc.gov/2024022183

Our books may be purchased in bulk for promotional, educational, or business use. Please contact your local bookseller or the Macmillan Corporate and Premium Sales Department at 1-800-221-7945, extension 5442, or by email at MacmillanSpecialMarkets@macmillan.com.

First Edition: 2024

10 9 8 7 6 5 4 3 2 1

For Eva, Guillermo, and Lucia—always

Tell me a story.
—Dennis O'Neil

*Some people become so expert at reading between the lines
they don't read the lines.*
—Margaret Millar

ALTER EGO

CHAPTER ONE

She'd been driving for what felt like forever.

Laura Gustines blinked her eyes, trying desperately to stay awake as she pulled her car off the Whitestone Bridge and onto the Van Wyck Expressway. She'd been on the road for almost eight hours—unexpected traffic and her own anxiety conspiring to derail her exit plans, a few nervous pit stops delaying it even further. But none of that mattered, she told herself. She'd gotten what she wanted. The final piece of the puzzle that would make her book truly sing.

She tapped her phone without looking down, her other hand on her battered Subaru's steering wheel. She squinted to make sure she was going the right way. It was well past midnight. She wanted to go home and sleep, but she needed to do one more thing.

She found the audio file on her voice recorder app. It was huge. The idea of losing it sent a jolt of panic through her entire body. In that file was the interview that would make her book—*Secret Identity*, a look at the women who had shaped comics but also been ignored—a cut above what she'd first envisioned.

When she pitched it to her agent, it was supposed to be a series of short biographies, spotlighting different women who'd made a meaningful mark in superhero graphic novels and comics. Folks like Karen Berger, Linda Fite, Trina Robbins, Patricia Highsmith, Ann Nocenti, Gail Simone, and Louise Simonson. She wanted to focus on mainstream comics, specifically the capes-and-tights genre, because it was popular, and Laura knew it'd pull in the casual reader in a way that maybe a more comprehensive tome wouldn't. But she hadn't expected to find anything newsworthy.

But then she'd discovered Carmen Valdez, a onetime comic book writer and acclaimed—if not bestselling—science-fiction novelist. Valdez had, at some point, not only written an issue of a little-known comic titled *The Legendary Lynx*—she'd also apparently co-created the character in secret. A character beloved by many hard-core fans, Gustines had discovered.

Gustines had also done the impossible. She'd found Valdez—specifically, where she lived, which few seemed to know. In a world where people routinely listed what they had for breakfast or their favorite bookstores, Carmen Valdez had disappeared completely. Though she ostensibly still worked in publishing, Valdez was a digital ghost—granting no interviews, making no public appearances, and fading into the ether of pop culture. Gustines had felt vindicated by just finding out where Valdez's home was: in Truro, on Cape Cod. Gustines had trekked out there to see if she could get the reclusive writer to admit that she, along with an editor named Harvey Stern, and artist Doug Detmer (a name only the most die-hard of die-hard comic fans would know) had created the character. It was a tale that had everything. Because this wasn't just a story of a ghostwriting fan. There was blood on the floor. There was a crime involved. And, if Laura did her reporting right, a lot of it could point to a deeper, more sinister problem involving the company that published *The Legendary Lynx*: a defunct outfit known as Triumph Comics, their dead CEO Jeffrey Carlyle, and someone named Dan Stephenson.

Stern had been murdered under mysterious circumstances around the time *The Legendary Lynx* launched, in 1975. Detmer died by his own hand later that same year. Stephenson, a shady business partner who worked with Carlyle, died in prison—serving time for Stern's death. Carlyle died of pancreatic cancer around 2007. Only Valdez remained, and she'd kept the truth—and her role in creating the Lynx—close to the vest for decades.

Not anymore. Laura had managed to sit down with the writer for a few hours, slowly collecting details that she knew had never been revealed to anyone. Now the story lived on Laura's phone, desperate to be heard.

Laura tapped the play button on the voice recorder app and watched as the file from her phone started to upload to the cloud. Laura let her tired mind wander for a second—to her, in her comfy pajamas, sipping a glass of pinot noir, listening to Carmen's interview again. Her only interview, Laura reminded herself. This was her shot. As Carmen's voice echoed through the car and into Laura's brain, she knew she couldn't mess this up.

"I created the Lynx. With Harvey at first, of course—but she was mine before then. The ideas. The biggest parts of her. They were mine. Harvey helped. Then Doug—Doug Detmer—brought her world to life.

"I'm just tired of being in the shadows. I'm old. I've done some great work. I've taken care of myself, my wife, my family—but I still feel incomplete. I still feel like there's an empty space on the shelf. And, I just want people to know. To know the character is mine. Well, ours. With Doug—of course. But mine. She comes from me. I created her. I held her in my mind long before I met Harvey Stern, or before our scripts were mailed to Doug. She was in my heart. And she's been gone for far too long."

Laura let out a long sigh. She was tired, too. She could feel her eyelids getting heavy. Could almost hear the comforting sound of her key sliding into her apartment's front door lock.

The car shook violently—the front of the car jerking to the left and slamming into the median, the screech of metal on metal cutting through Carmen's recorded confession. Laura felt her head swing along with the car, bashing into the driver's-side window. She heard a slight crackling sound on contact. Before she could start to look around, the car jerked again—this time from behind, as if an elephant were ramming into the right rear side. But it wasn't an animal—Laura knew that. In the corner of her vision she'd seen it. A large black SUV was now idling behind her. Lights off. Laura couldn't make out the model or license plate. She squinted as she tried to regain her composure, to push past the ache in her skull that wasn't a headache, but probably something worse—a concussion, at the very least. She ran a hand over her head and felt a wetness she knew hadn't been there before. Warm and sticky. Tiny shards of glass embedded in a mix of blood and hair. A brief gasp of surprise slipped out of her mouth.

"I just wanted to have a chance, honestly. A shot. No one at Triumph wanted to give me that. My boss—Carlyle—he had decided what I was. He said he had a plan for me. But he didn't consult me on that plan. And maybe I didn't want to be part of it. But he didn't want to be bothered with anything else. He was in charge, right?"

Laura groaned. She tried to move the car but got nothing in return except a low screeching sound that told her she wasn't going anywhere. Her eyes, slow and groggy, drifted up to her rearview. Who the hell was driving out here with their lights off? she wondered. Some drunk asshole, certainly. Well, she'd give him a piece of her mind once she found a way out of the damn—

The figure seemed to appear out of nothing—speckles of fog moving closer to create a wraith-like creature that floated toward Laura and her car. But Laura knew that couldn't be true. She blinked hard, trying to focus her blurry vision, and looked again. But the figure was still there—in black from head to toe: glasses, skullcap, mask, jacket, pants.

What the fuck was going on? she wondered.

This was bad. Laura felt her vision flicker out for a second. Felt a dull ache spread over her entire body. She needed a doctor.

She tried to reach for her phone, her eyes following the white charging cable that had been connected to her car's USB port. But it was gone.

Shunted out of her reach in the bumper-car madness of a few moments before. Laura unhooked her seat belt, hoping she could lunge forward and dig around for her cell—but was frozen by a sharp jab of pain in her side. She screamed—as much from surprise as from pain—and pulled back. She let out a few short breaths, intending to try again, when she felt a dark spot forming in her peripheral vision. She turned her head and noticed the figure again. This time much closer.

Laura lunged—felt her fingers wrapping around the worn white phone cord. She yanked at it roughly and heard it jangle under the seat. It was stuck. She cursed loudly, trying to avoid looking at the shape standing outside her car. But even then she saw the gloved black hand lifting the gun. Noticed the long cylinder screwed onto the end—the thing anyone who'd watched an episode of any crime show knew was a silencer. Laura Gustines felt a howling sob leave her mouth—an animalistic cry she wouldn't have even considered human if she wasn't hearing it now. The next sound, a soft *schtoop*—was followed by a crash, as the window shattered, sending shards of glass onto the empty passenger seat.

Laura Gustines wouldn't live to hear the second shot, which sent a silent bullet crashing into her forehead. The reporter's body slumped forward, her bloodied head landing on the steering wheel, making the car horn bleat once.

The figure moved quickly and quietly—opening the door, crouching down, and sliding their hand under the seat. They pulled out the phone and glanced at the display—which asked for an access code. A soft curse. Then the figure slid the phone into their back pocket and left the car. Only Laura Gustines remained, eyes still open and staring out into the rainy Queens evening. The last few seconds of Carmen Valdez's interview drifted through the destroyed car.

"I guess . . . I just don't want to be forgotten."

PART I

SECRET ORIGINS

6 THE LEGENDARY LYNX

More like "the Missing Lynx." This kitten-with-a-whip (er, grappling hook) was a marquee character for the ironically named Triumph Comics (because they're now defunct! Waka Waka!) But imagine newcomer Eliza Dushku ("Buffy the Vampire Slayer") in the domino mask on The WB! Or whaddabout Winona Ryder ("Mr. Deeds"), who is in need of a comeback role just like Lynxy herself. After all, who doesn't love an underdog story? Or is it undercat? Just, please Hollywood…leave the plot from 1993's "Charleston Chew Presents…" freebie issue on the cutting room floor. Nuff said! ■CW

Excerpt from MERLIN MAGAZINE #56 (March, 2002)—"Top Ten Forgotten Heroes That Would Make a Great Show" by Chris Ward, Staff Writer.

CHAPTER TWO

My name is Annie Bustamante and I'm about to get fired.

I was sitting on a panel deep in the bowels of the Jacob Javits Center for New York Comic Con, where I was supposed to talk about my latest comic book work—a series titled *The Renegade*, produced by a fly-by-night publisher named Blast Radius Comics. Seriously. That was the company's name.

New York Comic Con was, by its own definition, one of the largest "pop culture events" in the world, even just a few years after its debut. I looked down at my badge, hanging from a lanyard around my neck, the thin plastic card that carried so much weight. It had the word PRO emblazoned on it, a sign to all comers that I, Annie Bustamante, wasn't just one of the masses. I was a professional. I actually created stuff. Did anyone actually read the comics I drew? Let's just say I was glad I didn't have to share sales numbers to get a badge. Lucky me.

The panel room was small, all things considered—but it was packed. About three hundred people. I scanned the crowd in the hopes of finding a friendly face. There weren't any—mostly old and mostly white, with furrowed brows, quizzical looks, and a few blank faces staring into the void. I was seated between a handful of other Blast Radius creators—also mostly men, mostly white, and all of them older than me—that I'd met a few moments before. My editor, Victor Riesling, was standing behind a podium at the far end of the elevated stage. I felt a drop of sweat slide down my back. My lips felt dry. My vision was blurring at the edges. I took a deep breath. This would be fine, I told myself. Just fine. It ended up being the complete opposite of fine. It was a nightmare.

I'd gotten the gig writing and drawing *The Renegade* in the usual way—someone I knew reached out asking if I wanted to work on something. *The Renegade* was a comic book based on the hyper-violent, testosterone-heavy novels of a hack named Tom Gravins—no way that was his real name. They wanted me to take over for Gravins on the *Renegade* comic with an eye toward becoming the regular writer/artist.

I didn't really have much choice, all things considered. I was eating a dinner of microwave ramen as I read the email offer. I was desperate.

Plus, the email was from Danny.

Danny.

Danny had been smart. While I'd toiled away on the path of the starving freelancer, my childhood bestie had chosen the more stable route. He got his first break as an editorial intern in the hallowed halls of DC Comics, then parlayed that experience to becoming a full editor at Blast Radius Comics, *The Renegade*'s publisher. If the email hadn't been from Danny, I would've ignored it. I knew the source material was crap; plus, it was Blast Radius Comics. The name alone gave me hives. Still, it was Danny. I could remember sitting in the spill-out area at Glades Middle School during the summer, frantically flipping through stacks of Marvel trading cards—comparing character attributes, examining the artwork on the front of the cards in the way an archaeologist might look at a dinosaur fossil—and spitballing ideas for our next comic book project. Danny was the story guy, even then. My creative partner.

So I took the gig. I mean, the warning signs were there—the byzantine work-for-hire contract, the insanely urgent, suffocating deadlines that paired nicely with the copious notes from the licensor. I liked to think of myself as a pretty sturdy freelancer, but even I had my limits. Danny had done the initial outreach and had been the big allure on the project. But a few weeks into the job, I was reassigned to Riesling. The kind of comics guy who had more companies on his résumé than still existed. It went downhill fast. Just like this panel.

Things started to go sour as we hit the home stretch—the final ten minutes, when fans take turns sauntering up to a faulty mic to ask questions. Though I'd done my fair share of these before, I felt petrified. I had no connection to the source material. In fact, I hated it. I didn't want to be up here, defending my work. I wanted to be hiding at home, behind my art table, drawing feverishly to finish another assignment and shunt all of this from my mind. I saw Danny, standing off to the side of the panel, pacing nervously with each slide and comment. I should've felt a wave of relief at his familiar, warm face—but it made me feel worse. I wasn't just making a fool of myself in front of strangers and an editor I hated, but in front of Danny—whom I loved. Who'd known me my entire life. I caught sight of the Blast Radius PR guy, a relatively nice kid named Ron Barajas. He seemed skittish and amped in the way only PR people could be, nodding and smiling as if everything were *great, great*, a sure sign that things were actually Not Great At All.

I guess I'd been staring, because Barajas gave me a strange, emotive thumbs-up—and I snapped back to reality. I felt dizzy and grimy, regretting how I'd spent the time before the panel. I looked down the table, trying to find a sympathetic face, but I just saw strangers. Men who loved this kind of shit—sitting up onstage pontificating about how they tossed in that character cameo in issue number whatever, or that time they smelled Stan Lee's deodorant. They lived in the weeds, and this was where that was celebrated most. I was alone, the only woman onstage, which was fairly standard for these kinds of things. I tried to exude confidence, but that was gone. I'd made the mistake of downing a few drinks at the hotel bar before walking over to the Javits and I was starting to feel the dirty side of it—the headache at the edges of my vision, the drag on my voice. I thought I seemed okay when I got to the room, but now I wasn't so sure. Was I . . . slurring my words? I prayed for a few easy questions and a hasty exit. I got neither.

To be fair, I wasn't deluded. I knew my place in the hierarchy of comics. At best, I could be labeled a "rising star." But in reality, I was scrounging for any kind of work, taking gigs for low-rent publishers like Rampart Comics and Mercenary Press. It wasn't what I'd imagined when I was sitting in my mom's living room in Miami—sitting nose-to-nose with my best friend Danny Alvarez, cooking up our own Spider-Man, Batman, and X-Men stories. I liked to think I was pretty self-aware, but at this moment I had no concrete sense of where I stood in this crazy business.

My career, for whatever it was worth, was in a rut after a meteoric start when I took the *Renegade* gig. I was a "rising star," according to places like *Newsarama* and *Wizard Magazine: The Guide to Comics*. My art was called "dynamic and edgy," and fans seemed to really enjoy my work, particularly my gritty relaunch of a staid sixties superhero property, *T.H.U.N.D.E.R. Agents*, a U.N.-like group of heroes once created by the legendary Wally Wood.

The *T.H.U.N.D.E.R. Agents* assignment had taken me by surprise, though. I knew the Agents had been revamped by nearly every publisher over the decades in every which way—with none really resonating beyond the initial news blip. But the appeal of playing with established toys plus a steady paycheck made it hard to turn down. I had never expected it to be more than that. But suddenly it was. Readers were responding. The reviews were good, the sales were steady. It helped that I'd been paired with another "rising star" in writer Charlie Tomlinson, an acclaimed literary novelist looking to make their mark in comics. Tomlinson's thoughtful and meta story paired nicely with my art style—which owed a lot to masters like Toth, Detmer, and Buscema. We had a hit. For the first time ever, the Agents were giving the X-Men and the Justice League a run for their money. The publisher, a tiny house named New Wave Comics, was unprepared to handle the demand—and soon the bubble had burst, with Tomlinson quitting abruptly, citing editorial interference, leaving me to stand alone as the new "it" creator in comics. My next step was pivotal. But praise like that goes straight to your head. Mix it with a few too many cocktails and your own ego, and the end result is something akin to greed—and I took the next gig that made sense mathematically, not creatively. Enter *The Renegade*.

I thought I could fix the inherent problems in *The Renegade*. I thought that, through sheer force of will, I could make these testosterone-fueled stories matter. I mean, we'd done it before, right? I could make this book something special while paying my bills at the same time.

Well, wrong. I was dead wrong.

Though I'd been working on *The Renegade* for almost a year, this was my first in-person exposure to the intellectual property's vocal and often toxic fandom. Like I said, I knew I could draw the hell out of a *Renegade* comic, but what if some Rene-Groupie (that's seriously what they call themselves—I wish I were joking) came at me with some hyper-specific question about the novels?

But none of that really mattered. I was about to get fired.

And it wasn't a picayune fact that would get me fired. It was something much more predictable.

The man, probably pushing fifty and wearing a shirt two sizes too small, was dragging a torn bag with what appeared to be a highly de- tailed Renegade statue in it. He approached the microphone with a ner- vous energy. He cleared his throat. He tapped the mic. Then he let out a long, thoughtful sigh. I wanted to die. The slight headache had entered migraine territory. I was squinting to try to stifle the pain. The bright fluorescent lights were not helping. *Get me out of here, please.*

Finally, he spoke, first in a whisper—then, after another throat- clearing, louder.

"Miss, uh, miss Busta-bustaman? What is it?"

"Bustamante," I said, trying my best to be polite.

"Yes, Busamannay."

"Bustamante," I corrected him. I felt my face heat up. I could have— should have, probably—let it slide. *But it's my fucking name, dude.*

Either way, he ignored my correction and kept on trucking.

"What, uh, how do I say this? . . . What on earth, if you don't mind me asking, qualifies . . . uh . . . someone with, um, well, your experience . . . your . . . credentials, you know?" he stammered. "Someone who doesn't, well, have military training, or know much about hand-to-hand combat . . ."

I felt my pulse quicken and my eyes narrow. *I should've expected this*, I told myself. *This couldn't be a surprise to anyone, Annie.* Hell, Tom Gravins, the writer most associated with *The Renegade* comic book before I took over, postured as a man's man. Gravins claimed to have served in the Middle East, but I'd always thought it was bullshit. He talked tough online. He "kept it real" on his YouTube channel and podcast, where he dispensed his "hard-core" opinions on the industry, politics, and pop culture. It was painful, trust me. I'd listened to just enough to go from curious to nauseous. The Rene-Groupies loved and missed him, and they hated Blast Radius and Riesling for firing Gravins and then replacing their hero with me, a woman. I stopped myself from rubbing my temples and started to respond.

"Are you asking me what qualifies a woman to write and draw *The Renegade*?"

I didn't have to turn to my fellow panelists to know they'd all craned their heads to look at me. I could feel their stares boring into my skull.

The thing was, despite all the creepy incels and weirdos, coming here reminded me of why I love being surrounded by comics, anime, cartoons, movies, and more. Everywhere I looked, there were tattered books, costumes, giant images of buxom women plastered on ramshackle booths, long logo displays precariously hovering above them all, TV screens blaring trailers and video games and panels, and everything playing at peak volume to cut through the loud hum of the crowd. It tickled the back of my brain a bit, this immersion. If I closed my eyes for a second and let myself feel these things—what I saw, smelled, heard, it almost felt real. I wasn't a kid anymore, and it'd been a few decades since I really cared about comics, or considered creating them, a passion that didn't just pay my bills. Before my love for comics had been burned out of me, excised like some cancerous lump and replaced with an empty space.

Could I ever get that back? I wasn't sure.

After my combative answer, there'd been some yelling. I might have wondered aloud if the guy still lived with his mom, or if he was still a virgin. In the same sentence. Mercifully, the panel was shut down. I found myself swimming through the sweat-soaked masses of fans, editors, colleagues, writers, producers, readers, and vendors to get to my meeting with Riesling, who'd stormed off the stage in a huff. I knew it was over then.

How could it not be?

CHAPTER THREE

shouldn't be here," I muttered to myself, glancing down at my watch.

Nothing I'd said today had felt truer than those words. I didn't belong here anymore, if ever.

My head pounded and my mouth felt dry. I'd just left the panel and made a beeline to this meeting, without even thinking about how I was feeling. That's what comics did to you. You sacrificed everything—especially your own health—to get to the next thing, or to make sure the pages were uploaded and your editor was happy. It was a one-sided relationship, and comics weren't texting me back. Ever since I was a kid, I loved drawing—looking at the blank page, imagining what I wanted to see on it, and making it happen. I thought working in comics would be the dream—because what's better than getting paid to do what you love? But I didn't love it anymore. When adults used to ask me what I wanted to be when I grew up, I didn't hesitate: I wanted to draw comics. Because I thought that was it. But now—sweat running down my back, mouth dry, body aching—it felt like I'd taken a wrong turn somewhere.

Comics were in my blood, they defined who I was and would always be. Putting pen to paper and telling stories, blending pictures and words—it was magic. But superheroes? Those days were gone. Especially now. Especially since that conversation with Mami, a few years back. One of the few moments when I felt close to her.

If *The Renegade* fizzled out, as I fully expected it would, that door—to strange places, worlds, costumes, and ideas—was forever closed. Whatever hope I had of exploring Wakanda, the Fourth World, or the Savage Land was gone, shunted to another dimension out of my reach. I'd have to step away completely, accepting that part of my story was over. No superhero would ever engage my mind in the way those old comics had. Ever. I would grow up and move on. I'd leave my superhero friends behind.

Except one.

The cover caught my eye as I tried to dodge a large man dressed in a Booster Gold costume who seemed desperate to reach the restrooms across the way. I lost my balance for a second, then paused to collect myself. I looked up and realized I'd somehow stepped into a comic shop owner's booth. I took a deep breath and gave the tiny space a once-over. I was surrounded by . . . stuff. Long cardboard boxes packed with comics packed in plastic sleeves, T-shirts and posters lining the booth's makeshift back wall, valuable comics slabbed in plastic bricks, their value dependent on how they were "graded" by an independent company. It was a lot. The hum of the crowd flowing around the booth added to the sense of dread I'd felt, my overall mood notwithstanding.

That's when I saw it. That cover. The one I'd pored over as a kid, my eyes wide with wonder.

The image was of a woman, her back to a grimy redbrick wall—an array of guns pointed at her. She was definitely a superhero, but not the flying, cosmic kind—more of a street-level crime fighter. She wore a costume that resembled a disco tracksuit, mostly blue, with leopard-skin patterns down the middle of her shirt and pants, topped off by a domino mask that theoretically hid her identity. All the tropes were there, but there'd been something about this character that pulled me in when I first saw her. I looked at the logo that hung above the image of the woman—the stylized words calling out to me, a potent mix of nostalgia and power: *The Legendary Lynx.*

I snapped out of it for a second and looked at my watch. Yeah, gonna be late. But fuck it. Who was in a rush to get fired?

I stepped farther into the booth and motioned for the lone employee. He walked over, eyebrows raised in the universal *What do you need?* look.

"That book," I said, pointing to the first issue of *The Legendary Lynx.* "How much?"

The guy, stout, with a long graying brown beard, followed my finger with his eyes. "Oh, the Lynx? Uh, well—I can give it to you for twenty. Maybe fifteen? Or whatever your best offer is."

Best offer? Did this dude not understand what he had hanging in his own makeshift store? Probably not. I didn't really understand, either. But the book was calling me, and reminding me of another time—like a vision or dream. The first issue of *The Legendary Lynx* had been the first time I'd noticed not only the story and art—but the names attached. Artist Doug Detmer was unlike any of the over-detailed, exaggerated artists Danny seemed to fawn over in the nineties. Detmer's figures were lithe, dynamic, but also enamored with the power of cartooning. His stories moved and felt alive—with a visual energy I'd never seen before, and rarely saw after. I could still see the pencil-and-ink stains on my palms from tracing over Detmer's pages. I'd felt this weird, amorphous connection to the man. Like I could build him, bring him back to life just by channeling his work onto my own lined school paper. If only I'd known.

I handed the employee a ten and a five and watched as the burly man in a faded Defenders T-shirt rubbed the bills together before sliding them into his back pocket. Then he turned and reached for the copy of *The Legendary Lynx* #1. He handed the comic to me brusquely. It was encased in a plastic slip case and cardboard backing—bagged and boarded, as the kids say. Protected from the elements. This was the part I absolutely hated. The sealing away of the story, whether in a plastic bag or thick case, felt somehow antithetical to actually engaging with the art form. Comics were meant to be read, not embalmed. I didn't want to admire the comics I had, sealed away like some kind of four-color museum. I wanted to read the damn things. Experience the rush of a Frank Miller splash page or a Jack Kirby cover. Bop my head to Chris Claremont's purple prose. Try to wrap my head around a Steve Gerber story or pick my jaw up off the floor from a Kurt Busiek, Mark Waid, or Louise Simonson plot twist. Comics weren't a checklist. Not for me. They kept me going.

Or they had, once.

I thanked the dude, who was clearly nervous about being in a three-walled rickety room with a woman for this long, and stepped back into the chaos of the con floor. I held the comic up to the light and let myself admire it. I felt the nostalgia shoot through me like a powerful drug—every sense familiar, comfortable, and lived-in.

I couldn't help myself as I mouthed the words on the cover, decorated in that amazing retro style. The letters screamed at me—like a hand reaching out through a time vortex, pulling me backward.

THE LEGENDARY LYNX #1
"First Lethal Issue!"
PRESENTING TRIUMPH COMICS' NEXT SUPERSTAR—IN HER VERY OWN SERIES!
IT ALL STARTS HERE!
"BEHOLD—THE LYNX!"

God, she was so fucking cool.

Someone's bony shoulder slammed into mine, shaking me back into the sweat-soaked reality of New York Comic Con. Ugh.

I reflexively pulled out my BlackBerry and scanned my email. There was a message from Laura Gustines, a friend who worked as a book reviewer at the *New York Observer*. Every once in a while her editors let her write a story about comics—either breaking news or some half-baked trend piece. She was smart and could see the business from a big-picture perspective. So I liked keeping in touch with her. She could expense our drinks, too, so that was nice. Her note was brief—a news article Laura had found about a comic book collection, or "archive," as the story put it, belonging to a gentleman named Stuart Alford. Someone had stolen the whole collection.

Huh. Weird. I scrolled to the next email—from Mami.

"Anabel—checking on you. We need to talk. Are you okay? Dame una llamada, por favor, mijita."

I deleted the email.

I was not okay. But talking to Mami wouldn't help. I looked at the Lynx comic in my hand again. I smiled to myself and slipped the comic into my bag, tapping it gently, like a talisman. Maybe Claudia Calla, the Lynx's curious and haunted alter ego, could help me get through the next few hours.

I felt my phone vibrating in my bag and snaked my hand inside to grab it. I didn't bother to look at the number because I knew who it was. I'd basically manifested him.

"Danny, I'm on my way, bro," I said. "It's New York fucking Comic Con, okay? I'm surrounded by all of the X-Men, the Justice League, the Doom Patrol, and their extended family."

He responded with a dry chuckle on the other end, that was it. It meant he wasn't alone—which sealed it. I was done.

"I'll see you soon, okay? Don't worry," I said, flipping the phone shut.

I let my mind linger on him for a second. The sound of his laugh.

Danny.

The thud of the heavy double-doors slamming shut left me in the temporary darkness of the Javits Center's cavernous infrastructure, the *thoom* sound echoing, as if punctuating the end of something long and painful. I took a flight of stairs up and found a stretch of skyboxes—cramped rooms with views of the convention floor. I found the one labeled BLAST RADIUS with little fuss. This was it, I thought.

I paused before turning the doorknob. I pulled the cherry-red lipstick out of my bag and put a coat on my mouth while looking at my reflection in my BlackBerry screen, like a knight pulling a helmet over their face—battle armor, in preparation for what was to come. I pressed my lips together and reached for the door. I was ready now.

I stepped into the tiny Blast Radius "green room" and immediately made eye contact with Danny, who was seated at a tiny table a few feet from the door with my editor, Riesling, situated next to a buffet of snacks that looked like they'd been sitting there for years.

I dropped my bag at my feet and took the seat between Danny and Riesling. I leaned over and gave Danny a peck on the cheek. This might be New York City, but Miami rules always apply. I looked at his sharp blue eyes—probably for a few seconds longer than normal. He looked away before I did.

"Hey," I said, leaning back in my rickety plastic chair, not looking at Riesling. Fuck him.

"Hey," Danny responded.

"Glad you could join us," Riesling said, his tone snide. He had a smear of what had to be jelly on his mustard pants. I wished it a long, healthy life. If anyone deserved it, Riesling did.

I moved my gaze up to Riesling's puffy, pockmarked face—his bulbous red nose looking red and swollen, a side effect from drinking hard for years.

Who are you to judge? a voice asked in my head. I looked away from him.

This man was a bug, I thought. A fly buzzing around me—insignificant and obnoxious.

"So sorry," I said, not sounding sorry at all. "I didn't expect to run into ten thousand people on my way here. Who knew? Thanks for understanding. At least there are donuts, right?"

Riesling shook his head slowly, like an exhausted grandparent. Riesling was the kind of old-school asshole who normally loved this sort of back-and-forth—swinging his dick around, making sure people knew he was In Charge and a Very Important Person. But I'd learned over time that the best defense against a USDA-Approved Asshole was nothing—if you acted like you didn't give a shit, it'd make them angrier. So I parried by being the cool girl—aloof, distant, disinterested, and totally bored. It pissed him off. Would it get me more work with Blast Radius? Certainly not. Did I care? Not at all.

I did care about Danny, though, and I caught him looking at me—his gaze leaning into mine. I gave him a slow, warm smile in return. It made me think back to a few weeks before, his hand grazing mine, the sounds of the city around us. But I shook that away because this wasn't the place for that. There really wasn't a place for that. Danny was like family. We grew up together—two latchkey kids joined at the hip, from elementary school to college, experiencing everything together in tandem, trying to cobble together some kind of comic book life because it was the only thing that seemed to bring us joy. But here we were, on opposite sides of this flimsy round table, tucked above the Sturm und Drang of New York Comic Con, acting like we were about to negotiate Middle East peace. At some point, Danny and I, we'd hit a fork in the road—a familiar intersection where Art Street and Commerce Avenue crossed. A spot where most creatives have to pick a lane. The dream had to become profitable, as dreams rarely do. Danny and I were supposed to be on this side of the table together. Danny as the writer, me as the artist. What a wonderful story that would've been, huh? Two Miami kids taking the comic book world by storm. But sometimes the weight of the world breaks you down—bills, rent, survival—and those fun, romantic ideas are trumped by the dark clouds of reality. Danny chose the staff route. I still remember the phone conversation when he told me. We didn't speak for weeks after that. I felt betrayed and ashamed—that my closest friend, my creative partner, was taking the easy way out. What about our ideas? The characters we'd spent years crafting and refining? Erased before they could live—the worst fate for a comic book character.

But over time, I started to realize that it was his life. Who was I to dictate Danny's dreams to him? The only dreams I could control were my own—my dream of working in comics, of making a name for myself in this medium that I loved. Still, I was happy to see his face, the familiar mouth, the sad eyes.

I knew what his hopes were. He thought working on this book—
The Renegade—would be the spark that brought us back to that creative
place. Best-laid plans and all that. Literally a week after Danny hired me
to write and draw the comic book adaptation of this critically maligned
aggro comic book series, Riesling had stepped in. Power-mad, egotis-
tical, and creepy Riesling. He'd demanded to edit the book itself, with
Danny riding shotgun—so he could "learn a thing or two." I was amazed
people actually talked like that.

Riesling was the kind of old, grouchy comic book lifer that was far
too common in the industry, a crotchety know-it-all who spent more
time rattling off stories about how he once worked with so-and-so than
doing the actual work in front of him. If you knew everything, there was
little incentive to learn. And Victor Riesling was certain he'd already
seen and lived it all.

"Let's get to it," Riesling said, leaning forward. I didn't move. I just
watched.

"Sure, sounds good," I said flatly.

I leaned toward my bag and pulled out a thin manila folder. I opened
it and pulled out a stack of small papers. Anyone who'd worked a day in
an office could immediately see what they were, and that was the point.
Invoices. The unpaid kind.

"I brought these along in case you hadn't seen the emails I sent," I
said, my tone still neutral, as if I were making a food order or trying to
book a doctor's appointment. "I'm still owed for the last two issues, one
of which already came out. Just wanted—"

Riesling let out a short, dry laugh.

"You've got to be kidding me, Annie," Riesling said, looking down at
the invoices and rubbing his temples. "After what just happened, you're
gonna wave those in my face? You should be thankful anyone in this
industry wants to work with you at all. I certainly don't. Not after you
fucked this assignment up."

I thought I heard Danny start to say something, but my brain wasn't
processing it. I felt a roaring fire inside me start to burn, and I didn't have

time for anything else. My mouth—still smiling, still placid—twitched. I watched Riesling, head shaking, slide the invoices a few inches back across the table—away. As if that'd make them disappear. I felt like Jean Grey, the power of the Phoenix coursing through my molecules—a woman imbued with the all-powerful Phoenix Force, now also provided with what she'd always wanted: a target.

Listen, I was tough. I didn't need any man to tell me that. I could be cool. But I was not invulnerable. When I got mad, it was never good for those involved. Out of the corner of my eye, I could see Danny stiffen up—bracing for impact.

"Oh yeah?" I said, my eyes still on Riesling. "What part did I 'fuck up,' Victor? Was it turning the pages in on time every week, despite not getting paid? Maybe it was the time I went to HeroesCon on my own dime to promote the book, and never got reimbursed, despite you promising me Blast Radius would cover my trip? Or was it when you—"

"What are you trying to accomplish here?" Riesling said, his voice sharp but not raised. Then he turned to Danny, an incredulous look on his face. "I took your buddy's word here. He promised me, repeatedly, that you were a pro. Now I have to sit here and watch you perform?"

"She is a pro," Danny said. I could see the wheels turning in his pragmatic brain. *How much of a stand can I even take here?*

I reminded myself that Riesling was Danny's boss. That after I stormed out of here, he'd still have to answer to this prick. It didn't make me any less annoyed at Danny's flaccid defense. But I tossed him a bone, shooting Danny a quick wink that said, *Welcome to the brawl.*

"Yeah, really? She's a pro?" Riesling said to Danny, motioning toward me as if I were just a picture on his wall. "You got a lot to learn about this business, kid. Not sure I can even teach you. You wanna know a pro? Kirby. That's a pro. Neal Adams. That's a pro. John Buscema. Real men who knew how to do the work—they respected the people they worked for. They didn't complain, they—"

I couldn't help myself.

I laughed.

"I'm sorry, but are we talking about the same people?" I said, taking in a sharp breath, trying to stop myself from giggling more. "Neal Adams went up against DC Comics to properly credit the guys that created Superman. Kirby fought Marvel on getting his original art back—"

Riesling shook his head. He wasn't a point-by-point debater, obviously. He was used to people—younger, marginalized, less powerful—just deferring to him. Why get into a factual discussion when you were always right?

Riesling shrugged and pushed his chair back from the table. He scoffed.

"I'm done with this," Riesling said. "You're fired. Don't expect a dime from us. Send all the emails or lawyer letters you want, I'll drop them in the shredder, okay? That's it. I haven't dealt with a petulant brat like you in decades. Decades."

He started to get up, then stopped and turned to me. He raised his arm and, I shit you not, started waving a finger at me.

"This business—it's full of people like you," Riesling said, eyebrow raised. "Difficult. Obnoxious. Holier-than-thou. But the difference between you and people like Wally Wood, Doug Detmer, or Alex Toth? They could draw. They survived on talent. Even at their worst, they made art that you couldn't achieve on your best day, ever."

My brain froze. Only my body moved.

I got up with a start, as if electrocuted. Later, Danny would recount what he saw, but in that moment all I remembered was grabbing my stack of unpaid invoices in one swift movement and then hurling them at Riesling's face with the precision of a major league outfielder. The papers landed squarely on Riesling's fat, pock-chiseled face—spreading out like giant confetti pieces onto his lap and the stained NYCC indoor carpet. I'll never forget the *thwap* sound the papers made as they hit him.

"Fuck you," I said, my voice seething—the words coming out like a sharp hiss. I felt the tears welling up in my eyes and vowed not to let this prick see me cry.

I felt Danny reach for me, moving on instinct. I sidestepped and met his eyes.

"What the fuck is wrong with you, Danny?" I spat, no longer able to filter my thoughts before they jumped out of my mouth. "Were you just going to sit there forever?"

I didn't wait for him to respond. I couldn't even look at his expression—mouth open, eyes wide.

I grabbed my purse and made a beeline for the door as Riesling stammered, grabbing at the stack of papers like a confused kid chasing soap bubbles in the park. As I yanked the door open, I could hear Riesling, that sad sack of shit, trying to formulate a response, trying to win the battle—but it was over. For him, for Danny, and for me.

We just didn't know it yet.

CHAPTER FOUR

L ike us? How?"

I rolled my eyes. Why did I always have to explain things to Danny that were right in front of his face? Every. Damn. Time.

Danny was seated across from me on the maroon-carpeted floor of my crowded bedroom in my mom's two-story Kendall town house. We were alone in the house—or my mom was passed out in the other room. It didn't make a difference. We were doing what we usually did over the summer to avoid the sticky Miami heat—lie around and read stacks and stacks of comics, with breaks to watch hours and hours of television. We'd hand issues back and forth, sharing our insightful commentary as we went. It was a crash course in the medium we loved—a chance to immerse ourselves in every part of it, from the layouts to the cover design to the letters pages.

"This one's neat—it's the first time Spider-Man's black costume showed up," Danny would say, handing me an issue of *The Amazing Spider-Man.*

"Wasn't it in *Secret Wars,* though?" I'd reply, scanning the cover.

"Here, try this—*Crisis on Infinite Earths*," Danny said, sliding a yellow-and-gray comic cover over. I recognized the Flash immediately, but it was unlike any Flash cover I'd ever seen. The red-garbed hero looked . . . doomed?

I started to flip through it when Danny interrupted.

"What did you mean, 'like us'?"

I looked up at him and sighed.

"Danny, how can you be so dense? I mean, you know, Cuban, or Hispanic—like us," I said, putting the comic down. "I hardly ever see names like ours in the credits. I never see people like us, well, in the comics. Like the heroes."

Danny didn't respond. I could tell he was processing. He did this all the time.

Even at this age, I knew I was in love with Danny. Not in the strange, kissing way you'd see on TV—I was still a little weirded out by that, though I had kissed Humberto Salazar after lunch a few weeks back. It had been kind of gross, honestly.

No, I loved Danny in the way I was supposed to love my family. If my family wasn't made up of people I would be totally fine never seeing again. Messed-up people who I only interacted with because I had to. But Danny was something else.

Danny had been my first friend in kindergarten. I could still see him sliding over from one line of kids, sitting cross-legged on the floor, over to me—as I cried, for Mami to come back and get me, even if she would never do that kind of thing. As far as I knew, she was halfway to Bird Road, desperate to be rid of me for a few hours so she could dull her senses with a few mixed drinks. He'd introduced himself with an ease I would never master.

"Hi, I'm Danny. Do you want to be my friend?"

I did.

I needed a friend then, and would seemingly always need one. That didn't necessarily mean I'd always have one—or always have Danny.

We made a nice pair—even as kids, people would refer to us as a unit, with one name fading into the next—"Dannie." It also helped that we were stone-cold nerds, too. We only really had each other.

Danny had always been shy but, like every kid, had assumed school would always be like elementary—where there was some general parity and kindness blended in with the ribbing and play. Where kids could be mean but never needlessly cruel. But middle school was another story. Kids were almost teens, and they were jacked up on hormones and raw emotion. The sharp, cutting cruelty that presented itself to Danny on his first day at Glades Middle seemed to have shaken him, and I had a front-row seat to his withdrawal from everyone but me. Something cracked inside of him then—though I didn't realize it until much later. A little light was blown out. Danny kept his head down, desperate to avoid conflict—working hard to be Switzerland to all the varied cliques, crews, and friend circles. But no one was immune to the savagery of middle school, no matter how cool you were. Not even me.

Not that I was cool, mind you. Far from it. But I was an athlete, at least—which was my saving grace. I was a good swimmer and played soccer, I had that instant camaraderie that came with being on an official team, even if most of my teammates were stuck-up bitches trying to seem much older than they were. But that shell was good and needed. Even if I had to continually dodge questions from my teammates about "that Danny kid—he's weird. Are you really friends with him? Do you even like him?"

I hated myself a little when I'd shrug and explain that I'd just known him for a long time and felt bad for him. It wasn't a complete lie. Because it was the omission that revealed the entire picture. I did feel bad for Danny—in the way any friend would be sad if they saw someone they cared for being picked on, watched their friend step further and further into the void, like a hero being jettisoned into the Negative Zone, or lost to the Siege Perilous. But I also loved him, the way you loved your sibling, someone you just assumed would be part of your life forever. And because we shared a bond that I couldn't seem to find anywhere else.

I turned toward my lumpy futon bed—reaching for something under it, my face wincing.

"What are you doing, Annie?"

"Con calma, Danny," I said. "Gimme a second, okay?"

The short box, about half the size of a traditional long box of comics, slid out from under the bed with a hissing sound against the carpet. I threw the top off and began to flip through the comics with a tactile precision that seemed well practiced, like a veteran file clerk who knew just where the information they needed was.

I scoffed—that was my version of "Aha!"—and pulled out a comic. It had certainly seen better days—the front cover was torn in a corner and the spine was barely holding together. But it was mine. A comic I'd somehow found while snooping through my mom's stuff, on one of those Saturday mornings she slept away, probably still drunk from the night before.

I laid it down on the floor between us. I followed Danny's sharp blue eyes as he scanned it. *The Legendary Lynx* #11.

"What is this? I've never heard of this character," Danny said, eyes narrowing. "This isn't even a Marvel book, bro."

I frowned.

"Bro," I said, mocking him. "We were talking about this book, like, last week, remember?"

"Yeah, but just talking—you didn't bring it to school or anything."

"'Bring it to school'? Are you high, Danny?" I said, my voice incredulous. "These books are rare as hell. The company doesn't even exist anymore, and there hasn't been a new Lynx story in forever. I think Triumph went bankrupt or something."

"How do you know that?" Danny asked, a tinge of betrayal in his eyes. We did everything comic-book-related together. Now I was showing him that wasn't true. It stung him, I realized.

"Oh, uh, probably in *Comics Buyer's Guide* or something," I stammered. "Anyway, I'm showing it to you because of this—"

I flipped open the comic and pointed to the credits. They read:

WRITER: CARMEN VALDEZ
ART: DOUG DETMER

"So what?" Danny said with a shrug.

"No seas bobo, Danny," I said, trying to get him to look me in the eye. I mouthed, *So what?* in confusion before continuing. "Dude, there's a woman writing this character! And she's Hispanic, like us. In fact, I did some digging—and Carmen Valdez is Cuban. Can you believe that? A Cubana! From Miami, too. In comics. She's apparently missing, though. No one has any idea where she went. Imaginate the stories she could tell, bro."

Danny paused for a moment before speaking.

"That is cool," he said, nodding slowly. "I've never seen that before."

I tilted my head back and laughed. Then I leaned forward and gave Danny a tight hug.

"That's the point, pobrecito," I said, kissing him hard on the cheek. "That's the point."

Excerpt from *The Legendary Lynx* #4, published by Triumph Comics, 1975.

STILL FEEL DAZED. LIKE I'M ZOMBIE-WALKING THROUGH LIFE. LIKE I *LOST* SOMETHING ALONG THE WAY.

DAILY TRIUMPH

Where is the Lynx?

THE VOID WITHIN

BUT I'LL DO WHAT I ALWAYS DO--

CHALK IT UP TO MY BRAIN BEING *BROKEN* AND MOVE ON.

GOD...DON'T EVEN WANT TO *THINK* ABOUT WHAT'S GOING ON AT THE OFFICE...

NEED COFFEE. KEEP HAVING THAT SAME DREAM--OF LEAPING ACROSS THE ROOFTOPS, LIKE SOME SORT OF--

OhMYGOD...

WHAT?!

WHAT HAPPENED TO THE LEGENDARY LYNX?

HAS TRIUMPH CITY'S HERO BEEN WIPED FROM EXISTENCE--AND HER *OWN MEMORY?* FIND OUT MORE IN 30 (*OR SO*) DAYS, AS WE USHER IN A NEW ERA OF *THE LEGENDARY LYNX* IN

TiTANIC TRiUMPH FASHION!

CHAPTER FIVE

NOVEMBER 11, 2023-FOREST HILLS, NEW YORK

I woke up with a jolt.

The booming sound of an orchestra crashed into my dreams, pulling me into the waking world. I reached out my arm and slapped my ringing iPhone playing the theme to *Star Trek: Deep Space Nine* on my nightstand. It was normally soothing, but not today—first thing in the morning, at peak volume. Nothing could be good under those circumstances.

It took me a second to remember where I was. In my Forest Hills, Queens, apartment. A spacious three-bedroom off Austin Street and adjacent to an area known as Forest Hills Gardens—an insular, manufactured neighborhood that seemed to bask in its desire to stay cut off from the rest of the town. I'd been back for a few weeks, but it still felt unnatural to me. I stretched my body out on my way-too-comfortable, way-too-expensive, and way-too-big king-sized bed. I felt my bare skin rub against the four-hundred-thread-count sheets I'd treated myself to a few days ago. A worthy investment.

I felt a shiver run through me—a sign that the temperature outside my windows was lower than I'd become used to. November in New York was mostly pleasant, but I'd been away too long. Annie Bustamante, filmmaker and artist, raised on the humidity, tropical breezes, and powerful sun of Miami, had also spent a good chunk of her professional career in Los Angeles, dodging earthquakes, stuck in freeway traffic, and eating tofu scramble. I wasn't used to this anymore. November in New York was downright frigid. And honestly, I could be in my fiftieth year as a New Yorker and I'd never get used to the cold. Ever.

I missed L.A.—my friends, my restaurants, my contacts. I'd spent the better part of the pandemic there—a trip that I thought was going to be a few months turned into a few years. But after my career decided to do a cannonball into the pool, I knew we had to come back, even if moving cross-country was the kind of thing I wouldn't wish on my worst enemy. I just hadn't realized how much my entire being would dislike being back. I couldn't stand the subway. I felt surrounded by people at all times. And Jesus, so what if I wanted my bagel scooped out sometimes? Everything just felt so much harder here, and I was too old for that now. I don't know how I ever made it here to begin with. But that was a different New York, and a very different Annie Bustamante.

I reached over and grabbed my phone. I scrolled through my alerts and notifications—nothing urgent, no calls from my agent, no offers, no last-minute deadlines for work. Things were quiet. Too quiet, if I was being honest. But my agent, Gary, said it'd be like that for a stretch. That I needed "to let your reputation cool down" for a few months before I could start looking for work in earnest again. That was the Hollywood cycle, he said. You bomb, you disappear, you return with a chance at redemption. Except in my case my movie didn't even get a chance to fail.

I felt weird saying it, but after a handful of movies, it was the truth: I was a movie director—and I was in demand, sort of. I'd started out as a storyboard artist, laying out the imagery that the director and cinematographer would eventually shoot. But back then, with my limited free time, I started directing shorts. One of them, a dark little noir titled *Wild Town*, based on the Jim Thompson novel, got some actual attention and won a few awards. Some months later, I was flying solo on a major motion picture, directing the Cuban migrant drama *90 Miles*, followed by the moody sci-fi spy thriller *Dark Space*. Neither set the world on fire, but both were well received, and *Dark Space* even got a few special effects nominations. It all culminated with *Red Barry*, a reimagining of the pulp newspaper strip with a colorful thriller twist. I'd replaced the boring, steel-jawed cop protagonist with a woman—played by Jessica Chastain, no less—who'd actually turn and look at the viewer, creating a fourth wall–breaking story that seemed to hit at the right time. A time when people were tired of looking at Zoom squares or ordering masks online and were desperate to laugh and breathe on each other. It was a huge hit. I was nominated for a Best Director Oscar, which I happily lost to Ava DuVernay. I could've had my pick of movies or jobs. Sometimes, that's the worst position to be in.

But I thought I had that beat. Because I knew exactly what I wanted to do next. I created a new version of Miss Midnight, a minor Golden Age superhero that had fallen into the public domain. I pitched it to the studio as *Twin Peaks* meets *Daredevil*, and next thing I knew, I had a green light, a hotshot screenwriter, and interest from Rosario Dawson for the starring role. For the first time ever, I got to experience a film that was wholly my vision actualized. A trippy neo-noir mindfuck that harkened back to the eighties erotic thrillers I loved, but also spoke to what I thought the world was feeling today: paranoia, fear, lust, and doubt with a surrealist bow wrapped around it. I could almost taste the rush that would certainly come at that first screening.

But it never got there.

The movie was finished, though. Like, totally done. Music, effects, edits. But only a handful of prints survived, and the only version I had of *Miss Midnight* existed on my laptop. In this era of corporate restructuring, mass layoffs, and brand management, all it took to defeat my little movie was a clumsy post-merger consolidation followed by a hierarchical change at the studio, and suddenly my artsy superhero thriller looked more appealing as a tax write-off.

Yeah, they'd dumped my movie in the trash to save a few bucks come tax time.

It didn't help that I was hooking up with the screenwriter, either—Nate Dillon, a blond surfer type who'd worked on the last *Mission: Impossible* movie. My brain immediately recognized he was attractive, but it didn't really click for me until later. One of those relationships that happen by proximity rather than sparked by romance. We were just working together, nose-to-nose for weeks and months. Eventually it just seemed to make sense—of course we'd sleep together. Neither of us had the time or inclination to date, and we could even discuss work in lieu of pillow talk. It felt right at the time. But hindsight has a way of adding perspective.

I shuddered a bit at his "moderate Republican" views and carefully curated Rush playlists. He had a cute smile, though, and, well, you get it. None of it mattered now.

Gary had suggested a break. The conversation had come a few days after the news had broken—amid the social media backlash that seemed to engulf the discourse for a cycle or two. People were mad. I loved it. I was mad, too. Gary, with some prodding from the studio, had dissuaded me from commenting, but it didn't feel like a time to back away—it felt like a moment to harness that energy into something else. Into a movement that would save my movie. But that wasn't how Hollywood worked. When you were hot, you were hot. When you bombed, the mushroom cloud extended far and wide. I was toxic, and I would be for a while.

So, I decamped back to New York and this Forest Hills apartment I still owned, and just . . . stopped. It was only then that I realized how truly exhausted I was. Of everything. Writers. Actors. Producers. Budgets. I missed the simplicity, the directness of what had gotten me into the field in the first place—drawing. Putting pen to paper and making something *exist* just with my two hands. I didn't want a committee anymore. Or for a good long while, at least. I had some savings, but those would only last for a bit. Q rating or no, I needed to work and make a living. And for once in my life, I was at a point in my career where I

could say no—even if it was just a gut feeling, a sense that the project
might be difficult and Not Worth The Effort. It was a nice position to be
in, I had to admit. I let my sleepy eyes drift over my large bedroom, over
the collection of photos and original comic book art on the wall. I felt
my phone vibrate. I flipped it over and looked at the display. It was a text
message from an unknown number.

> Someone thinks you should download the Signal app. Click here
> for more info.

The message was followed by a hyperlink I was never going to click
on. I marked the text as junk and tossed the phone onto the other side of
the bed. I flopped back down, my eyes on the ceiling.

I felt a great sense of peace wash over me.

Then the banging started.

A soft thump at first. Then a series of louder thumps, closer
together—like someone pounding on the floor with a dulled hammer.
Then a machine-gun-like series of thumps. It was seven in the morning.
Someone was trying to destroy the floor of my nice, comfy apartment at
seven in the morning.

"Margot?" I yelled.

No response. I stood up, wrapped my robe around me and walked
out of the bedroom. I pivoted left and opened the door adjacent to my
room. There she was, Margot Bustamante, earbuds in, bouncing up and
down as if she were trapped inside one of those inflatable bounce-house
castles. Thirteen years old.

It was seven in the morning.

"Kiddo," I said, my voice flat.

Still dancing.

"Sweetheart, do you hear me?"

Dancing.

"Margot Stella Bustamante, are you receiving me?"

Margot paused and cocked her head, her sharp blue eyes wide and confused. She pulled one of her earbuds out.

"Did you say something, Mami?"

I couldn't help but smile and shake my head. I backed out of Margot's room slowly and watched as my beautiful daughter, her long black hair waving behind her, slid the earbud back in place and continued her melodic thumping.

I loved her so much.

Unflinching love from the moment that tiny, blood-coated, worm-like creature was painfully pulled out of my body. In the years since, that textbook love, which I expected, was replaced by something deep and true—a bond that could never be tampered with. Margot's birth—and being a single mother to her—had changed me, added an urgency and clarity to the powerful internal desperation I'd been feeling at the ignominious end of my comic book "career." Now it wasn't just about me, my ego, or my lifestyle—it was about someone else, and ensuring she survived and thrived.

I walked into the kitchen and breathed in the smell of the fresh coffee I'd programmed the night before. Margot's expression—her tender face—reminded me of how that fork in the road first appeared before me, just a few weeks after that meeting with Riesling. I'd spent the morning hunched over the toilet, throwing up. It hadn't been alcohol—the night before had been a rare dry evening. I doubted food poisoning, since I rarely seemed to eat actual "meals" in those days.

I still remembered the slow, dizzy walk to the pharmacy, followed by the mad rush back home to take the pregnancy test, and the utter lack of surprise when it came back positive. I'd been single for years, yes, but I wasn't a nun. While my shrinking circle of friends had their share of long, meaningful relationships that tended to end with tears that birthed new, lasting friendships, my track record was different. Relationships that began and ended intensely—first dates loaded with, *Wow, you, too?* conversations, mix CDs, strong drinks and the occasional drug, clumsy sex, capped by diminishing returns. It took me years of therapy and recovery to just realize and accept that my behavior was a by-product of a much bigger problem—my obsession with drinking. But the disease didn't excuse the antics. While I had many fond, blurry memories of my misspent early adulthood, I was very glad it was over.

But on that gray New York afternoon fourteen years ago, I knew right away. It felt almost fated, I guess. I was just glad I got to tell him.

I poured myself a large mug of coffee, asked Alexa to play some Oscar Peterson, and plopped down on my gray sectional couch. I let my mind continue to wander. Having Margot changed things. Not just in terms of my work, but everything. That day with the test, in particular. I knew I couldn't just stop drinking on my own like a normal person. I never had just one—I couldn't stop after a few, either. Drinking alone was commonplace—hell, I loved drinking alone. By the end, around the time of the Riesling meeting, my brain had very capably rationalized all the "nevers" I'd created for myself over the years. All the things I'd told myself were signs of a problem. How I'd never drink in the morning, or skip work because of a hangover. Or how I'd never miss important events—weddings, gatherings, family stuff—because I was too drunk. So, in my heart I knew I had a problem. But I also didn't want to deal with it immediately. I'd been doing just fine, right? I felt a pinch of pride at being such a good, functional alcoholic. Why stress over it too much? But Margot changed everything.

I remembered tapping on my beat-up computer, trying to figure out how to find the nearest AA meeting, when I got a call from my L.A.-based friend Kellye, a showrunner for courtroom procedural shows who was making a move into features. She was doing her first movie on the cheap—would I consider storyboarding? Kellye needed someone she trusted—someone who understood the synergy between narrative and visuals. My comic book background made me the first person Kellye thought of. But I needed to come out to L.A., like, yesterday.

"And, look, I know you're dealing with some shit—but I need you to do this and do it well," Kellye had said. "I believe in you, and I need you to make this work if you say yes. I don't care if you've never done this before. I know you can. It would mean a lot to me."

I believe in you.

I felt my eyes welling up as Kellye spoke, so I just said yes—worried I might start weeping on the line if I said anything more.

The change in scenery, in climate, and just working with another female professional . . . it was all exactly what I needed, when I needed it. I hadn't looked back since.

On some days, I loved the work, and couldn't believe this was my job. I got to make movies for a living, which was insane. I was even respected in the field, at least I thought I was. I showed up and was responsible. I got to work on some cool projects. I had actual fans. Was it the life I'd envisioned? Probably not. I was still processing what happened with *Miss Midnight.* I wasn't hunched over my drawing board trying to meet some insane deadline for meager pay. Now when I drew, it was for fun. The mortgage was paid, Margot's needs were met, and I was relatively happy. I mean, being a single mom was not easy, by any stretch, but it was by far the best thing I'd ever done. I'd learned, in sobriety, to be thankful for what I had—to appreciate the small things and take the bigger things incrementally. To not get too high or too low.

But this break hadn't been planned. And as soothing as it felt to be out of the rat race for a minute, moving an almost-teenager from L.A. to New York didn't come without its share of bumps and bruises. It involved new schools, new friends, and a rocky transition. If it had been up to me, I'd be doing award season press for *Miss Midnight* right now. I might still be dating Nate, too, whom I hadn't heard from in months. Yes, the work was exhausting—demanding and all-consuming, especially when the film was a big deal with lots of cooks in the kitchen. But I loved it. And forces outside of my control had taken it away from me. Now I had to figure out where I stood.

I hadn't forgotten about comics, but it certainly felt like comics had forgotten about me. At least, present-day Annie. The irony was, my run on *T.H.U.N.D.E.R. Agents* had become almost legendary—a cult classic that critics and podcasters pointed to as how to reboot a franchise correctly, up there with classics like *Batman: Year One* or *Watchmen*. But all that love, all that academic analysis and obsession, couldn't pay my electric bill.

Every once in a while, between film projects, I'd think about comics— about the original rush that came with that first batch of assignments in my twenties. If I was feeling really nostalgic, I'd send out a few emails— feelers to editors or fellow freelancers. But comics were cyclical, and most of my contacts had dried up. People had moved companies or left the industry. Some of my contemporaries worked in animation or in film, too, if they were still in entertainment. Unless you were a huge star in comics, the numbers just didn't add up.

Every now and again I'd hear from a company looking for a cover, or a backup story. If I had time, I'd consider it. Until I saw the page rate and figured it might not be worth the effort. It wasn't that I felt more important or better-than, it was a logistics and numbers game for me. I could spend a month writing and drawing a ten-page story for a few thousand dollars or I could start working on my next film project, or I could . . . do nothing. I'd priced myself out of the industry I loved, and comics weren't desperate to have me back. It was still the question I got the most on social media, according to Margot: When was I coming back? What project would I want to tackle? What would it take? But it all felt like a train I'd missed—if my one claim to fame was an under-the-radar take on a property most had forgotten, I just didn't have it in me to work on something that would be over-edited and forced into a bigger picture I didn't understand.

It was my choice, to be clear. At my peak, I'd been a talented, versatile, and reliable monthly artist. The kind of team member editors dreamed of. People loved *T.H.U.N.D.E.R. Agents*. People wanted me to work in comics again—I got messages about it regularly. And even without the right contacts, all it would take would be a call from my agent to set up a meeting. I wasn't a nobody.

But did I want to go back to that world?

I took another long sip of my coffee and closed my eyes, letting

Peterson's virtuoso piano whisk me away. It had all happened so fast. The panel. The meeting with Riesling. The pregnancy and the new career were welcome distractions to what had become a Thing with a capital *T*. Thankfully, social media was still a tiny demon hatching from its egg when that particular shit hit the fan. There was no Twitter firestorm. But there'd been enough smoke to screen me as I scampered off to greener pastures.

Comics had chewed me up and spit me out, and at the moment I wasn't sure I wanted to go for another twelve rounds. Kellye's call had been an off-ramp. I took it with gusto, with that tiny baby growing inside me—what choice did I have? My comics career was collateral damage.

Still, the idea floated around me like dusty debris after an explosion. I could just walk through it, let it fade away and settle. I wasn't in control of that anymore, and I'd built another life—a career where I was re-spected and admired and had actual fans who cared about my work and what I did next. I loved comics, but I wasn't in comics anymore.

That was okay, right?

I got up from the couch and walked into my cluttered office, which was down a long hallway that formed the spine of the apartment. I opened a tiny file cabinet next to my drawing table and pulled out a stuffed manila envelope. I opened it carefully. I flipped through a stack of comic-sized pages. Rough layouts—loose drawings that would even-tually get tightened up to resemble final comic book pages, if I had the time or inclination. My decade away from comics had been fully focused on movies and being a mom. Not a bad trade-off. While I hadn't been working on comics, I'd still been creating comics—just not on anything realistic or potentially profitable. Which meant it was a lot of fun. It was something I actually looked forward to.

Fun like the comics that made me run to the shop—the ones that I read as a kid, like Claremont's soap-operatic *X-Men*, or Mike Mignola's gothic horror *Hellboy*, or the trippy, self-reflective stories that sprang from Denny O'Neil and Denys Cowan's *The Question*, and the Hernan-dez Bros' punk rock saga, *Love & Rockets*.

Books that went above and beyond what was expected, to create something wholly new—that still managed to wink and nod at what came before. I wanted to do something like that. I'd tried, a bit, with *T.H.U.N.D.E.R. Agents*—and it'd worked. Just on a painful delay. Too late to salvage my career. But now, dancing on the grave of what was once a promising comic book career, I could do whatever I wanted. I wanted to take something I loved and tweak it and twist it into something completely new and mesmerizing. And, honestly—it was fun to do it on my own terms and time, too.

I spread out the rough layouts carefully on the table. One was a splash page—a large single panel. It featured a female character in a leopard-print jumpsuit crouched near the ground, looking up to see another woman, younger, with blond hair, staring down at her. She was wearing a similar costume—but it felt more modern, like something you'd see on television, on shows like *Arrow* or *Daredevil*. Behind both women was a third character—an otherworldly creature that seemed to be pure dark energy. The rough layout only hinted at what I'd would eventually draw, but the structure was there. It was a turning point on a page in a story that no one but I knew existed, because it didn't exist. It was a drawing based on a document on my laptop. I could drag it to the trash and no one would feel a tremor.

I let out a brief sigh as I lined up another action page next to the splash.

This was how I blew off steam, my stress relief. Working on a story that would never exist or see print. But that was the point, unlike *Miss Midnight*. This was a story I was in complete control of—story, art, letters, colors. A story that I could craft at my own pace. Pure fan fiction. It was a story that, in reality, I would never officially be allowed to create. My agent, a fast-talking lifer named Gary Ackerman, had said as much the one time I'd mustered the courage to ask him. "Too obscure, Annie," he'd hissed before moving along to the next thing on his agenda.

You'd have to be well versed in comic book history to recognize the characters that were loosely drawn on the splash page. The woman crouching in the foreground of the page was Claudia Calla, otherwise known as the Lynx—star of the short-lived comic book series *The Legendary Lynx*, published by Triumph Comics in the 1970s. I loved the Lynx, of course—it held a special place in my heart. It was one of the first and few comics I could remember not only featuring a woman in the lead, but one that—at least for a brief time—was written by a woman, too. A Cuban woman like me, no less.

I probably spent way too much time wondering whatever happened to Carmen Valdez and the Lynx. The comic book landscape was littered with short-lived series, defunct companies, or characters whose ownership rights were so tangled and complicated that the likelihood of reading a new adventure featuring them was close to nil. Not to mention how Valdez just disappeared after writing one issue of the Lynx comic and a few novels. She never did conventions or interviews, and had no social media footprint. She was an enigma. It just added to the allure and my love for the character. A love I'd made no bones about in any press that asked what could bring me back to comics. So, this was what I was doing. Drawing and writing my own Lynx story because I could, and because that was all it would ever be. My own private fan letter to a writer I'd never get to meet.

I was pretty far along, even just working in increments—between being on set, spiraling into a new state, parenting my kid, and everything else. The pages kept coming. Through the pandemic—during shutdowns, variants, and the stress and insanity that it brought, I'd sat at my table and drawn, or written pages for me to draw. The general idea was simple: I wanted to continue the stories I loved as a kid—with the same tone, but modernized and relevant. I wanted to boil down my passions to create the kind of comic book I wanted to read, loaded with social commentary, great characters, and fun, genre-bending adventure. Just a change of pace my brain desperately needed.

And boy, was it fun.

Working on this pretend book had become my secret joy—the one part of my life that had no expectations, no incoming notes or edicts, no corporate masters. I ran a finger along the edge of one of the pages, my eyes looking over my own pencil work. In terms of the process, we were in the early stages. The layouts needed to be tightened up into finished pencils, then inked, then scanned and colored. But instead of dreading the process, I was secretly relishing it. It meant more time in Claudia's world, playing with the Lynx and the characters that resided in Triumph City. I was building something from nothing by myself. In a way, it felt like I was trying to channel myself—a younger, more innocent version of me. I was sending her a message—letting her know that, hey, despite the rocky path—everything just might turn out fine.

I heard my phone ping in the other room.

I checked my email.

Right above a reminder about the anniversary of my friend Laura Gustines's death was a sender I didn't recognize. Bert Carlyle. The tone was brief and stilted, like someone who's unaccustomed to using email or even talking to other people. "Annie—heard much about you. Would love to connect. Thinking of a new comic book project—interested? Send some samples and let's talk. Best, BC."

The name was a blank in my mind, but Bert's email signature was the opposite. The words sounded a blaring alarm in my head.

"Chief Executive Officer—Triumph Entertainment."

House ad for *The Legendary Lynx*, published in Triumph Comics titles in 1975.

CHAPTER SIX

I did the only thing that came to mind when contacted by a complete stranger—cyber-spiral.

I googled and searched and dug around.

There wasn't much to find. Bert Carlyle was apparently the only son of Jeffrey Carlyle, founder and owner of Triumph Comics—the ill-fated seventies comic publisher that was home to a number of now-forgotten superheroes—characters like The Freedom Alliance, Avatar, Graywolf, the Dusk, the Forgotten Five, the Eight Pillars . . . and the Lynx.

I swallowed hard, my eyes scanning over my laptop screen.

The Lynx.

Life was so fucking weird. But was it this weird?

I heard Margot step out of her room. I looked up and met her eyes. She seemed confused. I sure was.

"Mami . . . what are you doing?"

"I'm thinking. And, well—cyber-stalking. It's a thing I do."

"I know, but who's the lucky target this time? New job offer?" Margot said, tilting her head slightly, as if she were trying to get a clearer look at her mother—still in her bathrobe, sitting in a living room only lit by the sun, the laptop light illuminating her confused expression.

"Yeah, I think so? Honestly, I'm still trying to figure it out," I said, scrunching my nose. I patted the seat next to me on the couch. Margot plopped down beside me. "I just got an email from someone I don't know, and they are offering me work—but it's comic book work."

"You said you were done with comics," Margot responded.

"Not exactly."

"Well, that comics were done with you."

I nodded. Good girl. She knew Mami's speeches by heart.

"Right," I continued. "But this person—this guy named Bert— apparently represents a company I thought . . . didn't exist anymore? But they also own a character I really love—"

"The Lynx?" Margot said.

I let out a soft chuckle. "That obvious, huh?"

"Mami," Margot said with a scoff. "It's the only comic you still have. That box in your closet? Those are the only comics in the house, aside from those pages you're drawing that you think no one knows about."

"Okay, I'm going to skip ahead a few seconds past the part where you admit to rummaging around in my closet, but . . . yeah," I said, scanning our living room—unsure what I was trying to find. "I just wonder what I'd do if they offered me the Lynx. That would be . . . I don't know if I can say no to that. It'd be almost too perfect, like my mind manifested it or something."

"Do we need the money?" Margot asked, biting her bottom lip. She sounded like such an adult, I thought—and she was asking such an adult question. It broke my heart.

"No, sweetie—I mean, yes, money is good," I said. "But we're okay, for a little while. I wouldn't worry about it."

I knew this, of course, meant she would certainly worry about it.

"Then why can't you say yes?" Margot asked, frowning.

Here was the challenge with parenting, at least one of them: logic.

Kids saw things with a clarity that adults lost over time. Dulled by experience, tragedy, conflict, and society. But kids hadn't been fully shoved into the meat grinder of the real world yet. To them, life was about being happy and being kind. In many ways, I knew, I was learning as much from Margot as I was teaching her. This felt like one of those moments.

I opened my mouth to respond, but Margot continued.

"Mom, just reply to the email. Say you're curious to hear more," she said. "What's the harm? I mean, it could be cool, right? You love the Lynx."

"I guess you're right," I said, nodding.

Margot smiled and got up from the couch. I could hear her rummaging in the kitchen—the sprinkling of dry cereal into a ceramic bowl, a cup being pulled from the cupboard. I returned my attention to the laptop, still perched on my legs, and banged out a quick reply: "Hi Bert, nice to hear from you. Color me intrigued. Looking forward to hearing more. Best, Annie."

Thinking that was that, I started to close my laptop. But then I saw a bold email pop up at the top of my Gmail inbox. Bert had responded almost immediately. I skimmed the note. It was to the point. Bert wanted me to meet with him and someone named Arturo in Manhattan later this week.

I frowned. This was weird and moving fast—too fast. I was feeling whiplash—gear-shifting from my casual LiveJournal fan-fiction daydream to an actual meeting later this week. Was this Bert guy going to offer me the Lynx? Or was this just another grift—a small comic company trying to reassert itself via NFTs, AI, or an imaginary movie deal? A make-believe company that could only pay back-end and was going to launch via a crowdfunding campaign? The cash-grab mentality was rife in comics—and, not surprisingly, it was the talent that got the short end of the stick. All the risk, little reward. I was most definitely not interested in that. This whole thing had my Spidey-sense tingling.

I loved the Lynx. So it was certainly worth the train ride into Manhattan for a few hours to see just what might be on the table.

I replied to the email before I could talk myself out of it.

"Sounds great. Send details!"

I felt my mind flash back, as I closed my laptop—to another conversation I'd had with Kellye, years before she pulled me out of New York and toward Hollywood. I'd just landed the *Renegade* gig—my first work after *T.H.U.N.D.E.R. Agents*. My big follow-up. My chance to put a bigger stamp on the industry I loved, my way. I'd rationalized myself into accepting the job—I'd heard all the bad things about Blast Radius. But Danny was there and I was wanted—someone wanted me, Annie Bustamante, to revamp their character. That was worth something, right? I'd come to Kellye brimming with excitement, but left the call resentful—angry. It'd taken years of meetings and therapy to realize she had been right.

I thought about her words now, and felt my pulse quicken.

"What are you even saying? This is what I've always wanted," I'd told her, through gritted teeth.

"That's the problem," Kellye had said. "Because you want it so bad. Sometimes the worst thing that can happen to you is getting exactly what you want."

"But why?"

Kellye gave me a humorless smile.

"Because then you find out that what you've been dreaming of might be a nightmare instead."

CHAPTER SEVEN

Are you free tomorrow?"

I saw the response when I checked my phone, just a few minutes after sending my email. Bert worked fast, it seemed. My thumbs typed out a quick reply while I waited for Margot to finish getting dressed. By the time she was sliding on her sneakers, plans were set: Tomorrow, Serafina in midtown, high noon. *This is it, I guess.*

"So, you're doing it, right?" Margot asked as she stepped into the kitchen, grabbing a banana and tearing it open with the abandon only children have. "The Lynx thing?"

I gave a shrug in response as I slid into my light winter jacket.

"I'll take the meeting," I said, trying to play it cool. "I'm curious enough for that."

"Wow, Mami, who are you even kidding?" Margot said, eyebrows furrowed. "This could be Lynx-related, right? Imagine getting that shot? You need to do this."

Margot tossed the banana peel in the compost and walked out as I held the door.

"Look, I don't need to do anything," I said, not even convincing my-self. "We're not desperate for money. We have a good life. I like my work."

"I have a phone, Mami, I can read stuff on the Internet. I know people are upset about that *Miss Midnight* movie," Margot said, not flinching. "I hear you on the phone with Gary, too. We're on a pause, or whatever. I get it. But it's not like you just loved movies, right? It's not like, I dunno, you wake up from dreams of directing *Transformers Part Twelve*, right? Comics are what you do for fun. You grew up reading them. It's in your DNA—and Dad's."

The mention of her father floored me for a second. I grabbed her shoulder and enveloped her in a hug, planting a firm kiss on the top of her head. *God, this kid*, I thought. How did I create someone so much smarter and better than me? Sometimes it felt like we were the same—the fiery temper, the defiant attitude—but somehow, Margot was like the next model. Nuanced and strategic where I'd be chaotic and messy, understanding and thoughtful where I'd be resentful and emotional. She got all of that from her father. I felt a tightness in my chest.

I'd watched Margot grow so much over the past year—crawling closer and closer to being a teenager rather than a kid. I prayed that the transition didn't pull her too far from my reach. Since she was born, Margot had been my everything. I'm not dense enough to think that's really "healthy," per se, but here we are. But she was my constant—through job woes, loneliness, grief, and everything else. Margot got me out of bed, sober and living. My father died before I was born and my mother was a mess. I didn't understand that kind of love until it literally came from me. I'd always been jealous of friends who had that kind of dynamic with their parents—where they could tell them everything and anything, like besties. Or rely on them to pull them out of any kind of problem or jam. But now I knew, and it was the most important part of my life.

I hoped our dynamic was helping her, too, I thought as we walked out of our apartment and headed down Austin Street. No one would confuse us for the Gilmore Girls, but we were close. The second I found out I was pregnant, sitting in my apartment years before, I knew I had to change and that everything would be different. How often do we get those moments in life? All I knew, and still knew, was that I had to take care of Margot. Everything else had to wait. Romance was a distant afterthought, and even when I was dating—like the ill-advised thing with Nate—it always took a firm backseat to Margot.

A memory flooded my brain as if on cue, seeing an opening, some kind of primal response. A tender hand sliding over the scar on my face. Sharp blue eyes meeting mine in a dark room. Whispered words that would never be repeated. A long, meaningful kiss. A hurried exit. A half dozen drinks too many.

I shook it away fast.

"You okay?" Margot asked.

"Eh, I think so," I said, not meeting her gaze, feeling my eyes water. "Just a lot rolling around in my head."

"It's okay to be sad," Margot said flatly, as if she were reading a storefront sign. "I wish he was here, too."

I wanted to say something, but I couldn't. I draped an arm around Margot as we turned the corner toward the chaos and sounds of Queens Boulevard.

"How long are you going to be on this break?" Margot asked, clearly trying to change the subject, bless her heart. "Did Gary say when we should go back to L.A.?"

I didn't really have an answer to that. Gary hadn't given me much of a timetable. The fallout from the *Miss Midnight* shelving was still happening, and most of my usual industry contacts had gone silent. I'd done my part and been a good soldier, refusing the urge to unload via a hasty Instagram reel or tweet-thread. I knew as well as anyone it was a business, and sometimes companies make bad business decisions. But the studio's call to literally shred a year of my work and passion wasn't something I could just swallow and move on from. It stung, badly. And for Gary to then tell me I needed to wait quietly for the Hollywood gods to decide whether I was worthy to return didn't exactly sit well with me, either. Margot's joke about being the "it" director wasn't that far from the truth. But I needed for the bad stuff to cycle through, so I'd be seen as "Annie Bustamante, director of the Oscar-nominated *Red Barry*," not "Annie Bustamante, director of a movie the studio destroyed to save some money because it sucked so hard." Still, I wasn't rich—and I needed to provide. Maybe it was the best time to take a brief detour and work on comics.

Because I'm an anxious person and am programmed to think twenty steps ahead of the present moment, I wondered what would happen if this Lynx thing not only materialized, but took off. Assuming it was even a "Lynx thing." Could I juggle it all? Would I want to?

Those were Future Annie problems, for better or worse.

I'm not sure I'd classify Serafina as swanky, but it was certainly a type of midtown bistro I'd gotten used to over the last few weeks back in New York. It was a place where people "took meetings." Usually publishers or game companies rolling out the off-red carpet for potential talent or business partners. It was memorable if the meetings were good. The food was an afterthought.

I stepped out into the midday sun from the Manhattan-bound E train, making a right on Broadway. I walked the two blocks uptown from Fifty-Third Street and saw the familiar yellow awning. I was perpetually early, so I'd already given myself five imaginary minutes to wait at the front of the restaurant for the rest of the party to arrive. But I saw someone waving at me, the way a kid might wave at a parent while heading into school. The man was stout—pudgy, even—his thinning hair slicked back with too much product. As I drew closer, I got a look at his tired eyes—eyes that seemed to hover above an empty, forced smile. He stuck out a hand as I arrived at the outdoor table—his suit looking more rumpled than it should this early in the day, like a drunk rolling out of an alley to head home in the morning.

"Annie? Bert Carlyle. So wonderful to meet you."

After I shook his sweat-slicked hand and tried very hard not to wipe my palm on my skirt, Carlyle motioned for me to take the seat across from him.

"This is us," he said, as if I didn't gather that. There was another empty seat at the table.

"Arturo is running a few minutes late—you know these Hollywood types, right?"

I did, I was one of them. I wasn't sure Bert Carlyle could say the same.

I took my seat and smiled, watching as Carlyle fidgeted in his chair. God, this was going to be brutal. I was already praying for a tsunami to derail the meeting.

Carlyle placed both palms on the metal table and looked at me, his eyes homing in on mine in a way that wasn't creepy but was certainly odd. A forced intimacy that I could very much do without.

"I'm so glad you're here, Annie," he said. "So, so glad. This is going to be magic."

I shrugged and motioned to the utensils and water glasses on the table.

"Well, what . . . is this, then?" I asked. "I mean, I love a nice lunch as much as the next person, but I literally have no idea what we're talking about. I came because I recognized your name—actually, your company's name, but—"

He waved me off.

"We will get to that, don't you worry," he said with a dry laugh. "Trust me."

I did not trust him, but was curious enough to keep listening.

"I came across your name because in a few interviews you did, well, forever ago—back when you worked in comics—you said nice things about my father's work," Carlyle said. He pressed on, ignoring my raised eyebrow. Like his emails, Bert Carlyle didn't mince words. Or listen. "My father created a character—a female hero, a tough, no-nonsense badass woman called the Lynx. She's so cool. Gritty. Violent. The real deal, right?"

I opened my mouth to respond, but Carlyle ignored me. We were off to a great start.

"My father—a guy who just knew story, who just got comics, you know?" Carlyle said. "He dictated his idea to an editor on his payroll, and just, you know, told him what he wanted. He wanted a tough-talking, visceral, sexy, and intense woman—like, a real woman, yeah? And he wanted her in leopard stripes and claws and just—fucking shit up, okay?"

"Spots."

"What?"

"Leopards—and lynxes—have spots," I said, looking down at the napkin I was folding into oblivion.

"Right, whatever," Carlyle said. "My point is—my dad saw the future. He wanted to level the playing field, you know? Spotlight women. Give them agency. Really change comics, okay?"

I had, of course, heard this version of the Lynx's history before. Many times, actually. It made my stomach turn. The Lynx had been created by a man named Harvey Stern—a lowly editor at Triumph Comics. Harvey had also been murdered before the first issue of *The Legendary Lynx* was released. His collaborator, the acclaimed artist Doug Detmer, didn't fare any better, killing himself a few months later. The creative minds that had a hand in bringing the Lynx to life also shared a tragic throughline. They were not around to defend themselves or share their narrative. They were also not Jeffrey Carlyle, the blowhard founder of Triumph Comics who'd died of cancer about sixteen years ago. But Carlyle had managed to outlive Stern and Detmer, and the living and wealthy got to shape the narrative, whether they deserved to or not. Jeffrey Carlyle had not spared his son from hearing his own twisted version of events.

And, hey, I get it. Jeffrey Carlyle had owned Triumph Comics. It was in his best interests to create a narrative that involved him directly in the creative genesis of those characters. Otherwise, there might be a claim—like so many other comic creators from that period had made—that the

Lynx, or even Avatar and the Freedom Alliance or the Dusk, were not the property of Carlyle. Or whoever owned the IP now. I figured the younger Carlyle's smooth-talking spiel would get to that. Eventually.

"Look, Annie, I know we don't even know each other—but I think you get Triumph, okay? You get our characters," he said, waving off the waiter. "The Lynx has potential. Media potential. I've got investors knocking down my door. We're gonna go out with this in a big way. We're gonna get this baby optioned, produced, and on a streamer by next year, you feel me?"

This guy was a whole vibe, as Margot would say. I would wager that I, a director of multiple major motion pictures and a storyboard artist on a handful of others, knew a fair amount more than Bert Carlyle about how Hollywood worked. Getting stuff made was nowhere near as easy as he was intimating. But I nodded along, because I was still curious about where this was all going—and what my place in it was.

I didn't have to wait long.

The waiter returned, and Bert blurted out a quick order before the waiter looked at me, an apologetic expression on his face. I went with a simple salad. Bert waited for the server to move out of earshot for some reason, and then leaned closer, a conspiratorial look in his eyes.

"No one's gonna buy the film or TV rights to an old comic book character that showed up a dozen times and disappeared," Bert continued. He was wrong about that, but I bit my tongue. "Not without some source material. The Lynx needs a refresh. She needs a new look—an iconic appearance."

He took a gasping sip of water before continuing his rallying cry.

"The old comics aren't enough. We need new stories, new ideas, new visuals," he said. "And they have to be fuckin' huge. Big. Hits out of the gate. Sexy. But I've got a plan, Annie."

He moved his hands quickly—like someone setting up a Risk board before his friends showed up for game night.

"It's a multipronged approach," he said. "I want this to be, how do you say it—cross-platform? TV, games, novels, video games, streaming, podcasts, and . . . and . . ."

"And comics?" I asked, my head bobbing up and down with each syllable—as if to say, *Obviously?*

Bert pointed at me and nodded.

Then he actually said, "Ding ding ding," and I just about died.

"Yes, comics, that's where it all starts, right? You know the drill, eh?"

"Right."

After a bit, the food arrived, but Bert slid his plate aside. I wasn't sure if I should start pecking at my salad—it seemed like he was getting in the zone, some kind of hypnotic aggro-dance. Where was this "Arturo" person, anyway?

"I'm gonna make this happen. The Lynx is gonna be everywhere—it's going to kick the doors down for our other characters, like the Freedom Alliance, Graywolf, the Black Ghost, Carly Candela—all of them," Bert said, his manic eyes darting around, desperate and energized. Was he on something? God, I hoped so. It'd explain so much. "Hollywood is so, so primed for this—for us."

He grabbed his sandwich—a fancy-looking roast beef thing—and took a huge bite out of it. I couldn't look away as mustard started to dribble down his face. He wiped at it with his hand and then licked his fingers, still holding the sandwich in the other. I was fascinated. I guess people did eat like that outside of the confines of their own home and during daylight hours.

I'd met a lot of guys like him over the years. Executives eager to "build the brand" or "maximize the company's IP" or "get into some new markets" with . . . something. It was the something that was brushed off. The art, the creative process. That was the thing you paid for and forgot, then only cared about when it failed. Bert Carlyle wasn't really thinking about the comics—he was only interested in what might happen twenty steps down the road. At least that scumbag Riesling was a comic book lifer. He didn't get into the game to get rich. To be a creep? Sure. But not to get rich.

"That Thunder Warriors book you did—now, that was special," Bert said, nodding to himself. "Real good stuff—my people dug that. Heard you got some good reviews, too."

My people.

"*T.H.U.N.D.E.R. Agents*?" I said softly.

"Yeah, yeah, that—you took something old and dusty, made it look relevant. Now. Modern and edgy," he said. "That's the good stuff."

A little part of me died as he said "edgy." This was another well-worn path, and it wasn't exclusive to comics. So many times, executives—people who not only didn't create, but didn't really even engage with art—thought they knew what they wanted from a project. And, I'd learned, 90 percent of the time they actually had no idea what the property they were rebooting even was. What made it work, what connected it to fans. It was always much easier to knee-jerk and ask for something "gritty" or "edgy" or "ultra-dark." But making something more extreme didn't work—and there was a long line of failed projects as proof. But Bert was showing his ass. This, more than the clunky double-talk, proved to me he was a little fish set loose in a big pond. I really just wanted to stand up, say goodbye to Bert Carlyle, and call a car back to Queens.

But it was the Lynx. *The Legendary Lynx*, for God's sake.

I had to hear him out, right?

But I didn't have to do it on his timeline.

"I have questions," I said, cutting him off before he could keep bloviating. "And I need some clarity before we can really keep talking."

Carlyle stiffened. "Oh, well, of course—"

"Are you publishing comics?" I interjected. This was all I really wanted to know, and it would determine how interested I was in the rest of the meal, Arturo or not.

On paper, the question was silly. Who wouldn't want to make comics about the Lynx? But after listening to Bert Carlyle ramble on about TV and video games and every other form of media except NFTs and audiobooks, it kind of had to be asked. Where did I fit in?

"Yes, yes, of course," he said, wiping his mouth with a cloth napkin. "We're bringing Triumph Comics back in a huge way."

Bert dropped the *h* when he said "huge"—dragging the word out. *Yuuuuuge.*

"We've got deals with Diamond and Penguin Random House to distribute, we're talking to Amazon for digital now, too. It's all set up, the framework. If you join up with us, we'll be unstoppable. You're the voice we need. The last piece of the puzzle."

I tried not to sigh. *This guy thinks I'm a rube.*

"Does Triumph own the characters?"

There was a weird gagging sound and I thought I saw Carlyle choke on his water for a second. He composed himself quickly and responded.

"Oh, one hundred percent, of course. Wouldn't call you here if anything was in doubt," he said, nodding repeatedly. "Triumph has been out of the game, but we've kept all our records up to date. Jeffrey Carlyle created the entire Triumph universe—from Avatar to Zephyr. No question."

No question.

I waited a beat. You got the best tidbits when you just let other people talk, I'd learned. The silence seemed to lure Bert into expanding on the point.

"We have reams of documentation proving ownership, too, if it should ever come into question," Bert said, now picking at his teeth with his fingernail. "I'm not worried. Publishing is the setup. TV, movies—that's an IP game. You need characters. Characters people know and love. Like Lynx. I mean, you're a fan, no?"

"Oh, of course, huge fan," I said, trying to course-correct. All my alarms were going off and the red flags were waving fast, and I wanted Carlyle to understand I wasn't an easy get. But I also wanted to hear more. "I wasn't born yesterday. I know about comics and I know about Hollywood—and neither of them work the way you're describing. So can we pump the brakes on the sales pitch? First, tell me a little bit more about this new . . . company? How does it work?"

Bert nodded as he ripped another bite from his sandwich, trying to smile as he swallowed. I just looked down at my untouched salad and said a silent prayer as his chewing echoed in my ears.

"Good question, good question," he said with a laugh. "There's no fooling you, huh?"

I said nothing.

"Here's the deal—I'm the CEO and publisher of Triumph Enter-tainment. That's the parent company—all the characters are owned, one hundred percent, by that company," Carlyle said. "Now, I am just a part-owner in that company—I needed to take investors, you see? The comics-and-entertainment game is not cheap. And I couldn't just launch all this exciting stuff with my personal checkbook. My investors are chipping in to make this happen, and then we all reap the rewards together—once our media play hits."

Investors. Media play. Parent company. More buzzwords and bull-shit. Like movies and television and books, comics were always about the conflict of commerce and art. For every critical darling, there was a number-crunching accountant in the background tugging at the rug underneath it. Kirby's *New Gods* books were canceled, *Watchmen* se-quels existed, and Jean Grey had died and been reborn a half dozen times. Comics were a business and businesses existed to make money—especially when those businesses were owned by megacorporations with a bottom line and fiscal projections that could not be missed. More often than not, artistic victories were by-products of the business—not goals, per se.

"Who are they?" I asked. I didn't know anyone. Not anymore. But Bert Carlyle didn't, either.

"Who are who?" he asked.

"The investors, Bert. Stay with me."

He laughed nervously. "Jessica Doyle. Comes from tech. But she loves comics, publishing—big Superman fan, you know? She's wanted to get in on it forever. We talked, she liked the library of IP, and boom! We're in business. Now, if we can get you aboard—you can set the table. Put the pieces in place for us to really make this property sing. Your story—your art—will be the basis for everything else, Annie. TV, mov-ies, the whole nine yards. We need you. We're gonna be rich."

Oh God, I didn't think this could get sadder.

Before I could gather my things and get the hell out of there, Bert leaned forward, elbows on the table, a Joker-like smile on his face.

"So, are you in?" he asked. "We want you to work on a new Lynx comic—we're thinking of calling it . . . *The Lynx: Reborn*."

There it was. The offer. Or, the assignment, at least. It always came first, long before comic book people talked dollars and cents.

Carlyle spread his hands out in a strange *ta-da* motion, as if the word "reborn" had never been used by any IP anywhere to imply a new generation or new iteration of an idea.

I thought back to the pages I'd been drawing on a lark. The Lynx story I'd created just for myself was suddenly perfect for this—the real thing. My working title was equally simple, but much more effective: *The Lynx Returns!*

Carlyle seemed frozen in place, mouth agape—a strange, anticipatory smile plastered on it. It all hinged on this moment, to him; I let him linger there, getting a small kick out of it.

I was torn, of course. The twelve-year-old living inside my mind wanted to do this. Hell, I wanted to do this—I was doing "this" for free in my spare time. But there was a familiar buzzing in the back of my head, a dull alarm warning me that not everything was legit with Bert Carlyle, Triumph Entertainment, and this new take on the Lynx. But wasn't that comics, though? You chose the path of least risk. And here was a company—maybe even a real comic book company—that was willing to pay me something to create stories based on the character that brought me into the game to begin with. If not for the Lynx, I wasn't sure I'd even have considered drawing comics. I had to at least explore this, right? I could taste it—something so rare that it had to be tainted in some way: a passion project that would probably get made. So, what the hell, why not? But I was going to make him work for it.

"Sure, this could be fun," I said. "Assuming all the business stuff gets figured out."

I reached over my overpriced salad and shook Carlyle's hand.

Carlyle started to lean back, his every motion screaming, *Victory*. I half expected him to pull out a cigarette and take a drag. I couldn't let that stand.

"I have some requests. To begin with, I want to write it, too."

Carlyle's face blanched for a moment, then he composed himself.

"Oh, well, sure—we can talk about that. I mean, the art is a kind of writing," he sputtered. "But, sure, we can figure something out where you have input on the story—"

"'Art is a kind of writing'? Bert, do you hear yourself talking? Either I'm the sole writer or you get someone else for your 'edgy' reboot," I said. If I was going to do this, it had to be my way. The fleeting thought that I'd have to draw someone else's idea when I had my own brilliant take waiting for me at home didn't make sense. If I was going to work on the Lynx, I wanted to really pour myself into it. And, luckily for Bert Carlyle, I had already started. I wasn't going to come in like a mercenary collecting a paycheck, and I certainly wouldn't agree to anything if I couldn't write *and* draw it. Carlyle seemed to be jammed up somehow, so I kept talking.

"Bert, you seem nice and all—but I'm not some kid with a portfolio looking for a ten-page backup story to make my bones," I said with a laugh. "I was nominated for an Oscar. My run on *T.H.U.N.D.E.R. Agents* is up there with the best of the best. It won an Eisner Award. I love this character. You couldn't ask for a better person to do this. In fact, it feels like you need me more than I need you."

"Is it a dealbreaker?" Carlyle sputtered, his words squeaky and pleading.

"Yes," I said. "It one hundred percent is. It's not a *let's talk about it later* thing, either. I need to know, now. I'm fine walking. Are you fine with me walking?"

As Carlyle started to answer, a shadow fell over the table. We looked up to see a stout man with a scraggly beard, thick sunglasses, and clothes that made Bert Carlyle's style seem tailored. He was in his fifties, and when it clicked in my brain that this was the Arturo Carlyle was referring to, I almost jumped out of my skin.

"Arturo" was apparently Arturo Spinoza, one of the most beloved directors in modern film, probably the most secretive, and also one of the most controversial. God, would it have killed Carlyle to be a little more specific?

Arturo fucking Spinoza was here.

Arturo Spinoza, a director who was equal parts Brian De Palma, Francis Ford Coppola, and Michael Mann, who cut his teeth on a series of dark, sexy neo-noirs like *Miami Midnight*, *Keep Me in Your Heart*, and his most beloved film, the Hitchcockian masterpiece, *Kismet*. His movies were primal, visually alluring—the kind of films you watched over and over to make sure you didn't miss a shot or a nod to the greats. If I was being honest, he was one of my favorite directors ever—even the duds, like his ill-advised *Vertigo* remake and his tone-deaf adaptation of the 1980s television series *Hunter*, or even more reviled flops like *Downtown Deadbeats*. Either way, Spinoza created films about bad people doing bad things to each other, and they were mesmerizing and addictive—like sneaking a peek at a couple arguing next to you, or stumbling onto someone's diary. They felt voyeuristic and lurid in the best way. Spinoza had also worked with some of the biggest names—from Geena Davis to Richard Gere to Brad Pitt and Jennifer Lawrence. He was the kind of director actors had on their short list, and he'd built his own little troupe of actors who would follow him from feature to feature. He'd also created a mystique around himself that I, as a fan, found hypnotic. He never did interviews, he was rarely on camera, and made Steve Ditko seem like a social butterfly. He had it all—the reputation, the legend, and the work.

Until the bottom fell out.

I found it hard to contextualize the initial allegations against Spinoza because I never got a clear sense of them—even today, in the era of #MeToo, the rumors swirling around Spinoza felt nebulous and weird—and the director managed to dodge a full-throated cancellation at first. There were rumors of affairs—despite Spinoza's long-running marriage to his production partner, Ingrid—and casting couch stories. The hammer finally, concretely came down when an actor on Spinoza's most recent—

and last—big-budget film, the erotic neo-noir *The Remnants*, took him to task on social media—alleging a toxic work environment, sexist tirades, and a megalomaniacal approach to filmmaking that just wouldn't fly in this year of our Lord, 2023. It was then, as the Twitter Discourse took hold, that his career felt fully derailed. From the industry gossip that trickled down to me, which wasn't a whole lot, Spinoza was in the very early stages of a carefully curated comeback, choosing not to return to his roots of Hitchcockian crime and suspense, but instead pivoting to . . . the superhero genre. And maybe even television. It all seemed to line up now. Arturo Spinoza needed a win.

And he was standing right next to me.

Carlyle spoke first, motioning for Spinoza to take the open seat between us.

"Arturo—you made it. Wonderful," he said. "We were just talking about you."

The director remained silent, slithering into the seat without even a shrug of recognition.

The silence seemed to agitate Carlyle, who started scratching his right arm before Spinoza spoke, his voice soft, barely above a whisper.

"Why did you bring me here, Bert?"

Bert stammered a bit before calming himself.

"Annie Bustamante, comic book artist—she directs, you know, for movies now," he began.

Spinoza's gaze slid over to me, as if noticing I was there for the first time.

"Yes, you do good work. I was sad to hear about your last movie. Studios are so fucking stupid. I enjoyed your other film, *Red Barry*—I thought it was novel," he said, extending his hand. It felt cold to the touch. "A pleasure."

Novel.

Carlyle kept talking.

"And this is, well, a living legend—Arturo Spinoza. One of the best directors in history. Ever. One of my absolute favorite—"

Arturo raised a hand in disgust and waved it in Bert's general direction. "Please stop that," he said. "You're making me nauseous."

Carlyle wasn't wrong, though—as I watched Spinoza rub his temples in response to Bert's egregious ass-kissing.

Bert Carlyle, despite his Tweedle-Dum demeanor, had made one smart move: he'd snagged one of cinema's most evocative auteurs for what I had to assume was a bargain-basement price, to revitalize the Lynx on the silver screen. And, if you were being generous, you could make the case that Carlyle had snagged two amazing directors. Except it seemed like he didn't understand that, really.

I tried to keep my cool, and avoided looking at Spinoza—who seemed to be curling into himself across from me. Things had suddenly gone from interesting and maybe exciting to downright life-changing. Controversy aside, I didn't think I was on Spinoza's level. Not yet. I did good work—sometimes great work—but Spinoza was a name uttered along with Fincher, Cuarón, and Nolan. He directed the kind of movies I wanted to make—or would strive to make, if my career survived the *Miss Midnight* debacle. Being able to put our heads together on the Lynx felt like a dream in a dream. I just couldn't believe this was on the table. Arturo Spinoza was an auteur in a field that was now rife with franchises and celebrity-fueled projects, a singular voice in an ocean of sequels and remakes. His recent troubles notwithstanding—what was he doing *here*, working with a doofus like Bert Carlyle?

Arturo's eyes narrowed for a moment.

"Did Bert tell you I picked you for this?" he asked, his huge sunglasses sliding down the bridge of his nose, revealing dull brown eyes. "I wanted someone who *got* the character. Bert talks a nice game, but he doesn't get shit. He just spits out the same lines his daddy did in the press. I wanted someone who could nail an aesthetic, you see? A look. A feeling. Not some leather-bound weirdo brooding and hissing at everything. I want character. Conflict. Pathos minus psychosis. I don't want a novelty act. I don't want this to be a fanboy circle jerk. Mostly because, well—the Lynx has no fans. Just us. Maybe just you, Annie."

I took a long sip from my water, unable to formulate a response.

"I want someone to make Claudia—the Lynx—feel present, not cheesy. This isn't about money. Not for me. It's about story," he said, his eyes still burrowing into my soul. "I want someone who wants to be true to this character. Who might be able to elevate the material—which, honestly, I was surprised about. It was pretty good. It made me wonder who actually wrote it."

Carlyle interjected suddenly, surprising us. I'd almost forgotten he was there, so mesmerized by Arturo's call to arms.

"The Lynx was created by my father," he said flatly. "That is not in question."

Arturo rolled her eyes and returned his gaze to me.

"I want you for this," he said. "And I want to work with you. Not above you. You're the comics person. You know how these things work. I'm a filmmaker. I do that very, very well. We can bridge that gap and make something good—something that doesn't feel like a small piece in a huge puzzle for fans to speculate about. I want to make art."

I wanted to wince and blush simultaneously. Here was a man loaded with talent, who'd been mired in a series of bombs and controversy that almost obliterated his career. But I was a sucker for the late-career resurgence. Arturo Spinoza might have just one more great piece of work in him. Maybe I could help him achieve that—get over the finish line.

But something else bothered me. Something Spinoza said.

You're the comics person.

Except I wasn't. Maybe I wasn't Arturo Spinoza, but I wasn't some film student looking to shop my demo reel. I'd been nominated for an Oscar. People actually talked about *Red Barry* now—a comic strip that, before I made the movie, was all but forgotten. Was it possible to feel flattered and insulted all at once? If so, I was immersed in that feeling right now.

"I'm a filmmaker, too," I said, trying to keep my tone mellow and friendly. "So, I hope we can—if this happens, of course—find a way to pool our resources on everything. I'm not just a comic book artist. I haven't drawn a comic in over a decade, though I'm not rusty by any means."

I watched as Arturo started to respond, his mouth opening slowly—as if his face were a half step ahead of his brain. At the same time, Bert Carlyle was squirming—he was clearly not cool with me and a fading Hollywood director laying down the roadmap for Bert's last-ditch multimedia empire.

Bert interjected before Arturo could get a word in.

"This is all, this is magic, all good stuff. It's like we're building the plane mid-flight, you know?" Carlyle said. "And hey, I love me some indie cinema, Arturo—some dark, dangerous shit. Like, real film."

Annie watched as Arturo winced, not caring if Bert noticed or not.

"But we need the Lynx to be huge. A big film—tentpole stuff. Bigger than big," he continued. "We need this movie to matter. Like, *Jurassic Park* or *Iron Man*."

Arturo let out a long sigh.

"You cannot just—what is it—snap your fingers, you dolt, and create *Batman*," Arturo said, spitting each word out with a disdain that made me anxious and excited in equal measure. "That is not how art works. You create for yourself, you create with passion and love and hate and feeling, and then you hope it resonates. You cannot just follow a recipe and bake a movie. Are you a complete—"

I cut in, starting to feel bad for our boy Bert, who despite his oafish nature was still a person—and nobody deserved to be spoken to that way. My mind flashed back to the flurry of trade stories about Arturo Spinoza and his downfall. Guess he was still working on himself.

"So, who's writing the comic, then?"

Bert and Arturo looked at each other, confused.

"Well, Arturo, of course," Bert said. "We need that, uh, connective tissue. We need to be in lockstep—movie and comic in complete synergy. The film will complement the comic and vice versa. Everyone will love it."

I gritted my teeth and said a silent serenity prayer.

"Then I'm not up for this, with all due respect to you and Mr. Spinoza," I said, shifting my look from Bert to Arturo. "I have ideas for the comic, for the story and the art. I'm more than happy to contribute to the film—television or otherwise—as well. In fact, I think I should cowrite the adaptation, but I'm willing to discuss that later on. But my one dealbreaker is that I need to create the comic, completely and alone."

I looked at Arturo, whose expression had gone blank.

"I believe in you, Annie. This is why I asked Carlyle here to recruit you. I know your passion for this character. I can't make my film, my show, without you. You can create the comic, and I will take that to make something else. And you will help me with that, too," the director said with a sly grin. "It would be a disservice to you if I just told you what to draw. And I'd be a fool if I didn't use your skills to make a better film or show. We will put our heads together and make something great, I can feel it."

This was moving too fast.

Bert Carlyle spoke, desperate to fill the void of silence.

"It's gonna be you two—my two key people," he said, motioning toward me and Arturo with a hand. "You're gonna be breaking this story together—working eye to eye, eating and talking, like John and Paul when the Beatles were just starting. You listen to the Beatles, right?"

I didn't move or say anything. Arturo was glancing at his phone.

"You'll figure out the new take, the new Lynx. It'll be excellent," he said, talking more to himself than to me now. "We're gonna return Clara Callis to her glory. Mark my words."

He jabbed a finger on the table to emphasize his last sentence. I frowned.

"Claudia," I said.

"What?"

"Claudia Calla. That's the Lynx's secret identity."

Bert playfully elbowed Arturo, who looked like he wanted to turn to dust and blow away in the Manhattan breeze.

"See? She knows this stuff," Bert said, the shit-eating grin seemingly permanent now. "She's perfect for this."

Arturo shook his head in what seemed like despair.

"Let's get this going immediately," Bert said, looking at me. "Can you connect with Arturo tomorrow and meet up? Start brainstorming? Start drawing your pictures?"

Drawing your pictures.

I took a deep breath.

"If you can get me a contract, take some notes and revise, then get it back to me for signing before then, sure. But I don't imagine that's feasible," I said flatly. "I don't work on spec or before the ink is dry."

I looked at Bert as he stammered. I didn't want to enjoy taking this guy to task, but I was also not going to jump just because he wanted me to get to work. Your emergency doesn't increase my urgency, as the saying went. I hadn't even broached this project with my agent, who I was sure would have his own thoughts.

It was moving too fast.

A big, meaningful part of me wanted to run. Working on a comic book with a controversial director, for a fly-by-night operation desperate for attention? It just felt radioactive. But on the other hand . . . this was the Lynx. Arturo Spinoza. This might be my last, best shot at making a career in comics. On my terms.

So the journey would have to be on my terms, too.

I smiled warmly at Arturo and Bert and placed both my hands on the table.

"I think this could be fun. Let's get the business stuff buttoned up and we can do our thing," I said, standing up and extending a hand to Arturo, who took it slowly, looking up at my face in the midday sun. "I'm excited that we might get to work together."

Bert leaned over, and I tried not to laugh as I caught Arturo almost writhing out of his chair.

"We'll convince you, Annie," Bert said enthusiastically. "There's no way you can say no to this, trust me."

I tilted my head, trying to get a better look at this strange little man— this person I hadn't heard of until yesterday morning.

"Try to convince me, Bert," I said, a sharp smile on my face. "Just don't bullshit me."

I didn't wait for his response, instead pivoting away from the Serafina outdoor seating area and weaving through the Manhattan crowds down Broadway.

I could hear my phone vibrating as I turned on Fifty-Third Street. I figured it was Bert texting about a contract, or something equally desperate. Instead, it was a text—from an unknown number. I didn't even notice that part. I was focused on the message, in all-caps.

BE CAREFUL.

Excerpt from *The Lynx Returns!* #1, published by New Wave Comics, July 2024.

CHAPTER EIGHT

Annie, you're so good. Damn. How do you draw like that?"

I looked up from the piece of typing paper I'd been absent-mindedly sketching on. I hadn't even noticed Danny sidling up across from me. The Glades Middle School cafeteria was loud and bustling, even if kids could grab lunch and pretty much sit anywhere. I liked being here because it gave me cover—everyone was so caught up in their own stuff, I could just set up shop, have a quiet lunch, and doodle until it was time to go somewhere else.

I looked at my sketch—a shot of the X-Men, Marvel's team of mutant outcast heroes. It wasn't all of them—there wasn't enough paper for that. But it was the team I liked best. The original five: Beast, Cyclops, Iceman, Archangel, and Marvel Girl. I was an avid reader of the current series—*X-Factor*—that chronicled the reunited team's adventures. The book also featured the return of Marvel Girl, the heroine who'd died valiantly in the pages of *Uncanny X-Men* #137 as Phoenix. Her return had caused much drama, from what I could tell, but she was past that. I liked the characters and how naturally writer Louise

Simonson chronicled their dynamic. I loved her husband Walt's power-ful line work and panel-crushing layouts. I loved it all.

"Uh, thanks," I said, pulling the paper closer to me. "I didn't think you came to the cafeteria much."

"I needed something to drink and I only had a dollar," Danny said with a smirk. "And, hey, why don't you draw the real X-Men, though? These guys—they're boring."

I scoffed.

"Boring? Bro, X-Factor could destroy the X-Men. They're the origi-nals. The best. You know better. Don't go down this road."

Danny rolled his eyes.

"Whatever," he said, his fingers tapping down the edge of the paper and ending up on my hand, each brief tap like a hot jab from a lit ciga-rette. "I didn't know this was your new lunch spot."

I pulled my hand back.

"I like having some time to myself," I said.

Danny didn't seem to notice my slow recoil. He pulled his backpack onto the table and unzipped the green JanSport's main pocket.

"I wrote another story," he said. I watched as he pulled out a blue Mead notebook and plopped it on the damp table. He flipped through a few pages. "I read that Lynx comic again. It's really good, you know? It made me wonder what would've happened if there were more."

"More?"

"More stories," Danny said, as if what he was discussing was the most obvious thing in the world. "A continuation. We don't see much after the first bunch, right? Like, what would the comic be now? If, I dunno—Marvel or DC made it."

"It'd be boring," I said flatly.

"How do you know?"

"It's just not that kind of book," I said, recognizing my own lecturing tone. "The Triumph universe is small. The characters are weird. It'd just get . . . I dunno, consumed by something like Marvel."

Danny nodded to himself. He grabbed a few pages—all filled from top to bottom by his wispy scrawl—and tore them out of the notebook. He slid them over to me, folding them in half.

"Here," he said, so clearly trying to play it off—to keep it casual. "I thought, I don't know—maybe you would want to draw it? No big deal either way, I just . . ."

I saw Heather Sanchez out of the corner of my eye, approaching the table. I knew what would come next, and I hated the fact that my heart ached over it.

"Danny—hey, Danny? What the hell, bro?" Heather said, gripping Danny's shoulder. "What're you doing over here, slumming it with the nerd herd? We're sitting in the back. Come join us. Nestor got the new Pumpkins record. We're all taking turns listening to it."

Danny hesitated—turning to look at me for a second, then eyeing the papers he'd slid over. I knew what he was going to do, was even okay with it. But when he got up, a slight wave the only sign of recognition as he followed Heather away, the ache came anyway.

When he was out of sight, I opened the pages. Atop the story—if I could even call the grocery-style list of "things that need to happen" a story—was a mostly blank page, with a brief note from Danny—to me.

Hey Bustamante—
See if this gets you into drawing some Lynx stuff!!! It'll be sick. I'm gonna hit
Frank's Comics later—come with. Just us.
Later,

D

A smile spread across my face as I gently placed the letter into my own backpack. I pictured him sitting alone in the library, hastily scrawling the top note between periods.

I held my fingers over the folded notebook paper for what felt like forever.

CHAPTER NINE

"Are you nervous, Mami?"

Margot asked the question as we got up from our seats on the uptown A train. I turned to my daughter, wide-eyed and curious, as we stepped onto the platform. Sometimes kids, as they get older, start to seem and act like adults so damn much you almost forget that once upon a time they were basically kittens—depending on you for everything. Looking at her now, worry and care in her eyes, reminded me of that little baby I raised all by myself.

"I'm not nervous, sweetheart," I said, taking her hand. Normally she'd swat it away, but today she let me clutch her as we walked up toward the surface. "I'm curious. Maybe a little excited."

After a few days of what felt like endless back-and-forth, and over some of my agent's warnings, I put pen to paper on the contract with Triumph Entertainment. This was happening, I'd told myself before I electronically signed my name. I was going to create a new Lynx story, and I was going to write and draw it myself. It didn't feel as exciting as I'd imagined years before—reality rarely matches fantasy, across the board—but I was eager to get to work. Or, to keep working. My *Lynx Returns!* pages were no longer just a fun side project that would never see the light of day. Now I saw a little crack of sunlight. Nothing definite, but something. And that meant a lot.

We took a right as we got aboveground. Once upon a time, I had called Inwood home—before Margot, before *Renegade*, before a lot of things. I loved the neighborhood—still did. It felt like the front lines of the waning war between gentrified Manhattan and the blue-collar residents who'd been here first. But it was a fading skirmish—the result no longer in doubt. I led Margot down Payson and we found the building pretty easily—a nice-looking brownstone that seemed more residential than business. We walked into a cozy vestibule and I buzzed the number Carlyle had given me. Margot started to whistle as we waited. After a few more seconds, I buzzed again. A crackle of static introduced a familiar, ragged voice.

"Yeah?"

It was Spinoza's voice—but lower and hoarser than I remembered.

"Hey, Arturo . . . It's me—uh, Annie," I said, hesitation punctuating every word. "Annie Bustamante."

"Who?"

"We met at lunch with Bert—we're working on the comic together?"

A pause, then static.

"Right, right, right—come in."

Spinoza's voice was replaced by a loud buzz, followed by a metallic *clack*—I ushered Margot into a long hallway that led us to another, smaller door. This wasn't a business office—people lived here. I counted two names on the mailboxes outside of this door. Did Spinoza live here? Was this his bachelor crash pad? My mind fluttered back to the rumors and controversy. Surely Spinoza could afford nicer digs than this, unless he was in some kind of marital exile. I shoved the gossip away just as the interior door swung open.

I stared into almost complete darkness, my hand tightening around

Margot's. I could feel her tensing up. Maybe bringing her was a bad idea, but I didn't have a choice. She was off from school today and our usual sitter wasn't available. Parenting was all about tough calls like this.

I saw a face—a shape—cutting through the darkness. I let my eyes settle—allowed the sunlight from outside to illuminate the person before us—and made out Spinoza's bulky, rumpled frame. The sunglasses were gone, replaced by his muddy brown eyes and the dark, bruise-like bags underneath them. His mouth hung down in a frown that lacked intent—it was just there. In his hand was a large glass of milk.

"You brought your kid?" Spinoza said, looking at Margot.

"Yes, this is Margot," I said, ushering her in and toward a chair near the door. "I didn't have any child care, and—"

"We're off to a great start," Spinoza said, shaking his head as he turned around and took a long swig from the glass before placing it on a nearby table. "Come in, come in."

I wanted to strangle this guy, and I wasn't even three feet into his makeshift office, which, in the light, seemed like a twisted version of a bachelor pad. Food containers strewn around, Bill Evans on the stereo, the smell of dirty laundry. I leaned in to Margot and whispered in her ear.

"We won't be here long," I said.

"It's fine, Mami, just do your thing," she said, pulling her tablet out of her backpack. "I know the drill."

I felt a little bit of my heart crack. I wanted to hug her, bring her in tightly, and tell her I loved her, but this was all part of getting older, I guessed. She knew what to do.

I straightened up and turned to Spinoza.

"I think we need some ground rules before we start," I said, my voice shaking slightly, like it did when I was pissed. And I was very pissed.

Spinoza spun around, the half-empty glass of milk back in his hand.

"I don't work for you," I said, running my tongue over my teeth to slow my words down, trying to prevent a full-blown tirade. "I'm here to collaborate with you. And, like you," I said, motioning around the office-slash-crash pad, "I have a life. It includes my kid, who I will prioritize above anything else. So, please—do not make me feel bad for trying to balance everything. If this isn't going to work, I want to know now, before I actually start caring about the project."

Spinoza looked at his glass of milk, his eyebrows popping up in response—a lazy, lugubrious movement, but something.

"I apologize," he said slowly. "I'm a fat, cranky old man. I'm used to people just doing as I say. It's gotten me into trouble. You're right. That was rude of me."

He walked over to Margot and crouched down, his face close to hers.

"Hello, I am Arturo," he said, extending his hand. Margot looked at it closely before shaking it. "I'm sorry I was rude. What's your name?"

"Margot."

"Hello, Margot, it's nice to meet you," he said. "I'm looking forward to working with your mom. Thank you for letting her come here."

Margot looked at Spinoza, her eyes narrowing—as if to say, *Please, I'm not a baby.*

"My mom is talented. You're lucky she's here."

Spinoza stood up and nodded.

"I am, I am," he said.

Spinoza motioned to the large-ish space. I followed his hand, and allowed my eyes to get accustomed to the near-darkness. Lit candles illuminated a long, crowded working area. I noticed a small, cluttered cot at the far end of the room. I caught glimpses of movie posters, double-stacked bookshelves, the occasional photo, and perhaps a cat or two. Arturo Spinoza's office/apartment was a shrine to his career and ethos. Dark, brooding, spooky, and kind of sexy. I tried not to linger as I saw set photos from *The Woman from Prague*, or take in the rare Mondo poster of his arguably last "great" film, *Real Bad Things*. I could remember waiting in line on opening night for that one—eager to see what Spinoza would do with a real, honest-to-God all-star cast. Danes, Robbie, Washington, Harris. I'd loved every second of the twisted, queer, complex rural noir. But I'd been in the minority on that one. Pop culture had whizzed by Spinoza, had no room for his messy, character-driven tales of bad people

doing even worse stuff. They wanted capes, giant robots, franchise sequels, and celebrity-driven meme movies. So here we were—trying to
bring a little Spinoza and Bustamante to superheroes, because that was
the only path left.

"I liked that one."

Spinoza's words startled me, and I realized I'd been staring at the
poster for too long. I turned and smiled at him.

"I liked it a lot, too," I said. "I think it got a raw deal."

"Hopefully I'll live to see it 'reassessed,' or whatever the term is now,"
Spinoza said, now standing next to me, looking up at the poster. He
smelled of clove cigarettes and some cheap, pharmacy-bought cologne. I
felt a headache coming on.

I watched as the director continued down a long hall that began at
the far end of the office, turning right at the end. I picked up my pace
to catch up. We entered a less nostalgic space—an office, but one free of
decorations and mementos. A working room. Spinoza sat behind a small
gray desk. I saw stacks of yellow legal pads, all filled to the brim with
scribbles and diagrams—even a few sloppy Lynx drawings. Behind the
desk was a large whiteboard, words in various dry-erase marker colors
written sloppily, taking up almost the entire space.

LYNX—Who cares?!

WHAT IS THE CONFLICT?

NO GUNS—SHE USES HER WITS

>> Original story not by Stern?

CHANNEL DETMER!—SMOOTH, CLEAN, STARK

MODERN BUT CONNECTED—NEO-NOIR

"Just some notes," Spinoza said, following my eyes.

"No guns?" I asked.

"I detest them, hate them with a passion," Spinoza said, shaking his
head quickly. "They terrify me. My father killed himself with his own

pistol. It will haunt me forever. An escape from the pains of the real world—using such a crude device. Any hero I write—any person who is a star in my work—will feel the same way. I can't even bring myself to touch one."

It felt like the director was talking to himself more than me, so I moved on.

"And, huh, 'Channel Detmer,'" I said. "I support that."

"You would. You're his student, no? I don't mean literally, just that you seem to echo him in a way I wasn't expecting. Your art feels like his. Infused by it, you know?" Spinoza said, cracking his knuckles. "It's almost weird. In a good way."

I looked at Spinoza and wondered if he saw the concern in my eyes. The director had never seemed more frail to me in the short time I'd known him. Large and deflated, like a pile of dirty sheets cloaked by a black sweater, folding into himself in this cramped, sterile room—the opposite of the pantheon we'd just walked through. Spinoza looked ill, like a vampire waiting for dawn.

"I love his art. Everything about it. His camera angles, his line work, his use of Zip-A-Tone for shadows—all of it. I wanted to live in Doug Detmer's world," I said, as much to Spinoza as to myself. I felt something catch in my throat. "I wish I'd met him. I used to trace his work when I was a kid. It felt burned into my brain."

Spinoza nodded.

"Funny how the stuff that works us up as kids never loses that power," he said, nodding to himself. "It's a primal thing. Like blood. Like an infection we can never cure."

Spinoza let out a series of wet coughs, wiping at his mouth with the back of his hand.

"Sad story, that one," he said, the words sounding like a long wheeze. "Killed himself, right?"

I nodded.

Spinoza let out a slow sigh.

"Well? You're here to work, right?" he asked. "Let's talk. Big-picture."

I took a seat across from Spinoza. The director cut to the chase.

"I know you love my movies, and I appreciate you for that. Not a lot of people seem to like me—or my work—these days. It's been a humbling time. I want to get back to that. To making my own movies. But to get there, I need something. I need a hit," he said, not meeting my gaze. "Because a hit makes money. I'm old, and I want to make the kind of movies I want to make. I want Coppola wine money—the kind of cash I can parlay into my own stuff. Marvel money. Big-budget money. The deal I've got with Triumph is modest, but the backend is fucking great. Not those imaginary percentage points that get litigated to death. I mean gross box office. Nothing 'after expenses'—hard cash as it comes in. I want this to be the last project I do for someone else."

I didn't say anything. In situations like these, when someone is just unloading on you, it's better to listen. Not because Arturo Spinoza was my friend—mostly because I was a curious woman and this all felt like juicy, useful intel. And I felt bad for this man, despite him clearly being an egomaniac and potentially a creep and asshole. It was always interesting to see how people reacted to their privilege being yanked away. Some were humbled. Some pushed back. Arturo Spinoza was doubling down.

"Spinoza's toxic, Annie—trust me," Gary had said, his usual high-speed chatter slowed to a drawl. "His rep is shot. If you're on a pause, he's flatlined. There's something bubbling under there—I dunno if it's a big, concrete controversy, or some drama on that show he was on, but he's just DOA. Anyone that hires him now is doing it because they don't understand what's coming or because they're desperate."

"That show" had been Spinoza's first, much-ballyhooed shift from film to television. A Prohibition-era mob story that also featured vampires named *Blood Oath*. It'd locked on with a streamer fast, even snagging that actress from *The Boys* in the lead role. But as soon as it started, the plug was pulled, followed by a terse statement from the studio and a subsequent disappearing act from Spinoza. The silence afterward was deafening. His name hadn't graced the trades for months, almost a year. I'd been in Hollywood long enough to know that wasn't a good sign.

I trusted Gary—he was a good agent: honest, kindhearted, and savvy. He'd done right by me and had taken me on as a client when I wasn't on anyone's radar. But I knew myself, too—and even after a decade-plus in recovery, I knew my habits—especially the bad ones. I knew the kind of people I was pulled in by, and Spinoza fit the bill: complicated, brusque, and challenging men—surly creatives who rarely, if ever, loved you back. In my heart of hearts, I liked to think I was easygoing. That my kindness and warmth could tame even the most fearsome beast. Maybe that was true. But just because a tiger let you pet them once didn't mean they wouldn't bite your hand off the next time.

"Why're you doing this?"

Spinoza's question pulled me back to the moment.

"You're . . . what? Late forties?" Spinoza asked. "You've got a name. Hell, even I'd heard of you, and I'm out of those circles. But you're respected. People like your movies. Even with your latest film getting tossed, you're on the upswing, and I'm a has-been. You probably make a nice living doing what you do. So . . . why this? Trying to capture something you missed the first time around?"

"Well, I . . ." I stopped myself. I had to think. *Do I play it cool, or do I just tell this guy what's really on my mind?* "No, you're right—I guess. I want to give this another shot. I never thought the Lynx would be free."

Spinoza let out a quick laugh and leaned over the small desk.

"The Lynx . . . will never be free," he said, his eyes narrowing conspiratorially. "We're doing this under the gun, sweetie. We won't get the credit we deserve. We're gonna get so many notes our noses will bleed. It's the game. And that Bert guy? Total clown. Couldn't turn a camera on if you put a gun to his head. Probably thinks black-and-white film is a genre. He's a fool. It's not even his money driving this. But he has an, ahem, vision that we have to humor while we do what we want—what we need. And I need a hit. I need to get back on the map. Just long enough to be able to get paid and do what I want for the rest of my life."

I let my eyes linger on Arturo Spinoza. The scraggly, unkempt beard—more gray than black. The bleary, bloodshot eyes. The frumpy clothing and jittery movements. Arturo Spinoza was a man on his last chance. "Desperate" wasn't the word. No, this was past that. "Hopeless"?

"I'm not interested in doing what Bert wants, either," I said, slowly, as if talking to a tantrum-y child. "I want to do something good. I've done something good. It exists."

Spinoza made a questioning grunt.

I pulled out my phone and tapped the photo app. A few more taps. Then I slid it across the desk to him, hoping the older man at least knew how to side-scroll.

"What's this?"

"*The Lynx Returns!*" I said, unable to hide the pride in my voice—for this secret project I never thought I'd actually get paid to create. "I've been working on it since, well, the pandemic. Between my real gigs. For fun. I never thought it'd be anything. But then this happened."

I watched as Spinoza gingerly scrolled through my camera roll—pausing at each new page of inked artwork. Zooming in on panels. He lingered over a scene where Claudia Calla awakens—and shambles to her bathroom, only to find the Lynx staring back at her from the other side of the mirror. I loved that scene. It evoked everything I wanted this fantasy project to be—meta, suspenseful, and modern. I didn't want to negate what came before—I wanted to embrace it, and bring the Lynx back to life.

"This is good . . . very good," Spinoza said. "Moody. Weird. Nonlinear. I like that you're hinting at resolving a mystery that fans might want—but I think it could work for new people. Like me. Huh. You're really talented. And here I was worried your drawing skills might have atrophied while you were winning Oscars."

"Just nominated," I said. I felt my face flush.

He handed my phone back to me. "You didn't tell Bert about this, did you?"

"No," I said. "I wanted to make sure you were into it, too."

"Good, good. Be careful with him. He's a snake. Stupid, but a snake," Spinoza said before pulling out a vape pen. He let out a long puff of smoke. "Bert doesn't even do email. He doesn't like any kind of paper trail. Ask for a contract? Mention your agent? Send him a DocuSign or whatever the fuck? Guy will lose his mind. Both of his remaining brain cells will destroy each other. Don't even get me started on his business partners."

I cackled. After a moment, Spinoza joined along. I felt myself being pulled in by this man's coarse, ragged charm.

"But you didn't answer my question—why are you doing this?" Spinoza asked with a snort. "Lots of people like old comics. Spider-Man. Superman. Wonder Woman. All that shit. What makes this special for you? What makes it personal?"

I felt my eyes watering. Not from laughter this time. From something else. Something I wasn't ready to mention.

I turned toward the hallway, toward the room where Margot sat. I didn't want Spinoza to see my eyes redden, or hear my voice choking up. It'd give me away.

"I was my daughter's age when I discovered this character," I said. "When I learned about her—and the people who worked on it. Not just the creation—I know Carlyle's dad and Harvey Stern started the book— but one of the issues was written by a woman. A Cuban woman, like me. She was from Miami, like me. It just felt so surreal, that rush of identification. That a person who shared my background had made it, you know? Had done the work I was already dreaming of. It felt so special, like a secret . . . and just like . . . I felt seen. That doesn't happen a lot. It meant so much to me then. I just want to pay it forward a little bit."

"You mean Valdez?" Spinoza said, straining to look at my face. "The woman?"

"Yeah, she wrote one of the later issues," I said. "I know she wrote some books after that—but she basically disappeared from comics."

Spinoza cleared his throat. I stopped talking and looked at him again.

"I'm going to be very careful about what I say right now, which is hard for me. I'm not known for being circumspect," he said, wincing. "And—look—I certainly appreciate your story. I felt the same way when I first saw Almodóvar's *Women on the Verge of a Nervous Breakdown*. It wasn't the kind of movie I wanted to make, mind you, but it showed me I could make my own kind of movies. It's important, identification. It's nice and fuzzy, and will sound good when we do some press, but . . ."

Spinoza let out a long sigh, as if bracing himself for something painful.

"You need to steer clear of the Valdez of it all," he said, not meeting my eyes. "It doesn't help you or me."

"I don't understand—what do you mean?"

His dark-brown eyes widened a bit as he spoke, each word a warning.

"You know the saying, 'Don't poke the bear,' right?" Spinoza continued. "This is one of those situations. If we poke this bear, it will bite back, and we might not survive the experience."

CHAPTER TEN

Wait, so you just come to school—then go home?"

I looked up at Danny, seated next to me in Mr. Rodriguez's chemistry class. It was early in the afternoon at Southwest Miami Senior High School and I was counting the minutes until the final bell. I'd said as much to Danny, my best friend, lab partner, confidant, and, now, annoyance.

"Bro, did we just meet?" I snapped. "You know my routines better than my own mami."

"It's just, Annie—you could be doing so much more," Danny said with a shake of his head. "Don't you wonder where I go after school?"

"Home?" I said with a shrug. I caught a glimpse of Mr. Rodriguez looking up from his papers, scanning the room to see where the tittering conversation was coming from. I lowered my voice to a frantic whisper. "To do your homework? I don't know."

Danny laughed, looking down at his open book but still talking to me out of the side of his mouth. The quiz was long over, but we were in that luxurious post-test period when not everyone had turned in their work. We smiled at each other. He was having fun giving me shit, and I wasn't complaining.

He turned to me quickly, that slight smile still on his face.

"You know that's not true, Annie," he said. He leaned forward slightly. I could feel his breath on my face. It smelled like spearmint gum and the cigarette he snuck after lunch. "I go to swim practice. I do soccer. I'm on the newspaper—"

How quickly things can change, I thought. Just a few short years ago, Danny was the pariah—the outcast who did nothing—while I was the one running to soccer practice after middle school. But something had happened, and now I was getting lectured by him on being more active.

"You are a fucking liar," I hissed, my eyes down, pretending to read the open book on my desk.

Danny leaned back in his chair, hands behind his back, stretching. I let myself admire him for a second. He'd gotten fit over the last few years. Lost the baby fat he'd collected over elementary school and beyond. Rugged-looking in an unintentional, unkempt way. His face bore the battle scars of puberty, but he still managed to make it work. I wondered what had happened over the last year or so—what switch had been flipped when it came to Danny Alvarez. From gross, annoying, but beloved best friend to unstoppable crush. I could feel my cheeks reddening and turned around in my chair, facing my JanSport backpack, unzipping it hastily, squinting to look inside.

I reached in and grabbed something small and plastic, then pulled it out and slid it down the table toward Danny. He looked at the cassette tape, palmed it, and hid it behind the table on his lap—flipping it over to examine the track listing, written in my sloppy, hurried cursive.

"What's this?" Danny said.

The bell rang. Our classmates started to gather their belongings and noisily make their way out of the classroom.

"A tape, fool," I said, trying to play it cool. "I heard a few songs that I thought you might like, so I copied them onto this tape. You listen to tapes, right?"

Danny's brow furrowed. He wasn't dumb. We'd never traded music this way. Sure, we'd hand each other albums. Or make suggestions of songs we were listening to. Danny had gotten me into the Beatles and Nirvana, for example. But not like this. Not a curated thing. A mixtape meant something. Implied something.

My mind flashed back to dancing around my tiny Kendall bedroom, the various CDs I'd carefully chosen stacked next to my giant stereo—the one I'd taken from my mami's room when she was out doing who knows what; with the two tape decks, CD player, and radio all in one. I'd spent hours crafting the mixtape—not only what songs to include, but the order. How one song fed into the next one to create a Greater Meaning and relay my deepest thoughts. I labored over how to maximize the space—how to make sure I didn't go over and cut a song off on one side, or leave too much space. The risky opening of "Scenes from an Italian Restaurant" paired with the haunting elegy of R.E.M.'s "Nightswimming" and the droning melody of Pavement's "Summer Babe (Winter Version)." The Pearl Jam ballad "Elderly Woman Behind the Counter in a Small Town" as the side two opener, with the Gin Blossoms' melancholy "Hey Jealousy" right after. The even riskier closer, two Beatles' songs—"I Will," paired with the unlisted "Her Majesty" to fill out the tape. I almost groaned when I remembered adding Jewel's sugary-folk ballad "You Were Meant for Me." I wanted to die now.

I knew I wasn't being subtle. But it was the kind of thing I couldn't say out loud. The bravery came easy when I was alone in my room, like I always was—left to my own devices by my mom, my friends, the world. My imagination was the only thing I had, it felt like. But now things were different. Now things were real.

"It's just . . . some songs. Some songs I think you'd like," I said, getting up from my chair in one jerky motion. "No big deal. If you don't want it, I can—"

Danny, still sitting, was looking at the tape—flipping the plastic case over in his hand. His eyes scanning the image on the mixtape's cover—a shot of Batman and the pale-skinned villain Nocturna, embracing—artist

Tom Mandrake's haunted line work making the image romantic and lurid all at once. It'd seemed so artsy and perfect to me when I cut-and-
taped it to the cassette's cardstock, but now seemed cheesy and desperate
and stupid. He looked like an archaeologist, I thought—some kind of
Indiana Jones type, trying to figure out what weird artifact from a lost
civilization he'd picked up.

"No, I wanna listen to it, of course," he said. "I just . . ."

"I gotta go," I said, waving as I backtracked toward the door. "I need
to finish that essay for Rosen and I just realized, I—well, see you later,
okay?"

He started to say something, but I was already a few paces out the
door.

Danny caught up to me after the last bell, as I desperately made my
way down D-Wing, toward the student parking lot and my friend Bea-
triz's barely functional Saturn. Bea was not patient, I knew. She wanted
to get the hell out as quickly as possible. If I wasn't waiting by the car five
minutes after school let out, I'd have to figure out my own way home. I
caught sight of Danny a split second before he noticed me waiting at the
end of the poorly lit hallway.

"Are you okay?" he asked.

"I'm fine," I said with an almost imperceptible nod. "Why?"

"Why?" he asked with a scoff. "Bro, you got all weird on me—and you
just darted off. I thought we were going to have lunch. I had to sit with
Norwich and Ryan—with the other drama kids. It was weird."

"You love the drama kids, Danny," I said dismissively. "Don't pretend."

I didn't meet his eyes—couldn't meet them—as we walked toward
the parking lot, Miami's droning heat covering us like a flannel blanket
on a blistering beach.

"And I wasn't acting weird," I said, my voice distant and small, as if I
were trying to convince myself of something. I spun around, backpedal-
ing toward Bea's waiting car. "I hope you like the tape."

I felt his hand wrap around my wrist, gently tugging me back. I was
surprised and thrilled at the same time.

"Annie," he said, his eyes serious and focused. "We need to talk."

I started to respond, tried to say something—but the words didn't form. Something inside me refused to let them come to life. I just shrugged and backed away.

"I gotta go, Danny," I said. "I'll see you tomorrow, okay?"

I pulled my hand free, waving lazily before turning and running to Bea's car; she was waiting behind the wheel.

As I buckled myself in and the car wove around to the far end of the lot, I watched Danny standing there—his eyes on the car, his confused, longing expression unchanged.

CHAPTER ELEVEN

The Triumph Entertainment "offices" were located in a nondescript loft-slash-office space in SoHo, on Crosby Street between Broome and Grand. If you didn't know the offices were there, you'd never figure it out—there was no signage, no names on mailboxes, nothing. I felt like I was walking into a void of some kind—sterile and bright.

The meeting with Spinoza had left me with a weird feeling in the pit of my stomach. I'd taken Margot out for ice cream, as a reward for putting up with that weirdo. We didn't talk about work, which was a relief—we just chatted and laughed. But underneath, my mind was working overtime—Spinoza's warning on loop, the words bouncing off the inside of my skull like a giant bass drum.

You need to steer clear of the Valdez of it all.

I thought of Carmen Valdez. She must be in her seventies by now, at least, I thought. But no one had heard from her in what felt like forever. If Spinoza was "reclusive," Carmen Valdez was a ghost—she made Steve Ditko and Bill Watterson seem almost social. It reminded me of my friend Laura—she'd been working on a book about the lost women in comics before she died. When she'd told me about the project, I'd been so in the weeds on *Red Barry* I only had the capacity to have a few minutes of social conversation before my mental screen saver kicked in.

It doesn't help you or me.

I thought about the text messages. "BE CAREFUL" and the Signal app request. On their own, they could've been written off as spam or mistakes. But paired with Spinoza's warning?

The office's bright lights still felt almost offensive as I stepped off the elevator and took a long sip of my coffee. The front desk was empty. The only hint that this was a place where comics might be made at some point was a piece of paper taped to the glass entryway—TRIUMPH ENTERTAINMENT. Not even a logo. Behind the front desk were another set of equally generic glass doors and a line of cubicles, printers, desks, and myriad other "workplace" things that had the personality of an Office Depot. I fought back the urge to yell, *Anybody out there?* I wondered if it'd echo.

After five minutes and most of my coffee, I figured no one could know I was here, sitting alone in this lobby. I pulled out my phone to shoot Bert Carlyle an email. He'd called demanding this meeting. Our boy Bert felt it was truly essential for me, Annie Bustamante, just a few days into this confusing project, to meet Triumph Entertainment's main investor. I'd said sure, because how do you even say no to this? It felt so weird. My mind flipped back to Spinoza and bears and bites.

Before I started typing, I caught sight of Bert's familiar, slouched form walking through the main doors, a strange, glazed look on his face. He approached me with his hand outstretched.

"Annie, hey, so glad you could make it," Carlyle said as we shook. "I know you and Arturo were jamming yesterday—making some magic, right? What'd you guys accomplish? Anything cool? Want to riff with me a bit?"

I couldn't think of anything I wanted to do less than "riff" or "jam" with Bert Carlyle, a man who'd never broken a sweat working on anything.

I didn't even really want to be here, in this strange building—not when I could actually be working on this book Triumph had hired me to create. But there was something else, too—a gnawing curiosity that I couldn't easily silence. It had gotten me in trouble before.

"It's early, Bert," I said with a dismissive wave. "We'll share when we have something concrete that you can actually read."

Bert nodded, as if trying to convince himself that what I was saying was, indeed, the best plan.

"Totally, totally, I get it," he said, stepping in front of me and motioning for me to take a left and walk through another cubicle farm. "But I want you to know, Annie, and I've told Arturo this—I want you two to treat me like a partner. We're in this together. We're working on this together. It's an us, not a you or him, understand?"

I really wanted to smile, if to just calm this poor sad man down, but I could only muster a pained wince. It'd have to do.

"For sure," I said, my teeth gleaming. "I hear you."

"Excellent," Carlyle said as he opened a door at the end of the cubicle cluster. He motioned for me to walk into a medium-sized, blandly decorated conference room. "Come in."

Though my comics career had been fleeting—a spark instead of a well-kept flame—I'd seen my fair share of comic book company offices. I'd wandered the halls of most of the ones based in New York and a few in Los Angeles, and if there was one thing they had in common, it was décor—they were all tricked out with wall-sized murals of powerful characters, framed pictures of notable comic book covers, and plenty of memorabilia. The office was home, where you celebrated your successes and pretended that working in comics was just a blast. But Triumph Entertainment had none of those things.

"Is this, like, a WeWork or something?" I asked.

Carlyle's mildly disgusted expression told me all I needed to know, but I didn't regret the question.

I saw someone in the periphery of my vision, at the far end of the room, seated at the table.

"No, I mean, we are renting this space," he said with an exaggerated shrug. "But it's not—well, it's not that."

I nodded. I was already done. I'd spent a chunk of time going back and forth with Spinoza the day before, a person I could safely label "difficult," and now here I was, in some unremarkable office across town, waiting to meet with someone else. I just wanted to be at my art table, drawing more Lynx pages, living the actual goddamn dream, instead of talking about it.

The person at the far end of the room moved, and I turned to face them—a woman, a tall, blond woman with sharp features—dressed in a fashionable black business suit. She was stunning, frankly. If I'd met her years before, I would've said she looked like a character from an Arturo Spinoza film, like a young Rebecca De Mornay—maybe the best friend in *Kismet* or the femme fatale in *Miami Midnight*. Her beauty notwithstanding, she had a fluidity of movement that made her seem timeless—her manner felt classic and curated. She was standing in front of her seat at the end of the long table now, a curt, dry smile on her face. I suddenly felt really weird and awkward, because here was this elegant being, waiting like a normal person for me to introduce myself.

"Oh hey, sorry, I'm Annie," I said, walking over and extending my hand. The woman felt warm to the touch, her green eyes were light—almost transparent. I found myself staring. "Sorry, I'm just . . . I'm just really tired. But you must be—"

"Jessica Doyle," the woman said. Her voice was low—not a guttural sound, but a husky, bass-like voice that threw me off. For a split second I thought she might be putting me on, but that felt too weird, even for this clown show.

"Annie Bustamante, nice to meet you."

Doyle's grip was powerful—intentionally so, as if she were trying to prove to me how strong she was, but I didn't play those games. I pulled my hand back as quickly as I could.

"Quite the grip there," I said with a smirk, playfully massaging my hand. No one reacted.

"Let's sit," Carlyle said, motioning for me to take a seat on Doyle's left. Carlyle sauntered to the other side of the table. "We have much to discuss, ladies."

"How was your meeting?" Doyle asked, again with that deep, low-throttle voice. I tried not to laugh—it'd be rude, right? Right.

"Meeting?" I asked.

"With our friend," Doyle said in that deep baritone again. "Spinoza."

It felt almost intimate, like she'd set me up on a date with him or something. I shook my head and responded.

"Oh right—well, it was fine," I said, Spinoza's warning echoing in my mind again. "We just talked big-picture stuff—it's still early days, you know? We have to get into a rhythm."

Doyle nodded as she took her seat. I had to admit I was utterly fascinated by this strange woman, like a creature chipped out of marble come to life. She seemed so put-together, so controlled. What was lurking inside her head? Did I even want to know?

I was snapped back to reality by the sound of Bert Carlyle playfully slapping his hand onto the surface of the conference room table.

"I am so damn glad we're all here," he said, that stupid grin back on his face. "This is the beginning of a new era for Triumph—for the characters my dad created, the company he founded. This is what he always wanted. I can feel it."

Doyle gave me another dry, empty smile—then started to talk, her low voice fluctuating slightly with each sentence.

"We're glad you made the time to meet with us this morning," she said, looking up at me briefly as she spoke. "We believe a great deal in what we're doing here at Triumph, and I think you're a big part of that."

She motioned to Carlyle.

"When Bert came to me with his plan, to reinvigorate the IP his father created and bring it to a new, larger audience, I was intrigued," she continued, meeting Carlyle's hungry eyes, then looking back at me. "My background is in the tech field—I've started companies, been on boards, invested in every kind of product. But what really moves me as a person is story. Character. Engaging with things that make me feel something else."

I tried to smile, even though I had no fucking clue where this was heading. This lady was speaking in generalities. I mean, if you were a person on the planet earth, you probably liked story and character—it was all we consumed. Jessica Doyle felt like an enigma—someone's idea of the mercurial investor looking to make great art. She also didn't seem to laugh, or know how to—always a big red flag for me. I watched her take another breath before she spoke again.

"Look at Marvel—at DC. Triumph could be next in line," she said. "We have the tools—the team to match them, blow for blow. This time three years from now? We will be a completely different company. The landscape of comics and entertainment will be different."

I tried not to frown or give away anything I was feeling or thinking, because it was all snarky as hell. I mean, it was a nice pitch, sure—and it was, for me, the first twenty times I'd heard it. But a new comic book company swooping in and changing the industry was as tired a trope as the idea that comics were dying. I wondered if Jessica Doyle had ever read a comic for pleasure—outside of IP acquisition, multi-platform discussions, or pitch meetings.

"We're looking to transcend the genre of comics," Doyle continued. "We want to make prestige material—the kind of art that gets people excited for each episode or film. We want it all embedded in not just the pop culture, but culture, period."

I repeated the serenity prayer a few times in my head as I watched Doyle continue her speech. I'd interrupted a stadium's worth of people over the years to remind them that comics were a medium, not a genre— and I sure as hell wasn't going to do it one more time here. I was a good soldier, and I could suffer through this part. The suits were always a bitter pill in comics. You had to do the dance and kiss the ring to get to the fun part. The problem was, the fun part got smaller and smaller. You pitched, you begged, you cut corners, gave away rights, all for the chance to make comics. And as time rolled on, that part—the making-comics part—became harder and harder to do. But I needed to get past it—all that mattered was the work.

Then I saw Arturo Spinoza again, melting into himself in his tiny office, looking at me with those dark, baleful eyes. His warning again.

You need to steer clear of the Valdez of it all.

So I did something I'd eventually regret. I interrupted Jessica Doyle.

"Sorry, Jessica, but—Bert—did I hear you right? Are you seriously saying Jeffrey Carlyle personally created all the Triumph characters?" I asked. It was more a statement than a question—but a hammer connecting with a steel drum nonetheless.

Doyle's smile never wavered, but one of her eyes twitched momentarily. She glanced at Bert Carlyle before leaning back in her chair and turning her focus on me. I felt a shiver run through my body.

"It's not an opinion," she said, as if she were relaying the weather, not discussing IP ownership. "The copyrights and trademarks to all the Triumph library of IP are owned and controlled by Triumph Entertainment."

That's when I saw the fork in the road—one was the easy path, where I could just nod along, listen to Doyle and Carlyle, and then head home to my work—or another, more complicated trail, one that wasn't fully visible, but certainly fraught with more challenges and twists. I was never big on the easy path.

I let out a dry laugh.

"Well, look, we all know those are two different things," I said. "I mean, no one is disputing that, say, DC Comics owns Batman lock, stock, and barrel—but did a corporate brand create him? No. It was Bob Kane and Bill Finger. But what you're saying is a little different—you're saying Jeffrey Carlyle, who used to run this company, or some version of this company, created all the characters that were eventually published? I'm not trying to be combative—I'm genuinely curious if that's what you believe."

Doyle gave me that frigid smile again. I was clearly bothering her—I could tell, because Bert Carlyle looked like he was about to have a brain hemorrhage, flustering and fidgeting just outside my range of vision.

"Triumph Entertainment owns all the characters first published by Triumph Comics and credited to Jeffrey Carlyle as creator," Doyle said, as if she were reading off a teleprompter. "We are excited about what the future holds, and about a potential partnership with you to reinvigorate the Lynx."

Potential partnership.

Okay, now I was pissed off.

"Potential?" I asked.

Doyle raised an eyebrow.

"Well, we're only in the early stages—you said so yourself," she said, tilting her head slightly. "We're getting to know each other."

I looked down at my hands for a second before responding.

"I meant Arturo and I were in the early stages. My contract says we're official," I said, giving Doyle my own version of her Stepford smile. "And I understand that talking about things like this can be uncomfortable, but I'm a creator myself. I know intimately that there's a huge difference between owning a character and having created one. In fact, from what I know about the Lynx, her creation is very much in question—"

It was Doyle's turn to interrupt me.

"I don't have time to talk semantics with you," she said. "I'm not interested in doing it, either. What I am interested in, Annie, is the work. Your work. I want to know what you plan to do with our character. Sell me on it. That's what's going to make people care about the Lynx. Because, let's be honest—no one does now. At least, no one outside this room. So, does it matter who owns a character that no one cares about?"

We locked eyes, her pale green ones widening slightly.

I cleared my throat.

I reached for my bag and pulled out my sketchbook. I placed the Moleskine on the table and opened it up—slowly pulling out design after design—sketches of characters, the Lynx in action, Claudia Calla, her love interest Simon Upton, the streets of Triumph City. I ran my finger over a full-body sketch of the Lynx's new, more modern costume—a look that nodded to the past but felt like it was crackling with energy and verve. I tapped my finger on the image.

"This is the only character that would bring me back," I said, looking up at Doyle, then at Carlyle. "To comics. To this place that I love so much, but had to leave. Or, rather, was left by. When I read *The Legendary Lynx* as a kid—I felt seen. To read about this powerful woman, this crime fighter with a dark, tragic past—who's able to overcome that, to not only help her friends but also protect the people she cared about . . . and realize it was written, in part, by a Cuban woman, like me? That identification was huge. I felt less alone. Like, maybe the little sketches and story ideas I was doing in my spiral notebook meant something. Those stories—about Apparition, El Cid, the Lynx's origin . . . they felt so different from even the modern comics I was reading at the time. It's funny, my daughter reminded me that the only comics, the only comic books we have in our house—they're copies of the Lynx. It's always been the only comic that really mattered to me. My biggest regret, while I was living in Los Angeles, working in Hollywood with comics in my rearview, was that I never got to write a Lynx story. And now I will. And it's going to be a story worthy of the character. It's going to change lives."

I looked down at my hands for a second. I felt my heart racing, slowly returning to normal. I felt like I'd gone somewhere else—hopped on the Cosmic Treadmill and traveled to an alternate earth, where I was able to channel a version of myself that didn't really talk all that much. But this Annie—the Annie inside me, the young kid who lived and breathed comics and was obsessed with the Lynx—I loved her, and I wanted her to speak up.

Carlyle's face was more blank than usual. Doyle's expression unreadable. I felt a cold sweat begin to coat my skin.

Then Carlyle spoke, tapping one of my sketches. The big shot of the Lynx.

"This . . . this is fucking great," he said.

Doyle smiled. This time it felt genuine. Almost human.

"That was great, Annie, I could really feel it—feel the passion," she said. "I have to say—I was really touched by that. Now, I knew you were a get for us: You're a name. You've built a reputation for yourself in the film industry. But the thing I also discovered is that comic fans don't forget. People know you love this IP and world. Did Bert tell you that when we announced the formation of Triumph Entertainment, our socials were flooded with one request?"

"No, he didn't say anything," I said, feeling where this was going, but also wanting to hear it out loud. I was an artist. Ego is part of the drill.

"Everyone wanted you to tackle the Lynx," Doyle said, her eyebrows moving up and down like she was offering me a great deal on a used car—and she kind of was. "Your passion for the character is well known. I think this is a perfect moment for not just you—but also the brand. How often do dreams come true?"

Doyle's tale of a social media tidal wave was interesting, but also felt somewhat alien. I'd been off Twitter—well, most social media—for a few months. I found it exhausting and anxiety-inducing. The *Miss Midnight* drama hadn't helped, either—had in fact sped up my departure from the platform. It just wasn't great for my mental health. The bad outweighed the good. I leaned on Margot a lot to let me know if anything great or terrible was happening.

There was probably a lot to unpack there, in terms of my own anxiety and fight-or-flight instinct, and how the pandemic and my own movie being destroyed had probably exacerbated it. But that was a conversation to be had with my therapist, not android Jessica Doyle.

"I appreciate that," I said curtly. I wasn't sure what else there was to this meeting—and my gut told me it was time to leave. So that's what I did. I gave Carlyle and Doyle a smile and then stood up.

"This was nice. Thanks so much for taking the time, it was nice to meet you," I said, looking at Jessica, who seemed curious about my decision to stand and end her meeting. "And you both know I like this idea. I'm ready, and I obviously love the character. I'm willing to take a risk—I don't know anything about your company or what your plans are, beyond what Spinoza has told me, and—"

"What did he say?" Carlyle asked, his expression darkening. "Don't listen to his ver—"

I raised a hand slowly to pacify Bert.

"Oh, nothing bad, we've just talked about the project," I said with a shrug. "Ideas for the comic and how it can feed into his film, stuff like that. We're on the same page."

Carlyle stood up. He started to pat Doyle's shoulder, but she wiggled out of his ham-handed grasp. He moved around Doyle's seat and toward me, his smile emotionless, his eyes dead. Something had sent him down a dark path, and I wasn't sure what it was.

I reached for my bag but stopped cold when Doyle spoke.

"I wanted to discuss one more thing," she said.

I looked at her—tried to pull some sliver of information from her bland expression and came up empty.

I plopped back down.

"Sure," I said, swiveling my chair to face Doyle. That's when I noticed Carlyle had left the room. "What's up?"

She folded her hands on the table in front of her and seemed to be steeling herself for something—except it wasn't the way most people prepared for a difficult conversation, it was like someone's idea of how it went, or a bad daytime drama version of human interaction. That was the moment I realized something bad was coming. A second later, I knew exactly what it was.

"I don't know how to bring this up, Annie, so I'm just going to get straight to the point," Doyle said, her empty smile now just a straight line where her mouth once was. "I want to talk to you about Doug Detmer."

I had two options here: let it unfurl on its own, or put everything out on the table. I tended to try and be transparent with people, but my gut said something else.

You don't owe this woman anything.

So I put my shields up.

"Okay. . . ." I said hesitantly.

Doyle gave me that humorless smile again. At first I thought Jessica Doyle was just weird. Now I was pretty sure I couldn't stand her.

Doug Detmer was a classic, tragic comic book story. An artist's artist—beloved by his peers, feared by his editors, and forgotten by history. By the time Jeffrey Carlyle had handed him the assignment to visualize *The Legendary Lynx*, Detmer had burned every bridge in the industry—his exacting and combative nature winning him few friends. As the styles changed and the industry moved on, Detmer was left on the sidelines—even with a masterful line that evoked titans like Alex Toth and John Buscema. Shortly before the release of *The Legendary Lynx* #11, the sole issue written by Carmen Valdez, Detmer took his own life. The deaths of both Detmer and his Lynx co-creator, writer/editor Harvey Stern, had cast a dark cloud over the character for decades—for those who even knew who the Lynx was.

"Yes, the artist on *The Legendary Lynx*," Doyle said. She pulled out her phone and tapped a few things, then paused to look at the display. She spoke without looking up. "When were you going to tell us?"

You don't owe this woman anything.

"I don't need to tell you anything," I said. Now I was pissed. I stood up and swung my bag over my shoulder. I took in a slow breath before continuing. "And if this is how Triumph deals with—"

"Annie, you don't think this was relevant information?" Doyle asked, standing up to meet my stare. "That you—the writer and artist on the new Lynx project . . ."

She stammered a bit, shaking her head—as if trying to process the information herself.

"That you're Doug Detmer's daughter?"

CHAPTER TWELVE

Were you ever going to tell me, Mami?"

The words hung over the dinner table in Mami's dining room, the largest space in my childhood home. My words seemed to bounce off the room's peach walls, landing on the nice plates Mami dusted off for Noche Buena dinner. I didn't look at anyone seated around the table—not at Danny, though I could hear him clear his throat awkwardly, not at my mom's brother, Tio Raul, either—his eyes not even looking up from his Corona. I almost laughed as Mami's primo, Jesús, walked into the dining room—a shit-eating grin on his face, only to realize something was really wrong, the massive, steaming tray of lechon asado in his hands.

I opened my mouth to repeat the question, to really drill it into Mami, but I was met by her raised hand. It said more than she could vocalize: *Stop.*

So I did stop, but not without giving my mom a death stare—a look that screamed, *We will have words.* Mami looked down at her plate of food, as if to say, *Let's eat first,* then *we can talk.*

I took a long pull from my beer—my third beer of the night, which started just an hour ago. I knew Mami was a round or two ahead of me at this point.

I let myself be distracted by the food. The delicious food. The lechon was savory and soft, melting as it landed in my mouth. The mojito spread over it added a welcome tang of garlic and onion and flavor that seemed to fill the room. Mami's arroz y frijoles were the perfect complement—sturdy, basking in the sofrito base of vegetables, spices. I let myself disappear in it—wallowing in the comfort of my mother's cooking, one of the few things about her that made me feel safe. Everything else, every other thing she did for me, was a letdown. I listened to the rhythmic sounds of my Cuban family's Spanish, the way the sentences rang out or dragged on a few seconds too long, like a teasing refrain. I felt and heard the familiar creaks and aches of the old house. I wondered about what it had seen that I'd buried in my own memory—screaming matches, hands that hit too hard, all fueled by the same drink I was trying to use now, to dull the senses that would be screaming in pain otherwise. The holidays were a trip, man.

It was Noche Buena—Christmas Eve. It was a time to relax, not to stress. Tonight I'd crawl upstairs to my old bedroom, slide under my faded baby-blue sheets, and sleep until the Miami sunlight snuck in through my chipped, blood-red blinds. Or at least that's what I wanted. What actually happened was very different.

I was in my thirties—ostensibly an adult who could take care of herself. An artist, even—making my way in comics. Yet I'd never had a reason to look at my birth certificate. Not until very recently, at least.

It was a mundane thing that set it all into motion. Mundane and stupid. I'd lost my purse at a bar in midtown—one of those nameless faux-dive places that had electronic jukeboxes but still wanted you to think they could've hosted the Ramones. The whole night was a blur—just little vignettes popping up to remind me it happened at all. Dancing in the middle of the bar. A hurried run through the rain to a yellow cab. The jangling of keys as he tried to get them in the lock. More drinks. The sounds of Manhattan blaring through a partially opened window, through a grimy screen. A tangle of sheets and sweat. Then, in the early hours before dawn, as the pounding in my head woke me—I realized my purse was missing. I tiptoed around the unfamiliar studio apartment—desperate to avoid an encounter with the man who had seemed so mysterious and charming the night before. But I didn't have the capacity to be covert, and the next thing I knew, I was explaining that my purse was gone. I watched his expression morph from worry to relief. Not worry for me, mind you, worry for himself—then relief that it wasn't really his problem. The final scene played out as it had any number of times, with a hasty offer of cab fare and empty promises of a call to hang out again, as if we'd been hanging out to begin with. When I got outside, I had no actual idea where I was. My life had become an album track from *Exile in Guyville*.

I realized my purse was gone for good late that afternoon. I'd rapped on the bar door and was met by an employee, a young kid who couldn't have been over twenty-five. I saw a flash of recognition in his eyes even before I could ask about my bag.

Thus began the very not-fun process of applying for a new license in New York. But, not surprisingly, it's hard to get a new license when you don't have one to renew. I needed documentation of my identity—which meant calling my mami, who I didn't particularly get along with. Repeated calls over the following weeks got me nowhere. It was nothing really new—if something wasn't particularly important to Mami, it didn't register.

But the promised document never came. I was forced to request it myself.

A few weeks later, it arrived. I tore the envelope open, eager to resolve this administrative problem that had dominated my life for months. I didn't expect the document to do more than that. I didn't expect it to change my life.

I saw it under COUNTRY OF BIRTH, and below Mami's name, Inez Bustamante.

"Douglas J. Detmer."

It took me a split second to recognize the name. Another to get past the insanity of it. How was it possible? My mom had an affair with Doug Detmer, the artist and co-creator of one of my favorite comic book heroes? It felt surreal and like a painful, weird prank. But then the little details started bubbling up to the surface of my mind, and I started to believe—if not understand.

I knew my mother had spent time in New York in the 1970s—but she barely talked about it. She'd left Miami to get away, she'd told me—away from the heat, her family, everything. But all she'd found in the Big Apple were dead-end jobs, few real opportunities, and a winter she couldn't stand. Inez Bustamante had worked as a bartender, a waitress, and—briefly—an office manager for a building in the Lower East Side. The last bit lingered. Detmer had been based in New York, born and raised, before he took his own life in 1975.

I stood up and walked over to my barely functional iMac and tapped a few words into Google. Detmer's Wikipedia page popped up. It was sparse, but I found what I needed fast.

Before his death, Detmer had worked out of an expansive studio space in New York's Lower East Side. According to the police report, this is where Detmer took his own life.

I closed the window and spun my flimsy desk chair toward my bed and the room's only window—which looked out onto the hustle and bustle of Dyckman Street.

The coincidental detail wasn't a confirmation, but I didn't need that. I had it in the paper my mami had refused to send me. But what did it mean?

I'd never met my father—or gotten a name. All Mami told me was her side of the story—about how she'd returned home to Miami, defeated by New York and desperately homesick, only to find she was pregnant. The man was gone—but that wasn't the term Mami had used. "Se fue." He left. The burden of being my mami then fell on her completely. If only she'd succeeded, I often thought. She did work hard when she was sober and able to hold a job. I had vivid memories of her leaving me alone in our tiny apartment so she could take on grueling shifts at various restaurants and bars to make sure I was clothed and fed. But I also remembered strange men some mornings—who'd nod at me knowingly as they sipped a cafecito out of a My Little Pony cup that had been mine. Eventually she got married—to an old high school classmate who drank as much as she did but seemed to like her and didn't leer at me. They pooled their resources, and by the time I was eight or nine we were all able to move into a relatively nice Kendall town house. The house where I grew up, even after her husband left after a few years, pulled away by his own demons and vices.

The tumult of my childhood didn't leave a lot of room to ask about my biological father. It felt like a victory just to survive—to avoid getting yelled at, to manage to get Mami out of bed to take me to school. The big-picture stuff was just so daunting—and how would she react?

By the time I got older, the question of who my biological father was became more a curiosity than an emotional hole needing to be filled. I stopped asking Mami, because there was never a good time for a meaningful chat, so why bother? I resigned myself to never knowing.

But this piece of paper was something else. It explained the stack of comics my mami—who tended to stick to Michael Crichton and John Grisham novels when she chose to read at all—had in her closet, tucked away. It explained her disappointment when I told her I was moving to New York, and her staunch refusal to visit her only daughter. It went beyond laziness or a fear of a world outside of the Cuban American bubble of Miami. It explained the strange, pained expression she gave me when I showed off a drawing of the Lynx to her. The little moments seemed singular, but now, with the birth certificate feeling like a hot ember in my hands, came together to form something bigger. A deeper pain I could never fully understand.

"Mija, despiertate—Annie? Anabel, por dios . . ."

Mami's slow, slurred whispers filled my ears. I felt bloated and lethargic—but so was she, I recognized. After years of listening to it, I could pick out Mami's slightly slurred voice out of any lineup—could even gauge how drunk she was, down to the number of beverages. It wasn't lost on me that I was drunk, too—another generation affected by this disease.

It took me a moment to fully understand where I was—in the back room of Mami's house, in complete darkness, splayed out on the small couch in the corner of the space, surrounded by storage containers and things that couldn't find a place in the main house. It was late, I realized—and quiet, meaning everyone had left. It might even be Christmas by now, I considered.

"Why, Mami?" I asked, leaning into the argument to come, letting the alcohol fuel a bravery that I wouldn't have otherwise. I felt Mami's arms slide under mine, awkwardly trying to lift me to my feet, which was challenging when she could barely stand up herself. What had happened after I passed out? I wondered.

"Why didn't you tell me about him . . . ? About Detmer . . ."

"Annie, now is not the time," Mami responded in her stilted English—sounding sloshy and broken.

"When, then?" I asked, straightening up and turning around to face her. "How could you just hide that? Didn't you think I wanted to know?"

"I don't think about him at all," Mami said, looking at her hands, clenched tightly at her chest. "I don't think about him ever. I'm your mother, you shouldn't be questioning me like this, you—"

There it was. The trump card she pulled whenever she was on the defensive. As if the role of mother were like an honorary doctorate and not a full-time job. A job Mami had shirked time after time.

"I can question you," I said slowly, trying to focus my words and cut through the lingering haze of the drinks. "You're my mother, sure . . . but Detmer was my father . . . You both, well, you both fucked me up pretty badly. . . ."

I didn't regret my words, just watched as the bomb connected—as my mami's already twisted expression folded into itself, morphing into a look of rage and betrayal.

"Te di todo, Annie," she spat.

But she hadn't given me everything. We both knew this. Yet here we were, two generations of drunks, trying to poke and stab each other into submission—because it was the only way either of us was going to feel better about ourselves. That was the real tragedy, I'd come to realize years later, long after Mami was gone. Mami continued: "No necesitabas un padre. Especialmente uno que no existía."

I wanted to respond—to say I did need a dad, as much as I'd needed a mom. I needed people I could count on as a kid, people to relieve the burden I'd created for myself. No child should feel like the adult in the house—forced to keep things moving by sheer instinct and fear. But that had been my childhood—years spent trying to stay alive, because it didn't feel like anyone else cared about whether I did or not.

But I felt so tired. Maybe Mami was right, and I hadn't needed a father—especially one like Doug Detmer. I'd read enough about the man to realize he'd been difficult. Insanely talented but also impossible to keep working. He'd burned bridges with every major company and a few minor ones—from DC to Marvel to Charlton to Quality to Triumph. He'd illustrated masterful stories—elevating mediocre scripts and amplifying great ones. But he was a curmudgeon and a drunk, surly and prone to violent outbursts—a man so distraught by his own personal demons that he chose the darkest path to resolve it all. I would've run back to Miami, too, if I'd been Mami. I felt a pang of sympathy for her—mixed with a sad, pitying ache that just made me feel worse. She was my mother, after all. Her tactic worked. She was pushing the buttons she'd created.

I let Mami walk me down the hall to my childhood bedroom. Let her change my clothes, as if I were a helpless child—as if she ever did this when I was actually a child. I felt the cool pillow on my face as Mami gently laid me down on the tiny twin bed, her warm hand on my forehead. I let myself drift away—to another deep, empty sleep, as Mami spoke softly, the slight slur still in her own voice, too.

"Pobrecita," she said. "My poor, broken little girl."

CHAPTER THIRTEEN

You're kidding, right?"

Spinoza's words floated between us, like a cloud of smoke refusing to blow away.

"Why would I lie?" I asked, taking a sip of my coffee. We were back in Spinoza's workspace, just a few hours after my visit to the Triumph Entertainment offices. It'd been my first call as I exited the building. Spinoza's response had been swift: "We need to talk."

"It was a rhetorical question, Annie," Spinoza said with a slight sigh. "I'm just surprised by both sides of it. The fact that Jessica confronted you and the fact that it's true. How did you respond?"

"I was honest," I said. "I told them I was offended they felt the need to dig into my background. Doyle tried to play it off as standard protocol, but that felt like bullshit. Then I left, and here I am."

"You know what they're worried about, right?" Spinoza asked, leaning forward on his desk.

"They think I'm copying Detmer's style—the style that is so integral to the Lynx," I blurted out, interrupting Spinoza before he could answer his own prompt. "It's a veiled threat."

"I was thinking it had more to do with the character itself," he said. "They're worried you have a claim to the Lynx."

"Huh," I said. "I hadn't even thought of that."

Doug Detmer, as long as I'd known he was my biological father, had always felt like an enigma—an apparition of sorts. Not an actual part of my life. But there was some truth to what Spinoza said. Doug Detmer co-created the Lynx. And, as far as I knew, I was his only rightful heir.

"Those idiots probably shat themselves when they realized you were Detmer's daughter," Spinoza said, a crooked smile now decorating his round face. He waved a finger at me playfully. "I knew I liked you—not just because you're beautiful, of course. But you're smart as hell. Now I really like you."

The compliment landed wrong. Spinoza's expression had gone from conspiratorial to almost lurid. I tried to chalk it up as nothing and move on.

"I only found out . . . well, I found out a while ago," I said, unsure how much I trusted Spinoza. "It was hard to process. I was in a bad space at the time. But—"

Spinoza scoffed.

"Please, spare me the *I worked on myself and then the sun shone on my face for the first time* bullshit. I get it. Trust me," he said, his eyes rolling back slightly. "I just think it's fucking cool, you know? Your dad created the character we're working on now. It's like time travel. And how wild that you loved the character before you knew it was him. You're going to be writing and drawing this character that he helped bring to life. Hell, you even draw like him."

"I do not," I said defensively. "I wish people would stop saying that."

Spinoza wasn't the first to make the comparison. It wasn't a direct connection—not in the way, say, Neal Adams and early Bill Sienkiewicz's kinetic, dramatically detailed art looked similar. Or how Phil Jimenez's art evoked the hyper-dynamic grandeur of George Pérez. It was subtle, and it wasn't the kind of thing my own contemporaries picked up on.

"You do, though," Spinoza said. "You do draw like your dad."

"He's not my dad," I said. "I mean, his sperm had a hand in making me—but I never knew him. This whole thing . . . I loved the Lynx before I even knew Doug Detmer was anything more than a name on paper. So, getting to write and draw this was a dream apart from him. Our . . . relationship, well, it makes it all the more complicated."

Spinoza nodded. He opened a desk drawer and pulled out a vape pen. He showed it to me, as if to ask, *You mind?*, before taking a pull. A moment later he spoke.

"I'm bored with this now, to be honest," he said, holding the smoke in his mouth for a few seconds too long.

I wanted to respond but found myself grasping for words. Was Spinoza brutally honest or just a huge asshole?

"My guess is they didn't fire you?"

I shrugged. "I didn't stick around long enough to find out," I said.

Spinoza scratched his tangled, salt-and-pepper beard.

"Nah, bad news travels fast," he growled. "Your agent would've gotten an email within minutes. You're stuck with me for now."

The old director paused before continuing, tapping his chin with the vape pen.

"I will say, and you didn't hear this from me—you should look into who actually owns the copyright," Spinoza said.

"What do you mean?"

"That's exactly what I mean," he said, a thick eyebrow arching. "Just because Bert Carlyle says he owns Triumph Comics doesn't mean shit. It's easy to say and great for optics. But . . . does he?"

Spinoza leaned back in his creaky desk chair and pointed at me.

"But that's something to ponder on your own time, sweetie," he said. "For now, we talk story. And we talk about your idea. And we figure out how to make it better. Understand?"

I was still feeling lightheaded from the Carlyle and Doyle meeting—I didn't talk to many people about Doug Detmer. I wasn't really sure what made me want to talk to Spinoza about it, either. Did I see him as some kind of father figure? Doubtful. But the director was right about Carlyle's concerns about my own secret origin: The daughter of the

Lynx's dead co-creator wanted to work on the character? That would spell "lawsuit," for sure. But I would let Doyle and Carlyle play that card if they had it.

Now it was time to talk story.

"The rough idea, for my arc, for *The Lynx Returns!*, is about a person discovering who they really are. The truth about themselves," I said, sliding my palms over my skirt to straighten it out. "The Lynx is a lost character. Only a handful of people even know she exists. So I thought it would be interesting to make that literal. What if she—Claudia Calla—basically forgot she was the Lynx? Because someone wanted her to forget? And what if the pieces of that old, hidden life were starting to come out of the woodwork? In dreams, in her reflection, in visions. She feels like she's losing her mind—but something keeps tugging at her."

Spinoza licked his lips hastily.

"I like it. Very unsettling. Unreliable narrators are my thing. I can see this. I'm already more interested in this project just by talking to you," he said, tapping his vape pen on the desk. "We can really roll that out over the length of the film. She starts seeing things, feeling things . . . familiar emotions and reactions. She's wondering what the fuck is going on with her. Then we learn . . . what? That she forgot?"

"It was part of a plan," I continued, ignoring Spinoza's pitch-room enthusiasm for now. "Lynx doesn't have a lot of villains. She just wasn't around that long. Mr. Void is the big one, but it felt too obvious to use him. She fights this big, brutish villain named Diesel in the first issue—but I really liked one of the later villains, a telepathic character named Mindbender. She twists and alters reality and can drive people insane. I thought it would be interesting to have her do that to Lynx, to basically make her believe she was never a hero: To show her a different path. To erase her past, which in turn prevents her from being her true self."

Based on his blank expression, I could see I'd lost Spinoza.

"You still with me?"

Spinoza rubbed his eyes.

"I think so," he said, his voice sounding distant. "I'm just trying to think. There's something here. Something that deconstructs the Lynx to build her back up again. But do we want to say that? That feels trite."

"It's certainly been done to no end in comics—sometimes well, sometimes . . . not," I said. "But I think what clicks here is that the character—the Lynx herself—is lost. No one remembers her."

I thought of stories by legends like Alan Moore and Neil Gaiman and Grant Morrison—stories that lovingly, surgically exposed the insides of the superhero mythos to reveal what was underneath. If done well, it could give readers a new way of looking at their favorite characters, or revive forgotten heroes. If done poorly, it could read like overzealous fan service. For every instance of readers discovering Alec Holland wasn't, in fact, the Swamp Thing, but actually a giant, complicated plant creature—there were equal number of overly gritty, needlessly dark "reboots" of beloved four-color heroes that didn't land because of bad writing or poorly crafted artwork. I thought we could do it the right way.

"So what makes this version any different?" Spinoza said, a tinge of annoyance in his delivery. I felt my defenses go up and had to remind myself that this man—this acclaimed, if maligned director—wasn't a comics fan. He needed a guide into this world so he could create his own vision of my story on the screen. I had to sell him before I could sell the reader.

"It's not a grim story—it's a celebration. Of the quirky parts of comics but also a nod to Claudia's—and the Lynx's—perseverance. This character has outlived her creators. Has literally traveled through time," I said, my eyes widening. "She has clawed her way out of obscurity for this second chance. I think it's a story of a woman reclaiming who she is and pushing back against someone—or something—that's trying to program her to believe she's not that person."

Spinoza leaned back, his eyes set on me.

"Well, damn, that's good," he said.

Spinoza reached across his barren desk and grabbed a pen. He tapped it on a blank legal pad before starting to jot something down.

"I'm trying to wrap my head around how to make this work," he said, almost as if talking to himself. "How we make our work come together to create these two different things. Especially when our boss wants something completely different from both mediums."

I nodded. I did get it—I didn't need a tutorial on Bert Carlyle being an idiot.

"Listen, this is what interests me—aside from getting paid to make a TV show, and hopefully make a show that will fund the movies I actually want to make later on," Spinoza said, placing his hands down on the table. "I want to create a story about legacy. About the weight of our past. About making up for mistakes—or, at least, coming to terms with them. I think this is shit we all grapple with. 'Wow, I was an asshole twenty years ago—am I still a piece of shit?' That kind of thing. You get it, right? Anyway, I want to shoehorn that—my anxieties and dread about aging on this dying planet—into the fights-and-tights world. I want to take the tropes of the genre and talk about things we never see, because heroes are always young and vibrant and sexy as hell. I want to talk about a woman looking back further than she's looking ahead. Someone who's not sure she made all the right calls, and now she has to come to terms with her life and maybe start over. It's the kind of movie I wanted to make before I couldn't get a meeting anywhere. So now I want to make it here, because unless this is a hit, this may be my last work ever. But this is what I want to talk about. Can we do that?"

I felt a tingling all over my body, the electric shock of surprise at hearing my own ideas shared by someone else. I was frozen, unable to make a sound. But when I started talking, my words came out like a torrent.

"Yes, yes, that's what I want, too," I said. "I don't want to just . . . I dunno, do a low-rent Alan Moore riff on the Lynx. Moore has done it himself."

"I don't know what that means."

"I mean, I don't want to tear her apart unless that makes her a better character," Annie said. "I want to use the past as a tapestry, to show—"

Spinoza raised a hand. I went silent.

"That's cerebral plotty gunk, which is good. But we can get to that later," he said. "Let's talk primal stuff. What does this *feel* like? Why should we care about this woman who puts on tights and forgot who she was?"

I scrunched up my nose at Spinoza's comment. It was a good note, sure. I'd spent most of the time pecking away at *The Lynx Returns!*, thinking about the big beats. What happened. How it'd look. The big pieces of the story. But Spinoza was asking me to dig deeper. The only other collaboration I'd had that felt like this was with Danny.

"It's something I think we can all relate to—this idea that we have something in our past," I said, "something we can't touch. It might be good, or might be bad, but we can't see it. And we're worried about it. Why can't we see ourselves fully? What's missing?"

"Worried it might reach its hand out and scratch you," Spinoza said, not missing a beat.

Our eyes met for a second and I could see we were on the same page. I was jamming with Arturo fucking Spinoza. And I was holding my own, too. It was a good feeling. In all my time working in comics, my relationships with writers—or with creative partners, like editors, colorists, or whatever—were relegated to email and fleeting conversations at conventions, between book signings on the convention floor or between drinks at the bar. Nothing substantial. Not really. This felt like what I imagined music was like—playing your part and watching it blend together with someone else's to make harmony.

Spinoza inched forward, his eyes on me, and it was clear he wanted to talk about something else.

"What about the look—for the Lynx?" he said, back to his normal self now. "Were you thinking of changing it?"

"Well, it's complicated, right?" I said with a shrug. "I want to honor what Detmer did, you know—to have it feel like a continuation, but also make it feel like she—Claudia—was starting over. A soft reboot, sort of. So, the new costume is a symbol for that. It's the same but not the same."

Spinoza let out a long puff of smoke from his vape pen.

"Yeah, that feels right," he said. "There's so much baggage about this character that we need to start relatively fresh—"

"Baggage?" I asked.

Spinoza shrugged. "I don't know how much of this I'm even supposed to say," he said, resting his chin on his hands as he looked at me. Suddenly the director seemed very tired.

I waited in silence. I'd learned, over myriad business meetings and blind dates, that it was often better to let the other side feel like they had to fill a silence, instead of doing it for them.

"Has anything strange been happening?" Spinoza asked. The question felt so vague, so completely out of left field, that I needed a few extra seconds to just process the words he'd said, and to ponder if they'd been delivered in the right order.

"Strange?" I asked. "I mean, life is strange."

"I mean strange-strange—like, calls in the middle of the night, feeling like you're being followed," Spinoza said, tilting his head back and forth with each phrase. "That sort of thing."

I shook my head.

I was starting to like Spinoza more, but I wasn't sure I trusted him completely. Not yet. Plus, I wasn't sure about those text messages to begin with.

"What are you getting at?"

"I'd just—well, we need to be careful," Spinoza said. "Not only with clowns like Carlyle, but everyone he's associated with. And with this idea—this character. It's fraught."

"Fraught how?"

Spinoza winced. "Well, I think we're both about to find out."

A buzzing sound. We both looked down to Spinoza's desk and saw his phone vibrating. Before I could make out the name on the display, the director snatched his cell phone and started tapping at it feverishly. As if losing patience with that, he picked up the phone and put it to his ear. He began speaking in hushed, hurried tones, the anger spewing from his lips palpable and frightening.

"Listen, you have to let me do what I do," Spinoza said, his tone sharp and accusatory. "I know what I know, and you can't change that. Don't fuck with my shot. This is my career. I'm putting my reputation on the line. Let me do it my way, or you won't like what I have to say—out loud."

Spinoza tapped down on his phone one last time, then the iPhone slid out of his hand and slammed onto the floor. He didn't bother to pick it up. He glanced at me, as if noticing me for the first time.

"I think that's enough for today," he said, clearing his throat.

"What was that?" I asked.

Spinoza looked down at the floor, as if trying to locate his fallen phone.

"You don't want to know," he said, shaking his head, still looking down at the floor. He placed his hands on his legs and turned to face me, as if I hadn't just heard him threaten someone on the phone. "You're a mom, too. That must be hard. Having a kid. My family doesn't talk to me much. They don't need me. But your girl . . . she needs you, right?"

I nodded, unsure what else to say. The question was disturbing.

"The Lynx? The character. You love this character. Is that really it? That's why you'd ever say yes to this kind of project?" Spinoza asked. "And your daughter—she's never seen you work on this kind of thing. Does she read comics?"

"She does," I said, my words methodical—tactical. "She likes books by Raina Telgemeier. She likes some superhero stuff, like the Marvel movies. She knows more about current comics than I do. She likes fantasy novels, too."

"She knows you as a movie person who loves comics, right? She doesn't think of you as a comic book artist, right?" Spinoza asked, his tone soft—intimate. It was unsettling. "You want to show her who you really are, don't you?"

I felt myself pulling back—my entire body reacting to Spinoza's words, how this veritable stranger had nailed something I didn't even realize myself, like he'd plucked a thread out of my own soul.

"She will be proud of you, Annie," Spinoza said with a slow nod. "And she must love you already, I'm sure."

I didn't reply. I wasn't sure what to say. I got up hastily and nodded at the aging director. I felt like I was tingling—like all my muscles had fallen asleep.

Spinoza walked me to the door—his hand on my lower back, lingering a few seconds too long. I gently swatted it away. I turned to him and extended my hand. We shook.

"Let's meet later this week," Spinoza said. "And remember—be careful."

"What?"

Be careful.

Spinoza smiled instead of responding. I felt a wave of dizziness overtake me as he rushed me out of the office—a blend of confusion, elation, and . . . fear.

CHAPTER FOURTEEN

It was a Friday, so that meant we were drinking. Like Thursdays, some Wednesdays, and every Saturday. That was just college life, I supposed. Even if "college life" in Miami still involved living at home with your parents and commuting to school.

So we'd all gone to the bar, as we did. Most of my friends had made their way there after class. But I wasn't really good at "going to class" anymore. FIU bored me. It felt like high school continued—my dreams of going away to college dashed by my own laziness and the daunting costs that I knew my mami would just scoff at. It'd just felt easier to stay closer to home.

Closer to Danny.

Our crawl started at the Gables Pub—an unmemorable bar on Catalonia that had a half-decent patio, a solid beer selection, rude bartenders, and a jukebox that made up for most of it. It was dimly lit, reeked of stale weed, and sometimes featured loud emo bands desperate to be the next Weezer—except, c'mon. Weezer had always sucked. Everything after *Pinkerton*, at least.

I'd bummed a ride with Mike, a friend of this guy Pete who was in my English Lit 202 class with Professor Arnold. But Mike wasn't going to be my ride home. Danny would be there. Danny. He was like family. He'd look out for me.

By the time I got to the pub, I saw him tucked in a booth by the entrance, sitting with some of his friends from the blue tables—the metallic seats set up outside of FIU's Graham Center building. I knew most of them—José, Marlene, Alan, that annoying girl Patty, and some hipster doofus named Julio. But I just looked at Danny.

I sidled up next to him, giving him a quick peck on the cheek as greeting, standard Miami fare. But it always gave me a rush.

I'd already pre-gamed before arriving, so the night was blurry from the moment I sat down. Clinking glasses, complaints about class, gossip, music talk—it all felt the same. Familiar and comforting and fun. The liquor coated my stomach—I felt like my entire body was humming, tuning in to some other frequency.

After a few rounds, the musical chairs started as people stumbled toward the bathroom. The music got louder. The bar got more crowded. I smiled at Danny as he leaned over, his mouth near my neck.

"God, I am so bored," he said, his words stifling a laugh. "We talk about the same shit every night."

I turned to look at him, catching a drunken gleam in his eyes. He looked beautiful. Sleepy and shiny and pretty, all at once. I wanted to kiss him so badly then. It was the last moment before things went completely unmoored.

"Wait, seriously?" Alan asked, his tone flat and professional, but his expression giving him away. His pointed finger toggled between me and Danny across the table from him. "You two have never—well, you know?"

"What?" I asked, louder than I'd intended.

"C'mon, Annie, you weren't born yesterday," Alan said with a scoff. "The dance. The deed. Bumping and grinding."

I tossed a straw at him, missing his head by inches. He laughed. We were friends. This was how we all talked to each other. Crudely. With affection. Still, I could feel my face growing hot, could sense Danny fidgeting next to me. Was this making him uncomfortable? Was he repulsed by the idea?

Of course I hadn't slept with Danny, though. I hadn't slept with anyone.

Sure, there'd been boys. Kissing and touching and pulling and groping in various situations and places. Backseats of cars. At hotel room parties on South Beach. At eighties dance clubs downtown. I just hadn't—well, whatever.

"But you see the chemistry, don't you?" Alan was still talking. "You guys—you're either in love or you're siblings, and now I'm grossing myself out if you're siblings."

"Just give it a rest, bro," Danny said, his delivery humorless and pointed. Alan raised his hands in mock surrender.

"Oh, excuse me, Sir Danny, did I hit a nerve?" he said. "I'll leave it be."

"I bet you they like each other," Marlene said, interjecting herself, her sleepy smile sharpening. "I bet you they'd fuck if given the chance."

I heard a sharp gasp. It took me a minute to realize it was mine.

I felt Marlene leaning into my right side, could smell the cheap vodka on her breath. We were friends, mostly. I was friends with everyone at the table. But Marlene's joke felt like a pointed betrayal.

Alan and Marlene sized each other up, two mischief-makers. Game recognizing game. I felt goose bumps on my arm. Why wasn't I saying anything?

"This is getting annoying," Danny said, taking a last pull from his beer. An angry gulp. He wasn't a huge drinker. Not like me. Not then or later. He usually paced himself. Right now, though, I could tell he was drunk. And upset.

"Just say it, then," he said, looking right at Marlene. I could feel the crackle of sparks between them. I knew they had a history—a brief, sloppy one that didn't register on the relationship scale. I hated to call it friends with benefits because that would imply they were friends, and they weren't. They just happened to find each other attractive.

I'd never been jealous of Marlene. Danny was my best friend. He'd told me his feelings about everything—including her.

"Say what?" Marlene said, tilting her head playfully as she looked at Danny, my body stuck between them—watching a slow-moving amateur tennis match. "That I dare you? Well, okay—Danny, I dare you. I dare you both to get down to it and just have sex. Take a shot, go to your place and do it. You know you want to."

I started to open my mouth but waited instead. I was curious. What was Danny going to say here? How would he respond? I needed to know.

But he didn't respond. He stood up and left without a word.

As he made his way to the exit, Marlene yelled after him—a seething anger in her words.

"Ha, I knew it," she said. "You pussy."

She shook her head before finishing off her rum-and-Coke.

I just stared at her.

A few moments of silence passed.

I got up with a start, could feel all my friends' eyes on me. I tried to ignore them.

I moved around the table, saw Marlene watching me, eyes narrowed. As I turned the corner, I felt her warm hand wrap around my wrist. She yanked me back, her mouth close to my face, her voice a raspy, dragging whisper. I could smell the peach schnapps on her breath.

"Sometimes we get exactly what we want," she said, almost hissing each word. "And we don't know what to do with it."

I found him in the pub's tiny parking lot across the street, standing just outside the glare of a streetlamp. He was looking out onto the lot, as if he'd forgotten where he'd parked. But I knew that wasn't it.

He turned his face slightly at the sound of me approaching.

"You okay?" I asked, as if he'd just scraped his knee.

He shrugged and looked away. "They're assholes," he said.

I moved in closer and placed a hand on his arm. He seemed to bristle at the touch. I pulled back.

I had so many things I wanted to ask him, but the words seemed to crash together, unable to form full sentences. I was drunk and I was confused. But I knew I didn't want to be inside.

"You don't have to be out here with me, I'll be okay," he said, not looking at me. "I'll probably go home. Or just walk."

I started to pull away, but stopped myself. Everything felt raw—out in the open, vulnerable. If not now, then when?

"Why did you leave?" I asked. "Did the idea—was it a joke to you? Did you feel like it was . . . I don't know, bad?"

Danny turned around slowly, his expression softer—but still pained. I braced for his response.

"No, of course not—Annie, I just . . ." he said, looking at his feet. "I just don't want it to be like that. If that ever happens to us, I don't want it to be a fucking dare. I want it to mean something."

Our eyes met. We shared a smile. I slid my arm through his as we walked down Giralda toward Ponce de Leon, the Miami air thick and humid, like a warm blanket wrapping itself around us both.

I want it to mean something.

PART II

INFINITE CRISIS

DAILY TRIUMPH

TOP STORIES | TECH | MAGAZINE | CITY DESK | SPORTS | BUSINESS | ENTERTAINMENT | NATIONAL | STATE

LONGTIME REPORTER FOUND SLAIN

Staff photo by J. Craig

Daily Triumph veteran Simon Upton, brutally murdered by the Mindbender

Excerpt from *The Lynx Returns!* #2, published by New Wave Comics, August 2024.

CHAPTER FIFTEEN

FEBRUARY 10, 2009

The day started with a series of familiar, painful feelings—the cottony mouth, the headache that felt like an ax lodged in my skull, the panicked organizing of What Had Happened vs. What I Remembered—and the unfamiliar. Most prominent in the latter category was the sight of a man—not that it was strange for me to have unexpected hookups, but in this instance the man was on the floor—curled up by my bed, a towel tucked under his head. Next to him was a medium-sized plastic laundry bin. It took me a minute to realize it was Danny. And the bin was for me.

I felt a few memories flash before me. The dive bar excess of Rudy's in Hell's Kitchen. Danny trying to walk me home, dragging me into my own apartment. The feeling of his face pulling away as I tried to kiss him. Then a welcome, lasting void.

I rubbed my eyes roughly and felt the cool touch of the apartment's hardwood floors on my feet. I watched as Danny, in just boxers and his white undershirt, stretched out on the floor—wincing as he straightened up.

"How'd you sleep?" he asked.

"What are you doing here?"

Danny let out a quick, empty laugh.

"You don't remember," he said, more a statement than a question. "I found you drinking alone at Rudy's. I'd been looking all over for you."

"Well, you found me, I guess," I said, shaking my head—at myself, mostly. "Did you . . . did you get fired, too?"

Danny nodded, then paused.

"I quit," he said.

"You what?" I asked, leaning forward, ignoring the dizziness that swept over me.

"Riesling's an asshole," he said with a shrug. "I couldn't keep working for him."

But it was the words Danny chose to keep in reserve that mattered most. Danny had quit because of what Riesling had said to me. I felt a pang of guilt for calling him out in the green room, alongside a flush of admiration for this man.

"Damn, Danny," I said. I reached for the large glass of water on my nightstand and took a long sip. "I'm sorry."

"It's okay," he said, but his expression belied his words. "It was time to go."

I did a quick spot-check of myself, making sure I was decent. Somehow, I noticed, I'd changed into something before bed. I felt my body shudder at the thought of how that might have happened.

"I was drunker than I thought, I guess," I said.

"We made it home, but you woke up in the middle of the night," Danny said. "I had to help you to the bathroom."

I nodded, even though I didn't remember that. I wasn't surprised. My tolerance for alcohol seemed to have changed lately. Just a few drinks and I was worshipping the porcelain god, then blacking out. *A normal person would be worried*, I thought.

"Thanks," I said. I stood up, shakily at first, then with more control. Danny did, too.

"I should leave you to the rest of your day," Danny said. "I should probably . . . I dunno, look for a job or something."

I placed a hand on his chest and looked up at him, trying to smile but wincing because everything seemed to hurt now, inside and out. I hadn't fully processed the shame I was feeling, either. That my child-hood best friend had to basically drag me out of a bar and tuck me in because I was not a functional adult. I tried to defer the shame for a few hours, at least.

"Let me take a shower and I can take you out to breakfast, okay? I owe you that much," I said.

Danny opened his mouth to protest but I raised a hand to silence him.

"I won't hear anything but, *Sure, Annie, how nice of you*," I said.

"Sure, Annie, how nice of you."

"That's better," I said, pulling open a few drawers and collecting some items of clothing. "That wasn't so hard."

I could already feel myself breaking out into a cold sweat—the early gears of a rough, day-long hangover kicking into high gear. "Give me ten minutes and we can try to enjoy the outside world for a bit. There's a good bagel place on 207th Street I think you'll like."

Pile of fresh clothes in hand, I sidestepped Danny as he struggled to put on his own jeans and flannel shirt. I caught him watching me as I opened the door to my bedroom. Our eyes met.

"You kissed me."

Danny's words hovered between us as I swallowed a bite of a whole-wheat everything and cream cheese. We'd reached the outer edges of Inwood Hill Park, the sun relatively bright—offsetting the painful chill that seemed to have permeated the city this winter. I blinked a few times before responding.

"Sorry?"

"Are you asking me or telling me?" Danny asked, crumpling up his bagel wrapper and tossing it into a nearby trash bin. "I mean, it's fine—Annie, we're friends. You were drunk. I get it. We have a lot of, I dunno, unresolved stuff between us."

I took a hesitant sip of my large coffee, wincing as the hot liquid singed my lips.

"Danny, I—Okay, first off, I am sorry," I said, stopping for a moment and turning to face him. "I don't remember doing that. It is still not okay, even if we are friends, because we never laid down those ground rules. Are those even rules? Like, *We are cool to hook up with each other drunk?* What are you okay with? I don't know. It's not a big deal. Anyway, I made a mistake. I'm a mess. Now, that brings me to my first question . . . 'unresolved stuff'? The hell does that mean, Danny Alvarez? Because we almost fucked once, in college? Isn't that just what happens, right?"

Now it was Danny's turn to look sheepish. I could see his cheeks redden slightly, his eyes narrowing, too—a sign that he'd said too much. I thought it was cute. Even now.

"I just . . . how do I say this without acting like I'm twelve?"

"You're a man, everything you do is like you're twelve," I said with a chuckle.

"I just know you like me," he said, then immediately took a huge bite of his own sandwich, as if by doing so he'd exonerate himself from having to elaborate. Instead, he got a spray of coffee from my mouth.

"I like you? What?" I said, my voice more of a howl than speech. "Sorry, sorry, you just—what the hell, Danny? I like you? You were not kidding about—"

"Am I wrong?" Danny said, his expression serious now, as he took a step toward me. Not threatening, but closing ranks almost—as if it were something only I was supposed to hear. "I like to think I can tell, and you've been giving me signals since as far back as I can remember."

Before I could say anything else, Danny started to cough—a wet, drawn-out sound that made me feel instantly uneasy.

"You okay?"

He nodded, patting his chest gingerly. "Yeah, fine, just—I dunno, re-covering from last night," he said.

I let it go, plopping down on a nearby bench, on the edge of a small playground, and tried to watch the handful of small children play. I tapped the space next to me, motioning for Danny to sit. When he did, I continued.

"I didn't think you could tell," I said, not meeting Danny's stare, still looking at the playground, at the small dark-haired girl going down the slide headfirst. "I'd given up on that, you know?"

Danny said nothing.

I turned to look at him.

"But what's so weird about that? About you and me? Why is that crazy?" I asked. "What's scary about us?"

I could feel my eyes welling up, and I cursed the alcohol still mov-ing through my veins. Hated how raw I felt right now. Hated how my emotions had been in complete chaos for what felt like forever—but especially lately.

Now it was Danny's turn to look away. He leaned forward, elbows on his knees, and watched the same girl I had been looking at. But I could tell he was just trying to formulate a response. Danny was always careful. He was even-keeled, funny, calm, easygoing. Everything I wasn't—or wasn't naturally.

"What do you want me to say?" he said, still not looking at me. "You're my best friend. You know I love you, of course I do. But there's a lot go-ing on. I don't think I'm ready for something else."

I felt the words bubbling up, unable to stop them.

"Why not?" I said. "Why not more? Is it weird to even think that? I've had a crush on you since we were teenagers, Danny. You're just going to pretend like my feelings are something you can slide into a bag, then put in a box in your closet, hidden until you want to look at them again? I'm not a comic book."

Danny leaned back, still not looking at me, hands behind his head now as he stared up at the late morning sun.

"I want us to live our dreams," he said. I wasn't sure, but I thought I heard his voice cracking. Or had I imagined it? "I want us to make comics together. The kind of comics we read as kids. The kind of books that got us excited when we were sitting in the cafeteria trading issues and cards. You know what I mean? Like, really doing this work together. I thought Renegade would be it, but . . . I fucked that up. I feel responsible for what happened."

I sent a playful shove into Danny's shoulder.

"I got fired and you quit in solidarity," I said with a scoff. "I think you've paid whatever price there is to pay. And we tried. I mean, I know you were protecting me from more bullshit than I could ever imagine. It happens. We'll get to work on something soon."

I slid a few inches closer to Danny on the bench, draping an arm around him. He leaned into the hug, the warmth of his face next to mine.

"We'll do this," I said, my voice barely above a whisper, my mouth close to his ear. "We'll make something great."

He turned to me, his face closer than he'd intended, probably. We were inches apart, our breathing slow and jagged at once—a moment we both knew was coming but had danced around for too long.

His hand was touching my face, his delicate fingers sliding over my left temple—over the scar at the top of my cheek—the one I got while playing with him, when we were kids. Running around his backyard. The wound had long since healed, but the scar remained. His fingertips felt warm and electric on my face.

I hesitated for a split second before kissing him.

CHAPTER SIXTEEN

APPARITION wants you to download Signal.

stared at the text message and frowned. I couldn't chalk it up to spam anymore. I remembered Spinoza's warning—words that echoed the last mystery text I'd received just a few days prior.

BE CAREFUL.

I just happened to be looking at my phone while curled up on the couch with Margot, midway through what felt like our hundredth viewing of *Spirited Away*. I had my iPad on my lap, working on some digital layouts for *The Lynx Returns!* #2. I'd transfer them onto actual paper—with the pencil strokes in blue, or "blue lines"—and work off those later, turning them into usable pages. I put my digital pen to iPad and watched as the Lynx and her world appeared. I added more detail—tightening up the loose shapes and wiggles and turning them into actual set pieces and people. The look of the book was coming to life. The—God help me—vibe. I'd been working away at the story and art on my own for so long, I hadn't even considered anyone looking at it, much less liking it—let alone Arturo Spinoza. Even now, in my dimly lit living room, the sound of the movie and Margot's breathing lulled me into some kind of hypnotic state, where I could just zone out and create. It felt good. Like a muscle I'd ignored for too long. But then that damn text message.

APPARITION wants you to download Signal.

I felt a jolt of nerves. The same wobbly feeling I'd get while on a roller coaster, as it reached the apex of the wave, right before your stomach flipped and the whole thing went south. That sense that everything was going to change on the molecular level—and it might not be good. Before I could drill down on the thought, Margot turned to meet my gaze.

"What?"

"Nothing," I said. "Just lost my train of thought. You enjoying the movie?"

Margot shrugged and smiled at me, leaning her head on the couch cushions.

"You love this movie, Mami," she said, smiling. "It's why we watch it. It's like comfort food for you."

I laughed and turned my attention back to my iPad. I felt Margot inch closer, her face next to mine as she looked down at the page I was laying out.

"That her?" she asked. "Those shapes there?"

The page was a shot of Claudia Calla stepping into the bathroom and being surprised at her own reflection: the Lynx. It was a turning point in the story. The first clue that things were more complicated for mild-mannered Claudia. That there were many secrets left for her to unearth about herself and her role in it.

"Yup. That's our girl Claudia," I said. "The Legendary Lynx."

"I love that panel," Margot said, her finger hovering over the one that showed Claudia seeing the Lynx in her reflection. "I love how the figures mirror each other, and her expression—the surprise—is really perfect, Mami."

Spinoza had been right, I thought. I'd wanted this—for Margot to see me working in comics, actually working on them. I'd never thought it'd happen, not after so much time—Renegade, Danny, my film career. Whatever land mines awaited, I was grateful for Bert Carlyle's email. At least I thought so.

I watched Margot's smooth, familiar features aglow from the TV screen light. It was strange to see a version of myself at a different age. Because that's what Margot looked like to me—we had the same facial structure, expressions, despite our different moods and demeanors. If you looked at us, you knew immediately we were mother and daughter. I'd pored over pictures of myself around Margot's age. If I hadn't known that the pictures were of me, I would've guessed they were Margot. Everything except the eyes. In place of my deep dark brown eyes there were a pair of sharp, sky-blue ones.

I turned my attention back to the iPad. I'd laid out most of the second issue by now, and it was all flowing. I looked down at another file I'd brought up on my iPad—another character design—my take on the modern Lynx, after Claudia reclaimed her mantle and became Triumph City's defender once more. I actually liked it, and it took me a good while to appreciate my own work. Detmer would dig it, too, I thought. I'd found a way to honor the Lynx—to honor him, I realized—but also make it my own.

As the movie's end credits started to roll, I guided Margot to bed and tucked her in. I put my iPad away and stood in the middle of my living room. *I should feel tired*, I thought. It'd been a long week. But drawing had a way of energizing me—of making me want to run around outside and look at everything, absorbing every detail into my art brain.

Then my phone vibrated. It was that same message. Again. Whoever was sending these was persistent.

APPARITION wants you to download Signal.

I knew what Signal was—I had enough journalist friends, like Laura, who'd used it or apps like it—encrypted ways to communicate with sources or people you didn't want tracked. That wasn't what jumped out at me—it was the name, APPARITION.

If you knew the Lynx—knew the character and her world the way I did—you knew who Apparition was. Hilary Finch. The murdered heiress who appears to Claudia Calla at her sister's funeral—offering to train her to become a street-level vigilante. She returns to her former protégée years later—to ask for a favor: the Lynx's help in capturing the man who murdered her.

It was one of my favorites. I loved it not only because of the meaningful female friendship between the two heroes, one that bordered on romantic—at least as close as one could get in those Comics Code Authority days—but also because of how different it was. It showed *The Legendary Lynx* was willing to go weird, to tap into the supernatural and mystical in a way other crime fighters of the era didn't, and wouldn't until books like Frank Miller's *Daredevil* or the Doug Moench/Bill Sienkiewicz run on *Moon Knight*. The Lynx saga went all in and completely blew my mind.

Apparition.

I tapped the download link, which took me to a registration page. I followed the instructions and waited for the message to load. Finally, the message:

APPARITION: You have something that's mine.

I typed a quick response.

Who are you?

"Apparition" was active, the ellipses signaling that this was basically a live chat. A few moments later, a response.

APPARITION: Your murdered friend—Laura Gustines. Ever read
her book?

It was a trick question, I thought. Laura's book—a collection of
interviews titled *Secret Identity: A Look at the Lost Women Who Shaped
Comics*—had never been released. I knew this because Laura had mentioned the project to me a handful of times. Laura had died in a terrible
carjacking before she could finish it.

There is no book. Who is this?

APPARITION: I'm Apparition. A ghost that will
train you to be the Lynx.

Not funny.

APPARITION: Who's joking, Annie?

Deleting this now. Bye.

APPARITION: Before you do, look into your
friend's book. Open your eyes.

Who is this?

After a few minutes, it was clear "Apparition" wasn't going to respond.
I gritted my teeth and tried to ignore the texts, push them out of my
mind. It could've been anyone, I reasoned—an obsessive fan, a prankster,
hell, it could be Carlyle or Doyle testing my loyalty, or Spinoza un-
spooling some weird conspiracy. But none of that tracked. What did this
"Apparition" want from me? Laura Gustines was dead. Whatever she'd
been working on was lost to the world.

Wasn't it?

I groaned as I reached for my laptop. Now I was tired. But I was also
curious. And once I got started on something, it was nearly impossible
to derail me.

I googled "Secret Identity book Laura Gustines" and waited a second.

I found Laura's old author site, now inactive. Then I found an Amazon link that sent me to a 404 error page. This was going nowhere. Then something else—a brief interview on a site called the Comics Beat. I was familiar with the site and had probably spoken to them a half-dozen times over my comics career. The chat was between Laura and the site's owner / editor in chief, Heidi MacDonald. It was all over the place— mostly discussing Laura's role at the *Times* and her career as a comics critic—what graphic novels she liked to review, what she was reading, the general stuff. Not a lot about the book itself. Not until the end.

I wasn't sure what I'd been looking for—a kernel of a clue, a small glimmer of something I could file away and mull over. Something small, for sure. Nothing like this, though.

I read over Laura's quote. Twice. Three times.

COMICS BEAT: What else are you working on, outside of your day job at the *Times*?

GUSTINES: Well, I'm really excited about this project and, uh, I'm not really even sure I should be talking about it since we haven't announced it—but it's a book that started being about all the lost women of comics. You know, the creators and editors and other people who just seemed to be forgotten. And I was so happy with that. But as I drilled down deeper, I found a story that kind of exemplified it—my thesis. And as I kept writing, it made more and more sense to focus on that story, and have the others kind of serve as an echo, or a Greek chorus, em- phasizing what this story, well, teaches us. I'm heading to this one woman's house—this week—to talk about her work. She's basically disappeared—no one knew where she lived or what she was up to. She'd gone completely off the grid, but I'd found her, and she agreed to speak with me. I think she'll reveal some tidbits that I've only been able to piece together after years and years of research. Something that would uproot the perception of an entire company and character.

COMICS BEAT: Wow. Any clues you can share about the company? Is it an active publisher?

GUSTINES: I'm going to keep that to myself for now, but I will say that my hope is the book will reveal something even die-hard comic fans never knew—and shed a light on how some of these characters came to be. And, in a way, who has a claim to them.

I frowned.

If the creator Laura was talking about was Carmen Valdez—and there was little reason to think it wasn't—then she'd unearthed a secret within a secret. She'd not only tracked down one of comics' forgotten people—someone who'd intentionally disappeared from the landscape and was thought forever lost—but Laura had also unlocked a secret Valdez had maintained for decades, in the wake of whatever had happened with her and the Lynx. Laura had done what no one else had.

Had that killed her?

The thought appeared in my mind fully formed, like it'd been there all along, just waiting for me to look in its direction and dust it off.

It was a theory, I thought. I decided to test it.

I pulled out my phone and looked up Laura's obit. The "carjacking" had happened on October 10, 2018. I hopped to my mail app and looked up her email address. I had a few emails from her around that time:

Hey buuuuddy, so good to hear from you!!!! Things are hectic, for sure. Thanks for asking about the book, yeah—I'm heading out to do some research soon! Going up to Cape Cod tomorrow to interview someone. Fingers crossed this is the end, last final piece before I can send my MS to my editor. How's by you? How's Margot??? Kid keeps growing like a weed, huh? Give her a kiss from Auntie Laura!

The email was dated October 9, 2018.

My mouth felt dry.

I scrolled back and caught a glimpse of another, even earlier email from Laura—one about a comic book archive theft, belonging to some guy named Stuart Alford. It didn't seem related, but felt oddly important. I starred the email and moved it to my inbox.

I sat down on the edge of my bed and stared at my phone display. I couldn't tell for how long.

I found an old number I hadn't called in years.

Before I realized it, the phone was ringing.

"Annie?" the voice on the other end said, sounding hoarse and confused.

"Pete, hey, yeah—sorry to call so late," I said.

"It's fine—just gimme a second," Pete Fernandez said. "Not usually up this late."

Pete was an old Miami friend. We'd gone to high school together, drunk a ton in tandem and apart in college and beyond, tried to stay in touch, but ended up losing contact for years—until we both reconnected thanks to our mutual attempts at sobriety. He'd been through a lot—but I trusted him.

"How's Gracie?" I asked. Pete had a young daughter with his partner—in life and work—Kathy Bentley. I liked Kathy.

"She's good—typical four-year-old. Wants to do whatever she wants to do," Pete said. He sounded exhausted. I remembered those days. "Took forever to get to sleep. Kathy was just in there with her now."

A brief pause. Then Pete cleared his throat.

"But you didn't call to check in on me," he said.

"Pete, listen—I need a favor."

CHAPTER SEVENTEEN

My first portfolio review happened fairly early—before I'd even booked a paying gig—at a small convention in a hotel ballroom in Miami Beach. I'd waited in line for two hours to speak to an editor named Rich Berger—who, while seemingly unemployed, had long stints at companies like DC, Triumph, Valiant, and Rampart. By the time I'd gotten to the front of the line, it was almost dinnertime and the aging Berger looked like he was ready to be wheeled to the final session of shuffleboard on the front lawn. But the elderly editor seemed to light up when he saw my work—a sequence of Lynx pages I had hastily slapped together the week before the show. I hadn't even been sure I was going to attend, but Danny had insisted.

"You have to take a shot, Annie," I remembered him saying over and over. "You've got real talent. Not trying your best would be a waste."

I loved him for moments like that. Lightning bolts of true, unabashed friendship. Genuine caring.

"These are rough, I won't lie," Berger had said, repositioning his thick wire-frame glasses. I tried to follow his eyes and ignore the crumbs of food trapped in his thick gray mustache. "The perspective is wonky here." He tapped on the opening splash, where the Lynx was leaping into the night, her sometimes-partner Apparition floating beside her. "And I can't tell what happens between these panels." Tapping again. "The flow is off. You have to remember—you're telling the story. You're the director of the movie. If I can't understand what's happening by just looking at your art, you've failed. You understand?"

Our eyes met and I nodded. I could see this man actually cared about the craft, even after being eaten alive by the industry. I felt a kinship toward him, even though I wasn't yet fodder for comics myself. He cleared his throat. "But the energy is good. It feels like you've lived in this world. You know the name Detmer? Doug Detmer?"

I told him I did.

"Right, well, he's gone now, killed himself," Berger said with a pained shake of his head, the words delivered with the blunt precision only the aged could create. "But when he was around? He was the best. Total pain to work with. So painful you'd wonder why you hired him. But, man, guy could draw. You could smell the streets. Hear the cars honking. Feel the dirty wind of the city on your face. He was up there with Adams or Colan. Guys like Frank Miller—they took a page from Doug Detmer without even knowing."

I started to respond, but Berger pressed on.

"There's something here, something in these pages," he said, the words drifting away. "They feel like those. Not nearly as good, of course. You've got a long way to go. But you treat the line with the same . . . well, respect. You're trying to do more than crank something out. You want to create something lasting. He was like that. An asshole, a drunk, but a genius."

Berger's eyes lost their focus, and the older man seemed to be somewhere else.

"He created the Lynx," I said matter-of-factly, a sprinkling of pride in the words—as if throwing out the tidbit of knowledge would win me brownie points with this unemployed relic of a man. But somehow, that felt like a true victory—impressing a guy who actually worked on *The Legendary Lynx*. "With Harvey Stern, right? And Carlyle?"

Berger cleared his throat. He straightened up the pile of pages and handed them back to me quickly.

"Don't believe everything you read on the Internet," Berger said with a snarl. "Especially if it came out of Jeffrey Carlyle's mouth."

"I didn't mean to offend—" I stammered.

Berger shrugged as he stood up.

"Trust me, you're not even close. But as you get along in your career—if you stick with it—you'll soon discover that the history of these characters . . ." Berger said, motioning toward the Lynx pages with his chin. "It's written by the companies that own them, not by the people who actually created the characters. If you think Jeffrey Carlyle and Harvey Stern had more than a passing influence on the Lynx, you have a lot more to learn. I wish you well on that journey, kid."

As I took my pages back, I watched Berger slowly pull himself away from his seat. I heard the man behind me in line mumble something about how Berger was supposed to be here for another hour.

"I'm just taking a piss," Berger said, not looking at the man. "I'll be back."

I figured that was that, and started to turn away, tried to carve out the compliment Berger had paid me and leave the rest—the weird, uncomfortable, and confusing—behind. I felt sorry for this man, who'd clearly done so much for the medium, but was now a jaded, burned-out zombie just trying to make a living—forced to sit at conventions across the country rehashing old war stories he would rather forget. I was happy to leave.

But then Berger spoke again.

"What's your name?"

"Annie," I said. "Annie Bustamante."

Berger's eyes narrowed for a second.

"Are you from New York?" he asked. The question seemed to come from nowhere.

I shook my head.

"No, born and raised here in Miami," I said. "My mom was up there for a few years, before I was born, though. Inez."

Berger seemed to glaze over at the mention of my mom, as if returning to reality from a brief dream. He'd be dead in a few years, whatever secrets he'd collected over his life lost to time and age.

He looked at me again, raising a finger to point at the Lynx pages I was clutching to my chest.

"Well, listen, Annie Bustamante from Miami—keep drawing. I think you've got something here. Don't let anyone tell you otherwise."

I tried to respond, but he kept talking.

"And that character? The Lynx?" Berger said. "She's as much yours as anyone else's."

CHAPTER EIGHTEEN

I woke up thinking about Laura Gustines—and Carmen Valdez.

I'd had a dream where I was in California, visiting an older woman—who, in my mind, was Carmen, though I'd never met her—and she was lying in her bed. Her caretaker was nudging her to go to sleep, to ignore what was going on—there was a loud noise outside, like drilling. I was there, too, talking with her about comics. She implored me to help her up. I tried to, but then the dream ended and I awoke with a bubbling sense of dread no amount of coffee or good cheer could shake.

Margot could tell something was up as I sat across from her in the kitchen nook. I wasn't really great at hiding it, either, if we're being honest. She looked up at me between shovels of Cheerios, a novel carelessly cracked open on the table next to her. She reached out and placed a hand on mine.

"What's up?" she asked. "You've got that *the world is ending where do we go* vibe, Mami."

"Do I?"

"Yeah, to, like, a hundred," Margot said, frowning. "Would you like to share with the group?"

I made a clicking sound with my tongue.

"I don't know, I've just been feeling . . . strange about, well, something Spinoza said to me," I said, trying to find the right way to describe my anxiety to my daughter without, in turn, giving her anxiety. "It's just made me wonder about who actually . . . owns the Lynx?"

"Doesn't the company own her?" Margot asked innocently.

I started to respond when the buzz of my cell phone cut the moment short.

"Hello?"

"Hey, it's Pete," he said. "You got a minute?"

"I do," I responded, getting up from the table, leaving Margot with a soft pat on her hand. "Let me just get to my office."

I wove through our spacious living room and closed the door behind me.

"What's up? You work fast, Pete."

"I've gotten good at my job, what can I say," Pete said with a chuckle. "Okay, I don't have much, but what I do have is interesting."

I sat down at my desk and cracked open my laptop, the phone on speaker.

"What is it?"

I heard the sound of shuffling paper on the other end.

"So, it seems like your friend's book was ready to go—it was announced to the book trades via *Publishers Weekly* and *Publishers Marketplace*, so people knew it was coming. Not a lot of people, but book people and lawyers," Pete said. "That'll be relevant in a bit. Anyway, it was in the system—listed on Amazon, Barnes & Noble, everywhere. There was no cover yet, but the metadata existed and was public, so that meant a cover was coming soon."

I knew the basics of book publishing, even though it was quite different from the traditional comic book shop–driven system that superhero comics had used for decades.

"Was the book done?" I asked.

"Good question," Pete said. "Based on the initial announcement, I got for the name of her editor—lady named Yasmin Morris at Flatiron Books. I sent her an email but got a bounce-back."

"So, she's gone?"

Pete sighed.

"Annie, let me finish. People change jobs all the time, especially during the pandemic, and especially in publishing," Pete said. "This book was announced in 2017, and then crickets, except for a handful of interviews—particularly one with a comic trade site called Comics Beat. I emailed you the link—"

"I read it last night," I said. "Before we spoke."

"Either way, that interview—as you saw—seemed to imply Laura's book was changing. And she was heading to meet with someone for a pivotal interview."

"And she died shortly after it was posted," I said. "Also, she emailed me the day before she left—October ninth. The day before she died."

"Right," Pete said. "Again, her editor left the publisher, but I tracked her down."

"Yasmin Morris."

"Right, she's running a book-packaging company, whatever that means," Pete said. I heard the familiar wail of a young child in the background. The sound triggered a primal response in me to run and help. I didn't miss those days. "Look, I don't have a lot of time. I can hear Kathy losing what's left of her patience."

"I appreciate this," I said. "Just let me know what—"

"Don't start," Pete said. "I'm just helping a friend, okay? Back to Morris—she told me that Gustines was on a research trip and was on her way back from it when she got carjacked. Morris said she was going to interview one of the creators she planned to spotlight in the book. It was a big deal for Gustines, apparently."

"Did Morris say who? Did she say where Laura went?"

There was a moment or two of silence.

"That's what got weird," Pete said. "I asked her that this morning, point-blank. She was very chatty and friendly, even excited to be talking about the book and Laura, until I asked where Laura had been coming from. Yasmin seemed genuinely nervous when I pressed her on it, but I finally got her to say who she was visiting."

"Carmen Valdez," I said, knowing I was right before Pete confirmed it.

"Yes, exactly. See, you don't need me, Annie," Pete said. "From what I could piece together, Laura Gustines was in Cape Cod, heading back from a meeting with Carmen Valdez. She was the last person Laura spoke to before she died."

"A fact she basically made public in the interview before going to see Carmen Valdez," I said matter-of-factly. "Enough time for someone to . . . intercept her."

I could hear Pete take in a sharp breath.

"You're saying she was murdered?"

"I'm saying it could happen," I said, surprised at my own words. "And if it did happen, I want to find out what Carmen Valdez told her. Can you get me Yasmin's address?"

Another scream cut through the call.

"Look, Annie, I have to run. I just texted you her number and I'll get you her other info, too," Pete said, clearly more interested in our call than in dealing with a four-year-old's tantrum. "But be careful, okay? Having dealt with this stuff . . . all the time, well—it seems like someone didn't want whatever Valdez said to be made public in a book that was sure to be promoted like crazy and read by a lot of people in the business. Something seems way off here. These people—they wanted Carmen to stay hidden. And her secrets to stay buried."

Pete Fernandez's words hung over the rest of the day, and the one thought that seemed to stick in my mind was clear: I needed to talk to Carmen Valdez, and quickly.

If Carmen had a claim on the character—what did that say about Triumph's rush to get their version out there? Was I putting everything at risk by even considering a pilgrimage to Cape Cod? Probably. But I couldn't proceed as if everything were fine—not with what I knew now. I also had no idea where Carmen Valdez was, Cape Cod or not.

I replayed these thoughts as I dropped a few apples into my shopping cart at Trader Joe's.

"Mami? Mom?"

I turned to Margot, who was standing next to me, a hand on the shopping cart. "You know what? I think we should take a trip."

"Uh, okay. Where?"

"I'm thinking Cape Cod," I said with a laugh.

"What's there? I mean, it sounds nice, but, y'know . . ." Margot said with a shrug.

"Carmen Valdez," I said. It felt empowering to speak her name aloud. Like summoning strength from some lost spirit.

"Okay, Detective Bosch," Margot said sarcastically. "Get to the bottom of this whole thing, yeah?"

I smiled and gave her a playful shoulder-tap.

My phone buzzed. I looked at the display and saw an unknown number. I picked up.

"Hello?"

"Where are you?" Spinoza. "Annie? Are you there?"

"I'm . . . at the grocery store," I said. Spinoza sounded desperate—panicked. "What's up? Are you okay?"

"No, most definitely not okay," Spinoza said. I could hear clanging and some papers rustling on the other end. I pictured Spinoza darting around his spartan office.

"I don't get how you survive being so disconnected," Spinoza said. Before I could respond, he continued. "Just check your phone and call me back. I'm sure I'm not the only person that's looking to get in touch with you."

Spinoza clicked off. I looked at my phone display and noticed I had forty-five unread emails—which wasn't insane, considering the amount of newsletter, political campaign, and store emails I routinely got, but

I had checked my email before we got into the store less than twenty minutes ago. I felt a cloak of fear and anxiety fall over me. I clicked on the mail icon and scrolled through the messages.

The subject lines were jarring: "Wow, Annie!" "CONGRATS!!!" "Just saw the story . . ." "<no subject>" "Um . . ."

I was scared to click on any of them. Not like this. Not completely blind to what they were talking about. I felt a tug at my arm.

"Mami, are you okay?"

"I dunno, kiddo—but I think we need to leave."

Margot sat in the passenger seat of my compact car, scrolling through her own tablet while I processed just what the hell was going on.

A simple Google search had pointed me in the right direction. A story on the Hollywood news and gossip site *Deadline*: BREAKING NEWS: NEWLY FORMED TRIUMPH ENTERTAINMENT LAUNCHES AMBITIOUS FILM, PUBLISHING SLATE.

The brief story cut to the chase immediately, announcing the "rebirth" of "long-shuttered" comic book company Triumph Comics as "Triumph Entertainment."

The new company, headed by Jeffrey Carlyle's son, Bert, was intent on recapturing the original company's publishing success—I scoffed loudly—and translating it into a multi-platform media empire. All the buzzwords were there, even in just a handful of sentences. It wasn't the PR-speak that bothered me, that was par for the course—it was the details that were being unveiled, completely without my knowledge or sign-off.

The story went on to confirm that Triumph Entertainment's first order of business was to create a film based on "the company's most beloved character, the Legendary Lynx, created by Bert Carlyle's father, Jeffrey Carlyle, with help from artist Doug Detmer and the Triumph Comics bullpen of editors."

Another scoff.

"I can tell you're super-pissed," Margot said, "just based on the number of sighs and clicky sounds you make with your tongue."

I let out a dry laugh.

"It's this . . . announcement," I said, still scrolling. "It's basically talking about my project, but nothing's been confirmed on my end—and they've got the history of the character all wrong. Not to mention who her creators are. It's very weird, and it feels . . ."

Intentional.

I kept reading. The brief confirmed that the film *The Lethal Lynx* would be helmed by critically acclaimed and "controversial" film director Arturo Spinoza. The film—and any potential sequels—would be "thoughtfully paired" with a new comic book, marking the return of "fan-favorite" comic book artist/writer Annie Bustamante (director of the Oscar-nominated *Red Barry* and the recently shelved *Miss Midnight*), after a long stint working as a major film director and storyboard artist. The buzzwords seemed to glow on the screen. "Synergy." "Multiplatform." "Strategic rollout." And, hey, that was fine—but what got under my skin wasn't the garbled press-release language—it was the timing and method.

Just a few days ago, Jessica Doyle had revealed to me she knew I was Doug Detmer's daughter. It was clear Triumph Entertainment felt threatened somehow—as if I'd have a claim to the character because of my father.

I was furious.

I called my agent.

"Took you long enough," Gary said, skipping any kind of preamble.

"What the fuck, Gary?" I said, turning to Margot and mouthing a hurried *Sorry!*

"It's an old play," Gary said. I felt some comfort at his familiar, methodical voice—like a chess master setting up the pieces. "They talk first—announce the details on their terms, forcing you to either go along or go public and seem difficult. Doesn't work as well these days, at least not with notable celebrities or name authors, but they're betting that you want to do this bad enough that you'll swallow your pride and not make a fuss."

"So what do we do?"

Gary sighed. "Let's rewind to a few days ago, when good ol' Uncle Gary was very clear that this was not the best fit for—"

"Don't rub it in," I said. "It's unbecoming."

Gary laughed—a hearty no-worries laugh that just made me jealous. I couldn't remember the last time I'd laughed like that.

"Tell them I'm gone, that I don't want to do the comic anymore," I said, my hands shaking. I was trying to keep my voice calm and level because Margot was right there, but Margot had seen me in worse situations. She'd be fine. She was tougher than me. "They have a few days to get their ducks in a row before I go public, or they can reach out and have a sensible conversation. Those are their options."

There was a brief silence on the other end of the line.

"You sure you want to go hard? I mean, I don't disagree, I just want to do a quick spot-check. And, hey, you could use the money, right?"

"It's my only real card to play," I said. "Plus, I just promised my kid a weekend away, so I'll be out-of-pocket anyway."

I told Gary to let me know what they responded with and hung up the phone.

When it vibrated again, I just assumed it was Gary—calling back with some question or new detail—but it wasn't. It was another Signal alert.

APPARITION: Are you complicit with those lies?

I tapped out a reply.

I had nothing to do with that announcement.
APPARITION: Then do something about it.

I waited a beat, thinking of what to say. It could be anyone on the other end of this encrypted chat. Or no one. What was I getting into?

Like what?

APPARITION: Go to the Source Wall.

What? Where??

A few moments passed with nothing. Apparition wasn't online anymore.

The Source Wall. A trippy idea from Kirby's Fourth World comics—the basic source of, well, everything in the DC superhero universe. In this instance, though, it was a nod to me and a nod to who I was talking to. Or so I hoped.

I sent a quick text to Pete Fernandez. Then I slid my phone back into my pocket and looked at Margot, who was staring back—wide-eyed and worried.

"Mami, are you okay?"

I smiled. For the first time in a long time, it was a relaxed, genuine smile.

"I'm great, kiddo," I said, pulling her in for a hug. "I know what to do now."

CHAPTER NINETEEN

Where are you going?"

I'd woken up to Danny coughing. A soggy, loud cough that he clearly couldn't control. I saw him frozen mid-step in my bedroom—like a cat burglar who'd seen a light flicker on in another room.

It was early in the morning. A time of morning I was not used to seeing. Danny was in his boxers and nothing else. He had a pile of his wrinkled clothes in his hands. I rubbed my eyes. It was the clothes that gave him away. I'd been in this scenario too many times to not understand it, Danny or otherwise.

He was leaving.

"I—uh, I have to get going," Danny said.

"Where?" I asked, genuine curiosity in my voice. I wasn't mad—more perplexed than anything. "You're unemployed. I'm unemployed. Why not come back to bed?"

Danny's shoulders slumped.

I'd been half expecting this, honestly. After that hungover kiss in the park, I knew there was an expiration date on whatever was happening. But I wanted to enjoy it. This felt like I was being shortchanged somehow—something I really wanted to savor, even if for a limited time, was being yanked away early. Like a superhero forced to leave a date because the Fearsome Five were destroying Manhattan.

I'd even let myself pretend—to imagine some kind of fantasyland where it'd be more than this, more than a fleeting engagement. How could this not work out? I'd thought to myself, as we stumbled back to my apartment—stopping every few blocks, our mouths hungry and open and grazing over each other, our hands and bodies exploring and crashing into each other. It'd felt like it could last forever.

But he was leaving now.

"It's not a big deal," Danny said, pulling on his pants—trying to balance himself on the flimsy desk that dominated the corner of my tiny, cluttered bedroom. "I didn't want to wake you up."

Crates of comics and drawing supplies littered the floor. Art rested against walls, never to be hung. Half-empty glasses and dusty stacks of books and DVDs stationed on every free surface. A room—a life—in transit. Incomplete.

"Well, I'm awake," I said, hating the pleading in my voice. "Let's go get breakfast? Or try to go back to—"

"I have to go."

His voice didn't waver. The words were definitive and sliced through whatever ideas I had been trying to form about who we were, or what we could be together, creating a vast, empty void.

I let out a dry, unsurprised laugh. Humorless and dead.

"No jodas tanto, Danny. I know you too well for this act," I said, sitting up, the sheets wrapping around my naked body. "When did you get tired of it? What moment made you scared? I'm a big girl. I can take it."

He opened his mouth to reply, stopped, then started again.

"I'm sorry," he said. It sounded hollow. It was hollow.

"Then go," I said.

* * *

My moment of clarity came later, though. After a few weeks of wallowing over Danny, I decided enough was enough. I showered, changed into a nice outfit, and just . . . walked out. It didn't take long for me to find a bar, though I'd never, for the life of me, remember the place's name—but that wasn't important. I just wanted to feel something different—something that didn't occur inside my apartment or in my head.

I remembered sliding into a seat at the bar, which was mostly empty—not the kind of lively place I'd imagined or hoped for. I ordered a Seven and Seven, which I rarely drank—I was a vodka-and-soda girl, but tonight had to be different.

The blackout came slowly. Some call it a "brownout"—a muddy, shadowy loss of senses instead of everything suddenly going dark. I'd never experienced it before. Something new and scary.

I ordered another round and talked to a thin dude with the black hair and bent glasses sitting next to me. I could hear Warren Zevon on the jukebox—and talked to the man, named Steve, about it. I felt his hand tapping my shoulder, then resting on my back a second too long.

I wiggled away from his touch and pulled out my phone. I scrolled for a few seconds before my eyes could focus on the headline from a random comic book website. The news slammed into me like a baseball bat to my midsection. I gasped.

"Former Blast Radius editor Daniel Alvarez named EIC at indie start-up Spiral Comics."

He'd had a job all along.

I googled the company. They were based in Los Angeles. He was leaving.

I'm not proud of this, but I text-bombed him, my eyes blurring with what had to be tears.

Were you going to tell me??

LA, huh? Happy for you---I guess.

Thanks for the heads up.

You there?

Have a great life.

Fuck you.

I was hunched over the barstool, staring at the story now, sniffing and wiping my eyes hastily, not caring who was around—whatever was happening in the world outside of me and this screen.

I knew I should leave and go home. Take a shower, get some rest, think about what to do next. Process how I was feeling. I thought of the pregnancy test I'd taken the day before. The two lines that seemed to scream out at me and shake me to my very core.

I didn't care about long-term thinking. I felt pain and I wanted the pain to go away.

I drained the rest of my glass—a vodka soda this time—and motioned for the bartender, who seemed to hesitate for a split second. *These guys*, I thought, *fucking alcohol hall monitors.*

"Just fill it up," I slurred, sliding the glass across to the bartender— who complied.

"Hey."

I turned around slowly. It was the thin dude, sitting next to me, his hand on the back of my stool, his breath hot on my neck. Had we already been talking? I couldn't tell. He reminded me of Danny.

"Fuck him," I muttered to myself.

"What?"

"Nothing, nothing," I said, not even turning to face—Steve? I wasn't sure.

Thin Steve was showing me something—his palm up under the bar. I couldn't make it out, my eyes desperate for focus. It was a small baggie of white powder. I looked up at Thin Steve's face—a face I hadn't really noticed before. Long and lupine, his teeth bared in a smile. His eyes were dark—distant and black. If I'd been sober and seen this guy coming toward me on the street, I would've crossed to the other side.

But I wasn't sober—I was drunk and mad and I wanted to disappear.

The blurring got worse. A hasty walk to the bathroom. Dry lips on my mouth. Hands groping and grabbing, sliding under my shirt. My face close to a flimsy-dirty sink that smelled of hand soap and beer, the white powder shooting up my nose—Thin Steve watching hungrily as he took his turn, desperate for another bump. Then a fleeting glance at myself in the mirror. The dark circles under my eyes, my hair strewn and out of place, a smear of lipstick on the corner of my mouth.

It all felt so sad. The latest episode in a series of pathetic instances. My eyes dead and dull. It hit me hard. This needle in a haystack of bad choices stood out for one brief moment.

"No," I said, backing away from the mirror. Stumbling back. "No."

"Hey, what—yo, we're cool, right?" Thin Steve said, turning to face me, wiping at his nose. It was bleeding now, I saw.

"Oh fuck," he said, wiping his nose and looking at his fingers. I backed out of the tiny bathroom, heard the soft whine of the hinges.

I could feel the eyes of the bar's few patrons on me—the bartender's cranky mumble as I slapped a pair of twenties on the counter. I tripped over a tiny step before I fell out of the doorway into the Manhattan night—clutching the door to keep myself from hitting the pavement.

This was my life. This is how I'm going to die—drinking alone, in tiny rooms with strange people, doing terrible things to myself. To my body. To my spirit.

I was a broken person.

"No," I said to myself. A series of no's—each iteration growing louder as I walked down the street, each step focused and intentional, trying to overcome the dueling high from the coke and low from the drink. I felt outside of myself—but the hate and self-loathing were replaced by something else. A light—a sense of clarity.

I had to change. There was a good person in here, I knew. I had to become her—I had to reclaim this identity, this persona—if I wanted to survive. Like Claudia. Like the Lynx.

But I didn't know how to survive. Not yet.

PART III

REBOOT

Excerpt from *The Lynx Returns!* #2, published by New Wave Comics, August 2024.

CHAPTER TWENTY

I almost missed the call, as I ushered Margot into our apartment. Even after noticing it, I considered ignoring it when I saw it was a Face-Time. I regretted picking up the moment I saw her face.

"Hi, Jessica," I said.

"Annie, hey—" Jessica Doyle said, an empty, painted-on smile decorating her face. "How are you?"

I didn't have to wonder why Doyle was calling. If Gary was worth his salt, he'd called her and Carlyle within seconds of me hanging up with him. I'd quit, and this was the final nail in the coffin that was my relationship with Triumph Entertainment. I didn't feel bad, either. Quitting or being fired weren't new to me.

I motioned to Margot to head to the living room. Maybe Cape Cod wasn't in the cards today.

"Let's just get to it."

Doyle sighed.

"Well, I spoke to Gary. He seemed—well, very heated. He said you were extremely surprised by our announcement, and honestly, Annie— that makes me surprised. But after thinking it over—well, I think we've finally reached an impasse," she said. "I hope we can do this amicably and with little drama."

"That depends, doesn't it?" I asked with a shrug.

That smile again. Doyle wasn't rattled easily.

"Look, Annie, we all adore you—and your work," Doyle said, craning her head slightly, as if trying to get a better look at me. "But your vision just doesn't sync with ours, clearly. Us trying to make some noise about our big plans—that's standard practice in Hollywood. I thought someone of your stature and with your track record would understand that. You come from Hollywood as much as comics. But I guess I was wrong. We tried, believe me. We wanted this to work, in the same way you did."

"Why deal with someone who isn't a drone when you can juice them and get an announcement anyway, right?" I said, leaning into my phone. "You got what you wanted. My name attached to your company and your project. All I get is a lifetime of having to explain why it didn't work. And those answers are going to be very interesting, I can guarantee—"

Jessica raised a hand gently.

"Let's not get into threats, please. No one wins there. And I don't think I need to remind you that your contract included a pretty stringent NDA. Let's all move on from this and take it as a learning moment. I'm sure we all could have been better—more honest with each other," Doyle said, the words coming out robotically, as if read from a cue card. "And as a show of goodwill, you can keep your signing bonus and we can all part as friends."

I knew that by saying that, Jessica Doyle was confirming that this firing had everything to do with the Detmer incident. In their eyes, I'd lied to them—tried to pull a fast one on them by not revealing, up front, that Doug Detmer was my father. It created a major problem for Triumph—so much so that I became collateral damage. Maybe Spinoza was right—they saw me as a threat now.

"Additionally, we'll pay you for the time you put in. We'll also connect you with our PR firm so we can put our heads together on how best to message this externally, making sure we don't get any blowback," Doyle continued, as if going over a grocery list. "I'll reach out to Gary and—"

"What about my work?" I asked.

"Excuse me?"

"My art—my designs," I said. "The visuals I created. The look of the book and show. The stuff I shared with you—pages and pages of work. I'll be needing anything I sent to you back and a written confirmation from Triumph that it won't be used."

For a second I thought I heard Jessica gasp on the other side. I'd expected as much. This was the creative push and pull. I had been brought on to do work for hire, sure—but I'd also made sure Gary had inserted the right language to protect me—Triumph couldn't just use my designs or ideas without publishing them with my credit first, and I knew they had no intention of doing that if I wasn't there to finish the story. I'd been burned before, seen my work yanked away and reused, reworked, and mutated into something that was no longer mine. I wasn't going to stand for that. I was certain that Jessica hadn't bothered to read my contract, but I sure as hell had, and I made sure Gary and his team had, too. The text was there. If I got booted or left for cause, the artwork reverted to me. I couldn't really use it in any way outside of selling it to collectors—at least I didn't think so, since the Lynx wasn't my character. But the point was Triumph couldn't use it, either.

"Well," Doyle said after a long pause. Not an ignorant one, but a calculating delay. It told me that Doyle had an answer, she just wasn't sure if she should share it. "I can discuss it with Gary. I'm not sure what Bert's plans are, in terms of finding a new writer or artist—"

"I don't want my stuff used, period, end of story," I said, my eyes widening. "I do not want my ideas tied up in this comic, with all due respect. Can you confirm to me that won't happen? Right now, on this call?"

Doyle gave me a wan smile. "I'll talk to Gary," she said. "I'm sure we can work something out."

That wasn't enough, and Doyle's glazed response was pissing me off. I started to have doubts: Was the contract airtight? Was there a way for

Triumph to fuck me here? I started to feel the edges unraveling—all the hours of plotting, penciling, and inking were being pushed into a giant shredder. I would not allow my work to be stolen. I couldn't lose this.

Not like Carmen had.

I refused to let this sit.

"I'm calling Gary now, and I'll reiterate my preferences, per the contract," I said. I watched Doyle nod slowly. Watched as her finger seemed to inch toward her phone, trying to end the call.

"I have to go, Annie," Jessica said, her deep voice echoing through my phone as she tilted her head slightly—as if to say, *You went too far there, you ungrateful little bitch.* "It was really a pleasure. I'm so sad we couldn't figure it out. All my best to you."

Before I could respond, Jessica was gone—I was staring at my reflection.

I saw Margot creep back into the apartment's vestibule from the living room, a curious look on her face.

"That didn't sound good," she said, a sheepish expression on her face. "You okay?"

"It was fine," I said with a shrug. "They learned not to play hardball with Annie Bustamante."

Margot laughed. "I learned that at birth."

"Don't worry, I'll get another gig," I said, pulling her in for a tight hug and kissing the top of her head. "We'll be fine."

"I'm not worried about the money, Mami, you know that," she said. "I'm bummed—I really liked that story you were putting together. Those pages were great."

"Yeah, me, too, but I wanted to make sure they didn't use my stuff without me knowing," I said, more to myself than to Margot. "They shouldn't be able to tell my Lynx story."

"You should just do it yourself," Margot said, so casually that it almost seemed believable, the idea of me—Annie Bustamante—damning the torpedoes and writing and drawing my own Lynx comic.

But maybe I could do that?

I pondered it for a fleeting moment, letting the thought fade back into my subconscious. I couldn't, really. Could I? I stepped back and looked at my child—speeding faster and faster toward being a teenager, a young adult. Almost thirteen but already sharing more wisdom than I could spare.

I'd been sprinting for so long—meeting after meeting, hours and hours at the drawing table, literally immersing myself in this project— trying to bring myself closer to all these men who mattered in my life, like Danny and Doug Detmer, this mysterious man I never knew. Hell, I thought it'd bring me closer to the Lynx, the reason I was even working in comics at all. And now it was all gone. The reality was just now setting in, even if it was mostly my doing.

The Lynx.

No matter how desperately I clung to her—tried to tell this story, this adventure that felt imprinted on my brain—it still fizzled into noth- ing. Just another unfinished comic, untold saga—fodder for listicles and *Whatever happened to?*—style think pieces to get clicks.

But why did it have to be? I wondered.

"That art you created? That comic? It was so good. It's yours. No one can take that from you," Margot said, shaking me from my reverie, a steel in her delivery I'd never noticed before. "You can't just quit on that, Mami. You can't quit because some twerp in a suit thinks you don't know how to create a Lynx comic. You're probably the only person qualified to do it. It's literally in your blood."

"What are you saying, kiddo?"

"I'm saying, do your thing. Your own way," Margot said.

Margot's words haunted me hours later, as I tucked her into bed.

My first thought, the fight-or-flight response I tended to bring to everything, was to just move on. Let it go. Accept and pivot. It would be easy to just try to forget the Lynx. Forget Danny. Forget Laura Gus- tines and Carmen Valdez. Had it been a mistake to try to return to this industry, this place that had been so dangerous and toxic just a decade before? Perhaps.

I didn't realize where I was until I felt my finger sliding down the tattered, familiar cover to *The Legendary Lynx* #1. I was in my office now. The issue rested atop a stack of references I was using for my work on *The Lynx Returns!*—at least I had been.

Do your thing. Your own way.

I sat down at my drawing table and let my eyes look at the page—half drawn, the Lynx, or Claudia Calla rather, standing in her bedroom—the moonlight coming in from her window as she held up the mysterious uniform she'd uncovered, hidden in a corner of her home. This was the moment when our heroine, Claudia, remembers herself. Realizes who she is and was. A hero. And what she must do.

"Same here, Lynx," I whispered, leaning forward, the pencil doing what it always did.

I finished off the page and realized that it was close to two in the morning. I'd fallen into that almost trance-like state. The zone. Normally I would love this—because it meant I was connecting with the work. The story I'd created and jotted down after literally decades of thinking about it. Now it just felt bittersweet.

I looked at my phone. It was late, even for Gary, who was in Los Angeles. I called him anyway.

"I'm assuming this is an emergency?" Gary said. Based on the background noise, I figured I'd caught him at a dinner or some kind of social event.

"I need to talk something through, if you have a minute," I said.

"Look, I know you're torn up about this Lynx thing, but trust me—in terms of your bottom line, we will get you more lucrative work. I know it's scary, especially after the *Miss Midnight* stuff, but trust me—you're not toxic. We just need to give it time. I'm talking to Disney tomorrow. They're looking for someone to direct a new live-action *TailSpin* movie I think you'd be great for," Gary began. "And listen, you did the right thing by quitting. It was a sleazy operation, and—"

"Can I keep doing this?"

A pause.

"I'm going to ask the next logical question, Annie, even though I think I know what you're asking and it makes me worried," Gary said. "But . . . doing what?"

"This book. The Lynx. Who owns the rights?"

"Well, Triumph does," Gary said slowly, as if he were talking to a recalcitrant dog or toddler.

"How do we know?"

"I mean, who else would?"

"That's probably what they want us to believe."

"Annie, you're giving off real tinfoil-hat vibes here," Gary said with a dry laugh.

"It's not crazy," I said, feeling an unexpected energy course through me, as if suddenly imbued with the power cosmic—as if I'd finally collected the final gem on the Infinity Gauntlet. A palpable adrenaline. An excitement for the unknown. "Laura Gustines, a friend of mine, was going to interview this writer—Carmen Valdez—and blow the lid off it all with her book, and then she was killed. But my point is, the narrative that Jeffrey Carlyle created—"

"Annie, that's not how comics work—or entertainment, for that matter. You know that," Gary said. "Especially older, superhero comics. She probably signed a work-for-hire contract when she wrote for Triumph, so it's a dead issue."

"But what if she didn't?" I asked.

Gary sighed. I'd gotten used to that sound.

"What do you need from me, kid?"

"Well—I'm going to keep working on this. Let's figure out a way to publish it."

"Annie, you can't," Gary said, no longer trying to hide the exasperation. "I mean, I was going to call you tomorrow with this news, but we might as well talk now. But this company, this newsletter thing—kind of like Substack—is asking if you'd like to serialize a story with them.

The money is good. I imagine the oversight is minimal. If you wanna stay in this space, and do this—there are other ways. It might be the real break you need, while we wait for Hollywood to calm down. A profitable break."

"But I want to write a Lynx story."

"What?" Gary said. "Listen, just file off the serial numbers here. Do your own thing. Make it sing."

"I don't want to tell stories about, I dunno—the Feline Fury," I said, realizing how petulant I sounded. "It's not what I want."

Gary didn't understand. He couldn't. How could any rational person understand what I was grappling with? This desire to tell one kind of story—with one kind of character.

"Look, Gary, I'll let you go, it's late—even for you," I said. "Dig deeper into that offer. I might take you up on that."

Gary made a grunting sound of agreement before hanging up.

I stared at my phone display for a second before laying it face down on the drawing table.

Something was missing. And I didn't have a lot of time. I spun my chair around and reached for my laptop. I googled a name, "Harvey Stern."

I knew the broad strokes of Harvey's tragic narrative, capped by his sudden death in 1975. An editor on staff at Triumph Comics, Stern was asked by Jeffrey Carlyle to create a street-level female crime fighter based on a cat or cat-like animal, so the story went. Stern sequestered himself for days and returned with what would become the first six issues of *The Legendary Lynx*, after some fine-tuning from Carlyle and visuals from artist Doug Detmer.

So where did Carmen Valdez fit in? According to the record, Carmen had only written one issue—*The Legendary Lynx* #11. Ironically, it had been Detmer's final issue on art before he took his own life.

I googled "Carmen Valdez."

I wasn't sure I'd find anything I didn't already know, but it was worth a shot. I dug through the basic bio stuff—her brief career writing *The*

Legendary Lynx #11, a memoir graphic novel, then her pivot toward sci-fi prose. All the bios I found were short and to the point and seemed to hew to the accepted narrative: Carmen had worked at Triumph as Jeffrey Carlyle's secretary, got to write a comic, then drifted away from mainstream superhero action stories. The part that was left unsaid, the question Laura had tried to answer, was bigger: Where did Carmen Valdez disappear to? She hadn't done an interview in over a decade, and her last novel had come out before then.

"Where did you go?" I asked aloud, tapping at the keyboard.

I was on the eighth page of search results when I landed on a brief interview with a woman named Marion Price. From what I could tell, she was curating a museum exhibit for New York's Society of Illustrators on "Forgotten Heroes: Comic Book Creators Deserving Greater Recognition." I checked the date on the interview and cross-referenced the exhibit. It had never made it, apparently. Huh.

The interview itself was your usual PR-driven Q&A—"How does it feel to do this thing I am interviewing you about?" "Oh great, I love this thing." But midway through, I found a nugget—and the piece that had made it crop up in my search.

Q: Are there some creators you couldn't fit into the exhibit?
A: Oh sure. One in particular. I think the name Carmen Valdez doesn't mean a lot to comic book readers—she's more known as an author of novels now—but I think if we dig down, if we get into the weeds of the story, we'd learn her role in this lost history of comics is much more important than we first thought. I'm in the process of figuring out how to get access to a lost trove of historical documents that I think will really shed light on Carmen's career—as not just a writer, but really a trailblazer for women in superhero comics.

I started to type Marion's name into the search bar. Before I could finish, my phone buzzed with a text message.

Spinoza.

My office. Urgent. ASAP?

I let out an exasperated groan after reading it. I was already in a bad place—I didn't need Arturo Spinoza poking me. I dashed off a quick response before getting up from my desk to get ready for bed.

It's super late! Tonight doesn't work for me. I'm off the project anyway. 🧑

Spinoza replied almost immediately.

This is serious. We need to confer. Shit is hitting the fan. Now.

I was annoyed, my thumbs tapping my phone faster than I could think—my annoyance over, well, everything, fueling my response. I was tired of not being in control, and I wasn't going to be bossed around by a privileged has-been. No thank you.

Talk tomorrow. Good night.

I heard my phone vibrating as I walked toward my bedroom, but I ignored Spinoza. I just didn't care. I needed a break. I wanted to change into my pajamas, turn on my sound machine, and disconnect from the world for a few hours. I took a deep breath. I had a program. I had tools and resources to get me through challenging moments like this. Most importantly, I was certain of one thing:

I was not done with my story.

CHAPTER TWENTY-ONE

A fitful night's sleep did nothing for my mood. I woke up pissed.

I wasn't sure if I was just annoyed by, well, everything—Doyle's smug call, Spinoza's demanding texts, how a corporation had almost soured my entire relationship with my favorite comic book character—or if I was desperate for some kind of closure, but I felt like I was on to something. What that something was, I might never find out—but it was early, Margot was on her way to school, and the coffee was hot.

I flipped my laptop open and went to IMDb. I'd scoured Spinoza's page before—was already well versed in the director's varied and acclaimed cinematic output. But I was here for someone else. As expected, Doyle's credits were minimal. Executive producer on some never-released films, a producer credit for what was surely a free streamer movie. It felt like a dead end. Jessica Doyle was your typical investor, throwing money at a bunch of things and hoping one stuck. Then I saw something. It was Doyle's last credit. "Senior Executive Producer" on a never-finished film named *Overdose*, based on a middling memoir I'd given up on reading after a few chapters. The production company was named Decibel Entertainment. I'd never heard of them—which meant nothing, but the name buzzed around my brain. I jotted it down, unsure if it was anything.

I did another basic search: "Triumph Comics." "Bert Carlyle." "Jeffrey Carlyle." "Doug Detmer." I didn't find anything I hadn't memorized over the years. Triumph Comics had been a middling to poor publisher that folded in the late eighties, decades before the elder Carlyle died. Some Reddit users argued that characters like the Dusk, Black Ghost, Lynx, La Sombra, and Avatar were now in the public domain, but those arguments were smothered by the recent launch of Triumph Entertainment, spearheaded by Jeffrey's only son, Bert. I went back to the announcement.

There was nothing in the story that directly connected Triumph Comics, the company, to Triumph Entertainment outside of the name. My head tingled. Something wasn't right. I thought of Laura, and the book that would never be published, and Carmen Valdez, perhaps the co-creator of the Lynx, and Doug Detmer—dead by his own hand after drawing a comic written by Carmen. Where did Spinoza, with his shattered reputation, fit in? Had exile granted him a willingness to avert his eyes to something toxic in order to get paid? And where did I fit in—an artist who'd left comics, not looking back, only to get pulled into something that looked shiny and new on the surface—something that might be jagged and dangerous after all?

I decided to dig into Decibel, but came up with only a small placeholder website. But that was enough. It seemed that Decibel was owned by Doyle, with Carlyle as chief creative officer. They'd produced nothing, but that hadn't stopped the tiny company from trying to make waves—deal announcements, options, casting calls. Decibel tried really, really hard to be in the trades but didn't seem that keen on actually working. I scanned the tiny company's board of directors—which felt like a bit much for such a tiny operation—and didn't see any names I recognized. But I cross-referenced a few, like Grant Barrett and Rachel Kaminski. What I found seemed mundane enough—except for one name.

Marina Pestova. All the other board members had CVs with at least fleeting connections to the entertainment industry or tech. Pestova had nothing—she was a cipher. But I eventually realized I was looking in the wrong places. Pestova wasn't an entertainment person, or even a tech investor. According to a brief mention in a bigger story in *The Intercept* about the expansion of organized crime in Eastern Europe and Russia, she was married to Alex Pestova, a Russian oligarch with strong ties to the Putin government. Pestova's name felt out of place with the usual collection of Hollywood also-rans and never-weres that made up the Decibel board—a group that hadn't been updated, according to the site, in five years. Was it still relevant? I thought so.

I leaned back and let the information sit with me for a second. So, Jessica Doyle and Bert Carlyle worked at a tiny film production company that was tied—at least tangentially, a handful of years ago—to some potentially bad people. Now Doyle was investing in Triumph Entertainment, making hay over the company's vast IP library in an effort to launch a multi-platform media empire and, ostensibly, make a shit-ton of money. Those promises weren't just being made to the public, I thought. She would be making them to her business partners, too.

I swallowed hard.

I went back to the original Lynx announcement. The basics were all there. Annie Bustamante, after a huge social media push, was coming back to comics to relaunch the Legendary Lynx. Great, great. It felt like a nice story. The son of the Lynx's original co-creator, Jeffrey Carlyle, had revived Triumph as a multimedia company, with its eyes on the Lynx as the crown jewel of a cinematic empire to rival Marvel and DC. Hyperbolic, for sure. But that's what press releases are for. The release was sparse, which was understandable—there wasn't much to report. Hell, I hadn't even signed the contract at that point. I scrolled down to the comments on the story, which was on a comic book news site called *Popverse*. One posting stuck out. The username seemed to scream from the page.

CLAUDIACALLA_LIVES asked, "Are they reprinting the old

Lynx material? Seems like a good idea when you have such great IP, right?"

It was a weird, inside-baseball kind of question—but it got me thinking. Why *weren't* they reprinting the classic Detmer and Stern issues? What better way to reconnect readers to the source material? Was it possible they didn't fully have the rights yet?

My phone buzzed. I saw an email notification on my lock screen—from an address I didn't know, but immediately recognized:

simonupton@protonmail.com.

Simon Upton, Triumph City's best investigative reporter—Claudia Calla's beloved colleague, and a key supporting character in the Lynx stories.

While the email address was a deep cut, the subject line was not subtle: "READ THIS RIGHT NOW."

I opened the email. It was a forwarded newsletter from a website called SKTCHD. I scrolled down. At the bottom of what seemed like your basic website content roundup, I found the item. There was that name again.

Carmen Valdez.

The blurb was short but to the point. An obscure science fiction author and graphic novelist named Carmen Valdez had just filed suit against Triumph Entertainment, Bert Carlyle, and Jessica Doyle, claiming she had proof that she and Doug Detmer, with an assist from Harvey Stern, created the Legendary Lynx. I googled around for more coverage of the story, but found nothing. The original email was at least a day old.

I texted Arturo Spinoza.

Let's meet. Later today?

He responded almost immediately. A few minutes later, I was rushing to the subway.

CHAPTER TWENTY-TWO

APRIL 12, 2009

I'm going to be back in town for a few days. We should talk.

I awoke to the text from Danny and almost hurled my phone across the bedroom.

But I didn't. Instead, I lay in bed as the early morning sunlight crept in, almost enjoying the ability to awaken without a pounding headache and endless shame. I could get used to this.

I let my feet hit the floor and made myself a cup of coffee before responding. I considered calling my sponsor first, too. She'd warned me this moment was coming—that I needed to brace for how I'd react, to prevent myself from falling into the same patterns.

"Danny really represents your old life in a lot of ways," Sara had said just the night before, over coffee at a corner diner on Dyckman. "It doesn't mean he can't be in your life—but he'll have to return on your terms."

What were my terms? I wondered. Did I even want to see him?

I'd been sober for a month. Even if it felt like a lifetime, I knew my journey was only starting. Would I be putting it all at risk by seeing him?

I typed a response before I could answer the question.

We have a lot to talk about.

The first thing I noticed when I walked into the Whole Foods cafeteria in Columbus Circle was Danny. He looked tired, almost gaunt. His sharp blue eyes dulled and gray. As if he'd run a marathon the night before and come straight to work. He was seated at a table toward the back, the hustle and bustle of lunchtime midtown office drones putting together salads creating a low buzz that was strangely soothing. I sat across from him.

"You look like shit," I said.

"Thanks," he said with a smirk.

My eyebrows popped up, as if to say, *Let's get on with it.*

"It's good to see you," he said, clearly fumbling for the right words. But that wasn't my problem. He'd asked me to come here.

Danny cleared his throat, then took a sip from some kind of probiotic soda drink before talking.

"How have you been?"

"How have I been? I've been . . . fuck you, Danny," I said, unable to hold back my anger. "C'mon, bro—you can't just show up after ghosting me like that and expect us to catch up over sparkling kombucha or whatever you're drinking. So let me kick things off: What the fuck, why haven't you been in touch, and what the fuck?"

I watched Danny wince, but I didn't feel bad. He deserved this and had asked for it. A long silence lingered. I leaned forward to meet his drifting gaze.

"Seriously, that's your response? Nothing? Okay, then I'll just say it: I'm pregnant," I said, letting the words hammer him like a giant Looney Tunes mallet. I watched, waiting for his response, but his face was blank. "And it's yours."

He rubbed his eyes roughly before looking at me again. It felt like time was slowing to a crawl, as if we were both moving at superspeed, like the Flash and Reverse-Flash, caught in a struggle in the very speed force that powered them both—while the rest of the world trudged along at normal speed.

"Are you going to say anything?" I asked. "Ever?"

"I—uh, I wasn't expecting that," he said. It was honest, which, on some basic level, I appreciated—but it wasn't enough.

He looked more than tired, I thought. He looked ragged. I watched his eyes as they met mine. Could still smell his familiar cologne, predict his expressions. It hadn't been that long, I worried. The wounds were still raw. I wasn't sure I had the power to even deal with this right now. I wanted a drink so badly.

"I'm keeping it," I said matter-of-factly. "I'm sober, too. Four weeks. You know I never met my father—my mom kept that from me, because she was struggling with her own shit. I'm not going to do the same to my kid."

Danny nodded slowly. He understood how hard this was for me—not just the drinking, but the understanding of these painful cycles we get trapped in. He reached out a hand—palm-up—his fingers inches from mine.

"You will do it," he said, his voice hoarse—like he hadn't spoken in years. "You'll stay sober. I know it. Not just for this kid—but for yourself."

I placed my hand over his—felt his fingers wrap around it, tight and desperate, two damaged people clutching for purchase.

Excerpt from *The Lynx Returns!* #2, published by New Wave Comics, August 2024.

CHAPTER TWENTY-THREE

The words hovered in my mind's eye as I approached Arturo Spinoza's building. *Decibel Entertainment. Marina Pestova. Triumph Comics. Carmen Valdez.* Floating slowly, just a few inches out of reach—puzzle pieces desperate to click together, to form a bigger picture that I could finally understand. But something was missing, I knew, and I wasn't sure yet where to find it. Do I just show up at Carmen Valdez's door and explain who I am? To what end? I knew I wanted to keep telling my story—and the more I thought about it, the more the Lynx felt like a piece of me I wanted back, too. But surely that was madness.

Right?

All of this swirled around my head as I reached Spinoza's door, a half-empty Starbucks latte in hand. I'd cooled down a little bit since the night before—but I still felt angry and unmoored, frustrated that this dream opportunity—albeit one covered in land mines from the drop— had turned to dust. I buzzed the door. After a few moments, I buzzed it again. Nothing. I'd texted him before hopping on the 1 train north, trying to give the erratic director fair notice that I was coming in. Another buzz. Nothing. Was Spinoza pissed at me for refusing to jump into a cab at the drop of a hat? Well, fuck him, then.

This whole project—calling it that felt oddly generous—was a clear example of what happened when bad people owned cool shit, I thought as I jammed my thumb into the outside buzzer, letting it ring out for a good fifteen seconds.

What did Bert Carlyle know about the Lynx? Had he had meaningful conversations with his dad about the character before Jeffrey Carlyle died? Had he pored over the comics like I had—looking at every panel and page of Doug Detmer's art, desperate to emulate every line, every bit of shadow and contrast? Of course not. I'd had a bead on Carlyle the second I met him. He was a cliché. The kid who'd never struggled for anything in his life vying to grab hold of something he felt he deserved—characters his dad only tangentially created, if at all. The idea that the owner of a company had a creative say in all the characters his company owned was a fallacy that was still gobbled up and regurgitated by the mainstream press, even though giant holes could be poked through those narratives. I knew enough about comics, despite having been out of the grind for over a decade, to understand that even in 1975 the actual creative work was done by freelancers. Did Jeffrey Carlyle give his talent an idea? A germ to start from? Maybe—but did he do the work of cracking the story, or designing a costume? No. Way.

Someone came to the door, but I could tell immediately they had nothing to do with Spinoza—they gave me the standard *please don't talk to me* vibe most New Yorkers default to. I stepped aside as they walked out, then grabbed the door before it closed. Maybe Spinoza was asleep, I told myself.

I reached the top of the stairs and entered the fourth floor. Spinoza's office was right across the hall from the stairwell, and I knocked on the door gently. Nothing. I knocked again—harder this time, letting some of my frustration out on the generic office door. Still nothing.

Locked.

I pulled out my phone and started typing. After a few texts were sent—each one getting progressively more terse and angry—I knocked again. Nothing.

I tried the doorknob again.

I looked at my phone and realized I'd somehow missed a call—which now had an accompanying voice mail. I tapped on my call log and noticed it had come through from an unknown New York number a few minutes ago. It had to have been Spinoza. I felt a sharp chill run through me.

I listened to the message, immediately recognizing Spinoza's nasal drone—except this time it sounded different. Amplified. Nervous. Words slurring. Like the director had gotten hammered and then scrambled to send off one last message before passing out. It was worrisome. I had been sober for a while—and I knew how hard it was to maintain it. But even so, I still felt off-balance when I interacted with a decidedly drunk person—either in person or, in this case, hearing them on the other end of a call.

"You're quite the insolent one, aren't you? Huh? Well, now here I am, sitting alone in my office, hoping you'll have a change of heart. You. My partner. My creative partner," Spinoza said, his voice slurring again, dragging on every last syllable. "I just . . . well, I just wanted you to know our idea is dead, okay? They told me you'd left—which, hey, I can't blame you. But now? Now all we have are my ideas, and even those are dead. They're gutting it. I met with Carlyle and he said it was a no-go. 'Too complicated, too artsy-fartsy,' were his words, direct quote. They're a bunch of hacks, Annie, creative vampires."

A long pause after the word. Then a low, guttural cough. I thought I heard a gulping sound, but I could've been projecting.

"The worst part, Annie? These fuckers don't believe in art. I've met my share of moneybags dickheads who just leave you alone. They know the golden pot is at the end of the rainbow. They don't need to get involved. But Carlyle? He thinks he's some sort of Svengali. Stan Lee reborn, or some shit. He's not. He wants to leave a stamp on this thing, and if he were half as smart as he thinks he is, he'd leave two smart people with long track records alone to do their damn best work and bring life to a character no one even cared about yesterday. But with you gone . . . well, it's dead. Dead, dead, dead. Any chance I had of reviving my career—of recapturing even a sliver of that magic—it's gone."

Another pause. The sucking sound of a cigarette, a muffled moan that might've been a sob. I honestly didn't want to know. Then Spinoza continued.

"We need to stick together on this, Annie. We're family now. We're bonded. I don't think I'll be awake when you arrive tomorrow—don't want to be awake, or for you to see me . . . like this. The key to the office—it's under the mat. Go inside. I left something for you. You'll know what to do with it, Annie, you're smarter—better—than me," Spinoza said, his voice sounding frail and wispy. But it wasn't just the sound of Spinoza's voice that haunted me—would haunt me for a long time. It was the final words he spoke before the message ended.

"You're the last hope for this character, Annie . . . you have the real leverage here, my dear . . . because I'm as good as dead."

I crouched down in front of Spinoza's office door and found the key. I slid it into the door and then placed my hand on the knob. It turned.

I felt outside of my own body as I stepped into Spinoza's office, like the black energy being that leapt out of Negative Man of the Doom Patrol—a power that crackled with dark energy. Spinoza spoke a good game—but did he have proof of his vague intimations? That Triumph didn't actually own the Lynx? That felt almost too good to be true.

I frowned. Maybe Spinoza feared what I expected from Triumph. They'd hire some hack writer, who would then craft something flashy and mildly competent, Carlyle and Doyle would enthusiastically approve it, and they'd release something painfully average and mediocre to the masses, ensuring the Lynx would have a secure place atop the pile of failed comic book relaunches and reboots. The Lynx would be lost forever. A footnote with no future. No longer a hidden gem, but a spent cartridge. Something a handful of people might look back on fondly, if they even bothered to think about it. I didn't want that to happen. But the Russians? How did they fit into all of this? Where was the missing piece?

I'd wanted more for Claudia Calla—I wanted her to thrive and to remind the world why they needed someone like the Lynx. A woman who realized her power and potential and used it to help others like her. Especially these days—as our power, our own bodily autonomy, was being systematically stripped away and chipped at by those in power.

But was it even possible to do that now?

I thought back to one of my last conversations with Spinoza. What had he known then? What was the word he used?

Leverage.

I saw it then, peeking out from under a pile of papers on Spinoza's desk. A familiar, scratched-up, and well-worn MacBook Air. The Post-it note covering the familiar Apple logo made Spinoza's plan idiot-proof: ANNIE. I stopped for a second, sliding a finger over the smooth silver of the computer. Why did Spinoza want me to have this?

That's when I heard the footsteps.

It was the rushed patter that alarmed me. I was enough of a New Yorker to be able to drown out the noises of building life. Doors slamming. Elevator sounds. Muffled conversations. Loud, thumping music. But whoever was coming up the steps was doing it in a big hurry. And it sounded like they were stopping here on Spinoza's floor.

I grabbed the laptop and slid it into my purse. The footsteps were still coming, but slower now—*someone trying to find a specific door*, I thought. That meant they hadn't been here before. Which also meant they weren't supposed to be here. I looked around Spinoza's cramped office. There was only one way out, and it would mean crossing paths with whoever was coming in. That didn't feel like a good idea.

The tiny closet was embedded in a small hallway that led to the office's grimy bathroom, which clearly hadn't been cleaned in months. I could hear the doorknob turning in the main living area, the space with Spinoza's pantheon of posters and memorabilia. I opened the closet quietly.

It was mostly empty—some coats hanging flimsily and a few boxes of printer paper at the bottom. I stepped inside and curled myself up into a ball behind a small set of plastic shelves. It wouldn't hide me, that was for sure—but maybe whoever was coming in wouldn't look—

The creak of the front door swinging open. Slow, hesitant footsteps. A few in one direction, then a few more in another. They were inside, and they were looking for something. They were moving faster now. Inside the office, I heard papers rustling. A muttered curse.

A fist slamming on Spinoza's desk.

I tried to regulate my breathing. I didn't dare close my eyes, which had by now adapted to the relative dark of the tiny closet, but I tried to exist outside myself. To visualize what I would do next.

But what could I do?

The footsteps seemed to be moving faster now, as if the person was circling Spinoza's desk. I looked into my bag, at the laptop I'd hastily shoved in there, and took in a sharp breath.

Drawers slamming shut. More cursing, a low, unidentifiable voice.

More footsteps. Closer. I held my breath.

The footsteps stopped—not just outside the door, but close enough. Were they looking at the bathroom? Pondering the closet? I didn't have time to think about it.

There's no fucking way they don't open this door, I thought.

I leapt up and slammed the door open, hearing a low groan as it swung out fast—the thunk of contact as its shoddy wood connected with someone's body.

I looked back for a millisecond, to see the black-clad figure dropping awkwardly to the floor in the tight space between the closet and the opposite wall. Saw the mask on their face. The black beanie over their head.

The gun in their hand.

I turned and ran, my bag clutched tightly to my chest. I slammed the inner door between the main room and Spinoza's office shut, already hearing their footsteps behind me. Already knowing I was only a few paces ahead. I pulled stuff down—off shelves, tables, anything to just slow my pursuer for a moment. I got outside of the office and did something else—purely on instinct. I used the key Spinoza had pointed me toward and locked the door. My hands didn't fail me, and as I took two or three stairs at a time, I listened to the doorknob shake as whoever was on the other side tried to get out, then fumbled with the lock.

I made it outside, but that wasn't enough. Couldn't be enough. I kept running—hitting a fast sprint toward Dyckman. I made a sharp left. I found a crowded laundromat and stepped inside, huddling next to a set of machines, my body hidden from view, though I was able to look out a giant window.

I sat there for what felt like an eon. Watching every person that walked by. Every face. Looking for the person I'd seen in Spinoza's office—draped in black.

With a gun.

After a while, one of the employees came by and asked if I needed help. I waved them off gently, explaining I was waiting for a friend. That seemed to placate them long enough. I waited a bit longer. For my breathing to settle. For my fingers to unclench from around my bag.

What. The. Fuck.

After a few moments, I pulled out my phone and opened my Signal app. I messaged Apparition.

I want to talk to Carmen.

APPARITION: You say that like I can make it happen. But you seem to understand more.

APPARITION: . . . how's the project going?

I quit. I'm done with it.
Look---I think I'm in trouble. I think---I almost got hurt.

APPARITION: You need to be careful. This isn't a game.
APPARITION: You're only starting to see what you're up against.

CHAPTER TWENTY-FOUR

My hands were shaking as I pulled my vibrating phone out of my purse. I was in a state of disbelief—rewinding and replaying what had just happened over and over, as I tried to walk, just walk away—taking some cold comfort from the New York City crowds as I made my way downtown. Had this just happened? I kept asking myself. I was still processing. Someone had been in Spinoza's office, looking for the same laptop that I now had in my bag. If I'd arrived a few minutes later, I—

I didn't even want to think about it. I couldn't. I had to get home.

I looked at the phone display.

It was Gary. Shit.

"Hello?"

"Annie—you got a minute?"

"I—I guess so," I said, my words sounding choked off and distant.

"What's wrong? Are you okay?"

I didn't know what to say. I wasn't sure burdening Gary with this now would help, but I needed to talk to someone.

"I just—I had a scare, that's all," I said, curating the words carefully. "I'm in the city. It's . . . it's fine. I just need to get home."

A pause. I could tell Gary was running scenarios through his mind—what to say next, how to respond. But at his heart, Gary was a pragmatist. He pressed forward.

"Well, okay, but let me know if I can do anything? You sound really shaken up," he said. "I don't want to—"

"It's fine, just—what's going on?"

"I just got off the phone with our friends at Triumph. They're not happy."

"Okay," I said, not sure what else I could add—or if I even gave a shit at this point. I took in a long, deep breath. I needed to get home. Center myself. To sit in the dark for a minute.

Gary clicked his tongue before getting into it.

"From their perspective, they felt they had a handshake deal—that you knew what the terms were and had verbally been okay with them, on top of having a contract, so they didn't understand your issues with the announcement, which they saw as a formality. But, of course, the big breaking point for them came before—the Doug Detmer stuff. They felt you were being disingenuous, which—to them—put you in violation of the contract," he said. "They feel that voids any desire you might have to control how they use your artwork and concepts. They paid for it, it's theirs, and you lying to them allows them to do whatever they want. That's their take—which, look, is complete bullshit—but that's their story and they're sticking to it. They think it's best for everyone if you just drop your request and part amicably, with the understanding that they own that artwork and you can't use it in any way."

"If they're not going to honor the contract, why should I? I can just go public. Aren't they worried about that?" I asked. I could feel my face going hot. I didn't need this now.

"They don't seem worried. They don't seem to really be . . . how do I say it? 'Seasoned' when it comes to these kind of basic, end-of-contract discussions," Gary said. "Which is good and bad. That makes them wild cards. They could take you leaving badly and drag you over the coals if you make this hard on them. Wouldn't be the end of the world, but would certainly hurt your chances of getting more comics work."

"I may not want any more. And they can just fuck off," I half yelled as I turned down Broadway, the sound of blaring horns and the smell of a nearby food cart bombarding my senses. "I mean, I was doing just fine before they came along. Tell them the art is mine, I drew it and came up with it—I don't want any of my ideas showing up in whatever they do with Spinoza or whoever."

"They don't understand that," Gary said. I genuinely loved his grandfatherly, calming voice. It usually made me feel safe. But it wasn't working right now. "In their own clumsy, roundabout way, they still want you to do this—they somehow think you'll come back, sign a new deal, and keep working. As for Spinoza, well, they're having trouble with him, too. Have you spoken to him lately?"

I wasn't sure how much to tell Gary. Or anyone. Yet.

"I was supposed to meet up with him today, but he ghosted me," I said, dodging a stroller as I made my way east. "Look, Gary—I need to—"

"I get it, I'm almost done, and for what it's worth, I'm hearing from my side that he's out. Bailed. Not sure why, don't really want to know why. So, just brace for that. In terms of you, here's what we can do," he said. "I tell them clearly and without wiggle room that they can't use anything you contributed, okay? That, sure, they can be annoyed about the Detmer stuff, but this is a nonstarter for us. Either they shake our hands and we move away amicably, or we start considering our legal and publicity options. I'll downplay it, of course, we don't want them to think our finger is hovering over the red button—but the threat is there. How does that sound?"

"Marginally less terrible?"

"That's my fifteen percent talking," Gary said, and hung up.

He's out.

Had Spinoza already quit when he called me? There was no way to know. Not until I spoke to him. But before that, I needed to sit somewhere familiar.

I needed to feel safe.

I cracked open the laptop that night, after some takeout and a movie with Margot, who was mired in homework and preparing for a test at the end of the week. Sitting with her and just relaxing felt like such a welcome escape, the idea of doing anything relating to work or the Lynx felt almost improper. But once she was in bed, the laptop was all I could think about. But there was one thing I hadn't considered when I borrowed Spinoza's computer—any laptop worth its salt required a password. I sighed and closed the laptop. Why had Spinoza given me a laptop with no way of accessing the information?

Then the answer came back to me—in Spinoza's low growl.

Leverage.

Excerpt from *The Lynx Returns!* #3, published by New Wave Comics, September 2024.

CHAPTER TWENTY-FIVE

APRIL 12, 2009

S o, yeah—a lot has changed since you up and bailed," I said. I stood up and let my eyes scan the crowded Whole Foods cafeteria. "I didn't want you finding out ten years from now, or whatever, and resenting me. I know what that's like. You deserve to know, even if you've been a complete asshole. I'm leaving now."

His confused expression suddenly cleared up. If anyone could understand why I got sober, it would be Danny. But he didn't seem content to just let me go.

"Can I walk you to your train?"

I gave him a noncommittal shrug and we exited the mall and headed uptown.

"I'm not sure what you want me to say," Danny said after a few blocks of awkward silence.

"At this point, saying anything at all would be great," I said, shaking my head. "Just tell me what happened."

Danny let out a long sigh. He seemed shaky and unsure of himself.

"Annie, I needed this job," he said, looking at me closely. "I know I have a lot to answer for."

I stammered for a second—vacillating between keeping quiet and just saying what I knew I had to say.

"It's not just about the job, Danny," I said, frustration creeping into my voice. "It's how you did it. You just . . . left. And, look, you know I think you're talented—a good writer. You could do so many things. I don't get why you're locked into these dead-end editorial jobs where you're telling people what to do, people you could run circles around. You could do it yourself. It's not like you have this passion to be the next Archie Goodwin or Mark Gruenwald, you know? You were never dreaming of editing comics. You wanted to make them."

Danny's mouth formed a tight, thin line. I knew that face. He wasn't upset—not yet. He was thinking.

"Why don't we sit down? Can we do that?" he said. "There's a decent Mexican place on Ninth Avenue I used to love."

I didn't want to sit down. I wanted to have it out, even if it happened here on the street. But that was my temper talking. I nodded in agreement.

We walked a few more blocks in silence and found El Centro, a brightly decorated restaurant on the west side. The place was relatively empty, considering it was in that nether region between lunch and dinner. But that didn't matter as much in New York. We found a table near the entrance by the restaurant's giant windows and ordered.

I watched as the waitress wandered back toward the kitchen. When she was out of earshot, I turned to Danny.

"Okay, here we are," I said.

Danny leaned back in his chair and sighed.

"Look, Annie, what do you want me to say?" he asked. "I'm just not cut out for the freelance life. I'm not like you. I'm not a risk-taker. I like having a paycheck, health insurance, and knowing what I need to do each day."

I raised an eyebrow.

"Jesus, Annie, what do you want from me?" Danny said, exasperation glazing over his words. "Blood? We're friends, Annie. I know we—well, 'ended' is the wrong word—but we parted in a bad way, but I'm here. I want to be friends."

"Are you fucking kidding me?"

The question leapt off my lips, evading any kind of filters or second thoughts, sharp and direct.

Danny started to respond, but it was my turn to talk.

"You want to 'be friends'?" I said, using air quotes on the last two words. "Why would I ever be your friend again, Danny, after you treated me so shitty?"

I stood up and swung my bag over my shoulder, my eyes still locked on Danny, who seemed to sink into his seat.

"You know what, fuck this and fuck you," I said, giving him a dismissive wave. "This is unbelievable."

Danny started to get up, his hands raised—like someone bracing for a tidal wave to collapse on them.

"Wait, Annie, please—don't go," he said. "I—that wasn't the right thing to say. I'm sorry."

"Sorry, wow. Nice word, 'sorry.' That's a start, Danny," I said, still standing. "Apologizing."

"Please, let's talk," he said, sitting down slowly. I mirrored his movement, crossing my arms in my seat. "I don't want to screw this up again."

I slid a corn chip into my mouth and felt the pleasant crunch. I waited a few moments before responding.

"I'm not sure I want to be your friend, to be honest," I said, shaking my head. "And it pisses me off that you're trying to fast-forward to the resolution."

I didn't want to cry. I didn't care if he saw my eyes getting red or heard my voice crack. I needed this moment. I didn't want it to shrivel up and disappear, like some mirage in the distance.

"Look, I fucked up, okay? I get that," Danny said staring down at his place mat. "But I don't know what I can say to make up for it now. Any answer I give won't be enough. You'll still be upset."

"Are you listening to me? Any answer is better than what I have," I said, tilting my head. "Which is, like, nothing. You left me with nothing, Danny. I was at my lowest point and you just bailed."

"You did nothing wrong," Danny said, his voice sounding dry and spent. "I was in a bad place. It's me. I had been worried I was going to get fired from Blast Radius for weeks . . . maybe a month. I'd reached out to a friend of mine, guy I knew from working in the fan press forever ago. He offered me a gig on the spot. The only drag was it was in L.A. Then it all blew up at New York Comic Con. You seemed so brave in that room, Annie—just . . . powerful. You told Riesling to fuck off with . . . I dunno. I felt lucky to even know you. But I also felt like a spineless drone. Just sitting there and watching him berate you. So I quit. But I needed a job."

"That's what I don't understand," I said, leaning forward. Our food arrived and I lowered my voice to a whisper as the waitress set our plates down. "You were so desperate for work you needed to jump at the first opportunity?"

I watched as Danny took in a long breath, then looked around—in every direction but at me, the person who was literally screaming for his attention.

"I couldn't handle it," he said.

"Handle what?"

"I love you, Annie, you know that—or you should," he said, the grimace on his face already telling me that his words didn't fully match the thoughts he was struggling to vocalize. "I wanted you, too. But I—I can't do that now."

I scoffed and looked up at the ceiling.

"You 'can't do that now'?" I spat. "What—"

"I'm sick."

Everything froze for a second—like in a Marvel movie where the villain stops time, drinks in mid-spill, everyone caught between their words.

"What?" I asked, unable to formulate anything else.

Danny ran a hand through his hair and leaned into his palms, looking down at the table like a kid being lectured for misbehaving.

"It's nothing serious, I just . . . I need health insurance," he said, as if reading from a prompter. "It's a long story, okay? I just—I'm sorry I didn't talk to you about it."

I shook my head, as if trying to wake up from a vivid dream.

"Uhh, yeah, you think? First off, you could have said this—or some version of it long before—to me in person," I said. I could feel myself clenching, anxiety and worry coursing through me—clenching every muscle and joint. I knew Danny hated for anyone to worry about him. The fact he was saying anything proved it was serious. "Just tell me what's going on. What's wrong?"

"It's not anything life-threatening, okay? I don't even want to bog you down with it. You've got so much happening," he said with a slight wave of his hand. "I just couldn't afford—literally—to be without insurance. With the doctors and meds . . . it'd be too much."

"Don't brush me off. If it was no big deal, why couldn't you say something when I was calling, texting, and emailing to figure out if you were even alive?" I asked, my jaw tightening. I could feel my skin warming over as the anger spread through my bloodstream. "I had to learn about your new job from a story in, like, *Newsarama*! How do you think that felt? And now I'm finding out you're sick? What is happening, Danny?"

He reached a hand out to me. I pulled back.

"Don't touch me," I spat.

"I'm sorry," he said. "Okay? I am sorry. I should have talked to you. I messed up. I get that. I just want you to know I know. And I want to work on fixing it if it's even possible."

I couldn't respond. I felt torn. I was so angry with him right now. I wanted to throttle him, smash his face into the guacamole and make him beg for forgiveness. But now I was reeling, too—unable to believe how he was downplaying everything. What was wrong with him? I could barely get myself going each day—but did he need my help, too? I couldn't handle this.

"I mean, look at you," he said. "You've come so far, just in a few weeks. You're sober. Annie, that's huge. I can't even process the baby part of it, on so many levels. You're doing great, you're going to do great things in the future. I'm so proud of you. It's impressive. I'm so impressed by you. You don't need me."

He sounded like he was writing a goodbye note, and that gave me pause.

"I could've used a friend," I said. "I still can."

Danny sighed.

"You can trust me," Danny said—his eyes locked on me. I thought I caught a flicker of anger in his words, but ignored it. "You can trust me to know that I did what I did because I had no choice. I feel terrible about it, but I had no choice."

We ate in silence for a few minutes.

I stopped chewing—then slowly placed my burrito back on my plate. I looked up at him. The chasm between us felt so huge, endless.

"Danny, are you sure you're okay?"

His wan complexion looked positively ashen. He was sweating, too. His blue eyes looked unfocused and distant.

"Annie, I . . . I ju—"

Then he just fell over, like a slab of meat hitting the floor. Danny was on the floor, lying on his side, his entire body shaking—each spasm worse than the last.

I got up from my seat and moved toward him, my knees skidding on the restaurant's floor. I crouched down, reaching for him.

"Oh shit—shit, shit," I said. "Danny, are you there?"

His eyes fluttered. The spasming continued. His mouth was open. He was trying to talk.

"Danny, stay with me," I said, holding his head with one hand, my other hand digging through my purse. I could hear the restaurant react around me, our waitress was above me, saying something, asking something. I pulled out my phone and dialed 911. "Hey, uh, hi, I need an ambulance—my friend . . . he's . . . he's collapsed on the floor . . ."

I didn't finish the sentence.

CHAPTER TWENTY-SIX

It was a little past eight when Gary's call came in. I was in bed, huddled in my blankets, listening to a boygenius playlist Margot had made me—not awake but not asleep, either. I could hear Margot watching television in the living room while I sat here, still replaying what had happened a few hours before. Spinoza's office. The rush of adrenaline and fear as I ran down those steps. The pounding in my chest, the way I gasped for breath.

The gun.

I'd taken immediate precautions, but they'd done little to calm me down. I changed my routines. Finally scheduled that alarm system installation. Kept Margot close. But none of that could cool the burning fear—the sense that this was just the beginning.

"We need to talk," Gary said.

"Is . . . is everything okay?" I asked, drowsy. He was not the type to call this late unless everything was very much not okay.

"I just sent you a link. Read it. Call me back. Wow, this is . . . holy shit."

I hung up and clicked on the message icon on my phone. Gary had already sent the link.

It was to a *New York Post* story. The headline alone grabbed my attention: "Controversial filmmaker Arturo Spinoza spills dirt on newly formed media company."

Arturo Spinoza, the once–critically beloved director behind classics like *Blood Oath*, *Real Bad Things*, and *Kismet*, has revealed in a brief email statement to the *Post* a shocking allegation against his now-former employers, nascent media company Triumph Entertainment.

Spinoza, who was slated to be the showrunner of the first of what was envisioned as a slate of television shows based on Triumph's large library of comic book IP, has confirmed that he has parted ways with the studio, alleging improper work conditions and an even more startling revelation: the company might not actually own its marquee character, the Lynx. It is worth noting that Spinoza is not free of controversy himself—having been mostly silent on the work front after a number of allegations of impropriety and toxic behavior arose years ago.

"I realize this is a glaring allegation that they will immediately call into question, but it will seem prescient in the coming weeks, when more details come to light," Spinoza said in his lengthy email, which was received by the *Post* at seven this evening. "The principals of Triumph Entertainment—the mysterious shell company that claims ties to Triumph Comics, a long-defunct publisher that once launched characters like the Lynx, the Dusk, the Freedom Alliance, Avatar, Carly Candela, La Sombra, the Eight Pillars, and more into the world—are playing an elaborate game of smoke and mirrors, one that hopes to lull the world into thinking that they have the same creative and ownership rights over the material published by the original Triumph. But I know, firsthand, that this is not true. While I don't know the intricate details of their deception, I was told numerous times by Bert Carlyle, Triumph

Entertainment's beleaguered CEO, that the company hoped to vamp on the issue until all challenges were defeated—including the recent lawsuit filed by acclaimed science fiction novelist and comic book writer Carmen Valdez."

The timing of Spinoza's exposé is no coincidence. According to the director, he recently departed the project because his creative vision—crafted in tandem with veteran comic book creator and fellow film director Annie Bustamante—did not jibe with the company's get-rich-quick and profit-seeking strategy.

"Once we presented them with an actual story—with conflict, character, and a concrete evolution—they balked. They didn't want that. They just wanted sex, violence, explosions, and paint-by-numbers drama. Not for me. I'm glad to be on to my own projects, and I'm sure Annie feels the same way."

And I'm sure Annie feels the same way.
"Oh boy," I said.

I dialed Spinoza. No answer. I tried again, but it went straight to voice mail. I left a quick message—mentioning, as vaguely as I could, that I still needed the password to his damn laptop and exhorting Spinoza to call me back. I needed to talk to someone.

I opened the Signal app on my phone.

Guess you saw the Spinoza story.

APPARITION: Believe me yet?

Believe what?

APPARITION: The Lynx. Who created her.

I was really tired. Tired of mysterious tips and vague comments—from this faceless account, from Spinoza, from everyone. I decided to take a gamble.

> Does Carmen know you're doing this?
> Because you're certainly not her.

Whoever was on the other side of the conversation paused. A few moments passed. Then those familiar ellipses signaling someone was typing.

APPARITION: What gave me away?

> No one's seen or heard from Carmen in years.
> She wants to stay hidden. So, you must be her proxy.
> If she even knows you're doing this.

Another pause. I'd shifted the balance a bit. I waited a second before sending another message.

> I want to talk to Carmen. Help me find her.

APPARITION: I don't think that's a good idea.
APPARITION: Triumph is a house of cards.
Spinoza is right. But as long as no one has concrete
evidence, they can keep vamping.

> Where do I get the evidence?

APPARITION: We've both been looking for it.
APPARITION: But you've got more than I do—once
you unlock it.

I didn't know exactly what this person wanted, but I was starting to get closer to figuring out who they were. I pulled the covers around me, creating a protective sheet fort. Did Carmen have friends? Was there a way to find out? I searched for Harvey Stern again. His killer, Dan Stephenson, had been a hack comic book writer and editor who'd felt cheated by Stern—he'd also attacked another comic book editor, a woman named Marion Price. The name rang a bell. Then I remembered where I'd read it before. The article about the Society of Illustrators. The hints about Carmen. I shifted my search to her—the details were scant. She'd worked at Warren Publishing briefly in the 1970s, and for a small outfit named Bulwark, a company that seemed to release a bunch of comics for a year or two, then disappeared. A not-uncommon occurrence in comics then and today.

I managed to find a picture of Price—a group shot from a volleyball game being played in Central Park, between Warren and Triumph Comics. She was standing next to another woman—the only two in the shot. I knew immediately who the other woman was.

Carmen Valdez.

A group shot at a park event didn't guarantee Carmen and Marion were besties, but it was something. I needed that password if I was going to use anything Spinoza had—and, considering an armed maniac was after the same thing, I hoped whatever was on there was good. I texted the director a handful of questions, then called. Nothing. Something was bothering me—a low drone in the back of my head—something I hadn't looked at or wanted to since this all started. I kept tapping away at my phone screen.

The article about Triumph had intimated that Spinoza was disgraced in some way. Everything I'd read about the director seemed to qualify his controversy—vague innuendo that something bad had happened and people might be mad. But what was it? And did it have anything to do with what was happening now?

It didn't take long to find the story, but I could tell there had been some serious reputation repair at play. I'd heard of services that clean up the Internet for mentions of your name, and it felt odd to me that a story as terrible as this one didn't have a bigger footprint. And perhaps it had—a few years ago. But someone like Arturo Spinoza could afford a digital rehab. Still, those services could only hide so much.

It was a 2017 piece in *The Wrap*, one of the Hollywood trades—and it was brutal. Some of the broad strokes I was familiar with, but the devil is, well, you know. The piece was an anonymously sourced, deeply reported account of Spinoza's behavior on the set of his last major film, the critically panned erotic neo-noir *The Remnants*. The essay cited the director's abusive and harmful behavior—mostly toward the younger, female actors on set. The story painted a picture of a power-mad, self-styled auteur who'd never experienced any kind of pushback on his vision, much less his behavior. My stomach turned. My interactions with Spinoza had been mostly pleasant—if at times tense and overly familiar. But I'd never gotten a predatory vibe from him. Then again, men didn't behave universally toward women. He could still be a toxic asshole. Hell, sometimes it made sense to just assume someone in that kind of position was an asshole. I had certainly run into my share.

I did some more digging—a few follow-up pieces. The sudden cancellation of Spinoza's next film project, an adaptation of *Here Comes a Candle*. Well-crafted social media posts from the actors mentioned in the initial piece. A crisis PR firm–generated statement from Spinoza's team denying any allegations of bad behavior. Then . . . nothing. Spinoza disappeared—no interviews, no announcements, zippo. I did a quick search on the failed movie adaptation that would've been Spinoza's next project. I scanned the IMDb credits. A familiar name popped up.

Bert Carlyle. He was listed as one of a handful of producers. Decibel Entertainment was also listed as one of the film's production companies—in tandem with Spinoza's own Cold Spring Harbor Productions.

"Huh," I muttered to myself.

Decibel was funded by Jessica Doyle, and had a Russian oligarch on its board. Doyle funded Triumph Comics. On paper, it just looked like your usual *hire who you know*. Carlyle had worked with Spinoza before, so they brought him onto the Lynx. But why hadn't anyone mentioned this to me? I typed out a hasty text to Spinoza.

Know about your history with Bert and what
went down before. We need to talk.

I didn't expect a response. But it came seconds later.

Meet me somewhere.

I felt my face redden. Then I made some plans.

Excerpt from *The Lynx Returns!* #4, published by New Wave Comics, October 2024.

CHAPTER TWENTY-SEVEN

I turned away from the large window in the St. Vincent's Hospital waiting room, intent on returning to my seat and pondering what had just happened. It'd been a few hours since Danny was admitted, and I was still waiting for word from the nurses—anyone—that he would be okay. Not being his spouse or immediate family, I had no cards to play. I didn't expect any special treatment.

I also didn't expect to run into Danny, standing in the doorway, looking like he'd just been hit by a truck.

Our bodies collided in slow motion, like one of those car crash tutorials you saw in driver's ed. Danny stepped back—smiling wearily. He was also fully dressed. Despite not being a doctor, I was certain he shouldn't be up and about—much less ready to leave.

"Danny," I said. It was all I could muster.

"Hey, they told me I could find you here." His voice was raspy and tired. He looked gaunt—even more spent than when he collapsed, or when I saw him a few hours before.

I grabbed him by his arms and looked him over.

"What the hell are you doing?"

I felt him droop a bit under my hands.

"Annie, I'm fine," he said. "I just had an episode. I don't need to be here anymore. Thanks for your help, though—it could've been bad if I'd—"

"I am one hundred percent certain they did not just sign you out," I said, still looking at him, clutching him more tightly. "So, again—what the hell are you doing?"

Danny wiggled out of my grasp and stepped back.

"I don't need to be here."

"Actually, I would argue that point," I said. "You seemed pretty well fucked up a few hours ago. Now you're just fine and dandy?"

"I'm leaving," he said. "I signed myself out. I don't have time to be here, and I'm okay. I have some work to do, and I can't spend my entire trip in a New York hospital."

I could hear the familiar stubborn force to his voice. I wasn't going to change his mind. But I could also see Danny on the floor, his eyes rolling back into his head, the spasms: That wasn't just exhaustion from a busy work week. It was something more serious.

"What happened?"

Danny started to respond, but no noise left his mouth for a few seconds. Finally, his thoughts caught up with his body.

"It's a long story," he said. "But I'm fine. I really just want to go to my hotel room and rest, okay? Can we catch up tomorrow? I know we still need to hash out a lot of things. But I have to connect with some people while I'm in town for work. You remember Kellye? We're getting coffee tomorrow."

I was in recovery. My mother was a drunk, too. I knew all about white lies, tools for evading conflict—tools for escape. Danny might not be an alcoholic, but he was running the alcoholic playbook. He just wanted to get past me, to get away, to shut down. I could either try to keep him here, confront him, or let him go.

"I'm not letting you get past me until you explain what the hell is going on," I said, moving my body between him and the exit. I saw his back stiffen.

If Danny had been a child, he would've stomped his feet. Instead, he just clicked his tongue and looked away toward the visitors' area.

"I don't have time for this," he said, his voice husky and unnatural.

"You don't have time for what? Telling me why you almost died before we got our tab at dinner?" I said, stepping toward him, my eyes pleading. He didn't meet my stare. "That wasn't just an episode, okay? If you're really sick, don't you think you should stay here and see what's wrong?"

He turned to look at me, a humorless smile on his face.

"I know what's wrong," he said, his voice ice-cold. "I've known a long time. You can either let me walk past you, or I'll just turn around and find another way out. I'm leaving."

I didn't move.

He started to turn away, but stopped mid-stride, his expression softer now, almost nostalgic.

"Don't worry about me so much," he said, his voice muffled, like he was trying to swallow each word. "I'll see you tomorrow."

I didn't say anything. I felt my eyes watering and looked away. I didn't want him to see me like this. I didn't want to see him like this, either. He gave me a quick nod as he turned around.

My mind flashed back to that scene from *Amazing Fantasy* #15. The origins of Spider-Man. Where cocky teenager Peter Parker, in his home-made Spider-Man suit, stepped aside to allow a criminal to make his escape. What did he have to do? It wasn't his problem. He wanted fame and fortune, not sacrifice and pain.

A few pages later, tragedy would strike, and a lifelong lesson would be burned into Peter Parker's very soul.

CHAPTER TWENTY-EIGHT

I had made the mistake of thinking the Spinoza piece was a singular bomb the director chose to drop at a very specific time. But Triumph's response—calculated, well crafted, and honestly shocking—told me different. They'd known something was coming, and they hit back. Very hard.

I got the Google Alert as I stepped off the F train on Houston and made my way east. It wasn't to a story—not yet. It was an Instagram reel from a comic book fan account named @ComicBookBuzzBoy—and it featured what I assumed was the host's face in front of a headline that read "Fledgling Media Company Triumph Entertainment Unveils First-Ever Fully A.I. Comic Book Series."

I turned the audio on and caught a few seconds of the account's thoughts, which were harsh, as images of the Lynx—a rooftop shot by Doug Detmer, a less skilled illustration by Steve Tinsler, and character designs by me—popped up behind his floating head. God, I hated social media. The fact that this pseudo-pundit hated the pivot to AI wasn't the surprise—what was shocking was the move itself. I closed Instagram and looked up the actual story, forever more inclined to actually read than to listen or watch someone tell me what a story was. The piece was short—a regurgitated press release on *Gizmodo* with a fantastically gruesome headline: "Has-Been Publisher Triumph Entertainment Cements Its Notoriety by Deciding to Use AI to Create New Comic Book Series." Triumph had partnered with an AI company named CyberTransit to "generate" an all-new series of Lynx stories that would "evoke and expand on the world created by Jeffrey Carlyle, Harvey Stern, and Doug Detmer in 1975." Whatever humor I found in the corporate face-plant disappeared as I kept reading. A quote from Bert Carlyle was what broke me.

"By tapping into the vast library of Lynx comic book artwork— published and unpublished—we've managed to synthesize it all into one strong, powerful voice. One that can continue Clara Callas's story forever, under the watchful eye of Triumph Entertainment, the owners of the Lynx and her world."

God, he still couldn't even get the Lynx's secret identity right. I reread the quote, feeling like I'd missed something.

Published and unpublished.

"Motherfucker," I said, looking intently at my phone as I crossed Lafayette.

The one image that accompanied the story, and presumably the Triumph PR, was a mess—a sloppy, awkwardly posed, and just plain ugly image of the Lynx, now wearing what looked like fetish gear, leaping through a window down on an unsuspecting white lady. But there was something familiar about it. I enlarged the image. That's when I saw it. The layout—the camera angle—was mine. It was the look of one of the last pages I'd turned in to Triumph, before I'd quit. One of the many pieces of art I'd demanded they return and never use. But here it was— run through some cyborg meat grinder and turned into a Frankenstein monster of comic book art that didn't deserve to live.

They were using my art.

It would've been funny if it wasn't so sad. My worst nightmare was coming to life. Not only was I not going to be able to tell a story about this character—to create a proper continuation of her adventures and a fitting sequel to the stories that had meant so much to me as a kid—but they were handing the keys to a literal computer, to create an abomination of a story in a desperate attempt to generate headlines, attention, and—theoretically—money. It didn't matter if they were being excoriated in the press and online, because, knowing Bert Carlyle—he'd press on. He'd see it through because it was cheaper than hiring real talent, or having to deal with them. The story would flop, the Lynx would disappear, and that would be that.

And they were using my fucking art.

I almost kicked the door down as I stepped into Botanica, a dimly lit and musty basement bar on Houston. I had blurry memories of birthday parties and comic book–related events there and next door, at an even tinier watering hole named Milano's. But I hadn't stepped inside in over a decade. It felt like nothing had changed. Except it was slightly past rush hour and the venue was almost empty. Spinoza looked terrible. Hunched over a half-empty Guinness at the far end of the main room, draped in the pink of an overhead light. I pulled out a chair across from him. Only then did he look up at me, his eyes dark and glassy, an even more unruly salt-and-pepper beard decorating his aging face—his expression a foul grimace.

"You came."

"I'm here," I said, trying to hide my surprise at Spinoza's state. I waved my phone at him. "Did you see the latest?"

"Ah yes—Bert has sold his soul to Skynet."

Spinoza was going to be no help here, I realized. I'd just have to suffer through this, get what I needed, and leave. I felt jittery and panicked. Like someone was taking my very soul. And in a way—they were. Triumph was using my blood, sweat, and tears to create a zombie version of the Lynx, and I had no way of stopping them.

I tried to focus on Spinoza.

"Well, you summoned me, Dr. Strange—what's the deal?"

He waved me off. "I hope you've kept it secure."

"What do you mean?"

Spinoza looked around the bar, like an informant scanning a desolate alley. "I need you to have it, okay? The computer. I'm in a bad situation."

"I read the story—the *Post* email," I said. "The new one. What happened?"

"I flipped. It was a mistake. I had a tantrum," he said, licking his lips nervously, then taking a long thirsty sip of his beer—emptying the glass in a few gulps. "I called Carlyle's bluff, he called mine, then that happened. They've wiped us from the slate, announcing that AI garbage. We're no longer the conversation, and they're pissed at me. Which means I'm in deep, deep shit."

"Deep shit how?" I asked, leaning forward. "You quit. That's it. What else could there be?"

"You understand the term 'mutually-assured destruction'?"

"Of course," I said. "But what does it mean in this context?"

Spinoza sighed.

"Look, I've made mistakes. You did your homework finally, and got a sense of what my baggage is. I've behaved badly. All of this . . . the fame, the power, whatever you want to call it . . . it got to my head. I thought I was invincible. I did some bad things. I destroyed my life, myself . . . my family," Spinoza said, looking down at his hands. "Then . . . I dunno, then it all came apart. I thought it'd just go away—people would move on. Forgive and forget, you know? I had a drinking problem. Still do, I guess. But I'm not really sure what I need to do to get to work again. And Bert . . . well, Bert gave me work."

"What you have to do?" I interjected.

Spinoza looked up, his eyes red and misty.

"How long do I have to suffer before I can make movies again?"

I felt my entire body stiffen.

"It's not that easy," I said. "You hurt people. I mean, you probably shouldn't be in charge of a set, Arturo. Not until you get your shit together and do some serious work on yourself."

Spinoza scoffed.

"Listen to you—so high and mighty," he said, his voice sharp with disdain. "Do some work on myself? What are you, the behavior police? You've never said a cross word or made a mistake?"

I was taken aback. I'd expected contrition, not doubling down. But then again, it was the usual playbook for men like this.

"Everyone makes mistakes. Then you apologize and learn from them," I said, trying to keep my tone flat and neutral. "You don't demand forgiveness or, in your case . . . permission."

Spinoza's mouth hardened into a thin line.

"I didn't think you'd understand. Of course you wouldn't. Everything is an 'issue' now," he said, using air quotes to emphasize his distaste for the word. But the bite was gone. I could tell this was not a new conversation for the director, and his heart wasn't in it. He was walking over footprints in the sand. "My point is, Bert helped me when I needed help."

"With Decibel?" I asked.

Spinoza's eyes widened. He hadn't been expecting that.

"How do you know?"

"It's nothing a little Internet sleuthing couldn't uncover," I said. "I know the surface—but not the details."

"Well, suffice to say, I know where his bodies are buried, and he knows where mine are."

Then it clicked. The story about Spinoza wasn't just what I'd read. There was more. And Bert Carlyle was sitting on the info—salacious, concrete details that would obliterate what little was left of Spinoza's career.

"You shot first," I said, leaning forward. "But you missed."

"What?"

"You thought your email would sink the Lynx project," I said. "But it hasn't. Maybe it won't. And he's up to bat."

Spinoza nodded, then rubbed his eyes roughly.

"Yes, yes, Bert has enough stuff to destroy me. My career is over," he said, his voice hoarse and low. A broken man just biding his time before his cab arrived. "I mean . . . my kids will never speak to me. My wife will sue me again. And work? No one will work with me. I'll be making commercials in Thailand, if I'm lucky."

Poor baby, I thought.

"I don't expect your sympathy," he said before finishing his drink. He motioned to the bartender for another. "You don't owe me anything. We could've made something great together. But my talent doesn't matter anymore."

"That's your fault."

Spinoza looked up, confused.

"Stop acting like this happened to you—like some bolt of lightning came down from above and changed your life, made you into a temporary asshole," I said, feeling my fingernails digging into a napkin. *Fuck this guy*, I thought. *Fuck. This. Guy.* "You made your choices. You think you're the only person on the planet who can't hold his liquor? You think you're the only person who's ever said something they're ashamed of? Or done something their ashamed of? You're not. But people work on themselves. You're just sitting here feeling sorry for yourself, waiting for an angel to come down and absolve you because your sentence has expired. Dude, the only person you can blame is yourself."

I hadn't realized I was standing up until I felt the strap of my bag start to rest on my shoulder. Arturo wasn't looking up at me. His face was buried in his hands. I started to turn around, a tight knot growing larger in my stomach.

"Cvaldez1975."

"What?" I asked, looking back at Spinoza.

"That's the password," he said, falling back into his chair, as if his bones had been pulled out of his body and all that remained were squishy organs and blood. "For my computer. I hope you find something you can use."

I nodded. I really wanted to leave, but I had one more question.

"You mentioned you had stuff on Bert," I said. "What is it? Was it just that they don't own the Lynx?"

"I mean, they might—they might own the characters," Spinoza said, frowning to himself. "But I got the sense that they don't even know. But

I'll tell you this—the companies that won cases like this? Marvel, DC, you-name-it? They all had more of a paper trail. Their shit was airtight. I guarantee you our ol' pal Bert has no such thing. A few comics from the seventies doesn't give you ownership of jack shit. And I know for a fact all the files and paperwork for Triumph are gone. At least . . . Bert doesn't know where they are. And those files? Contracts, work-for-hire stuff, court filings. That's what you pull out to show your cards. So . . . if that doesn't exist . . . well, if they don't know where it exists . . ."

Spinoza trailed off, but I jumped on it.

"Wait a second—do you know where those documents are?"

Spinoza motioned for me to sit back down, so I did—taking my place across from him at the tiny table. He was glaring at me now, a glassy-eyed, foggy stare.

"Did you hear my question?" I asked. "Do you know where those documents are?"

Spinoza waited a beat. I watched him as the wheel in his head began to grind, trying to formulate a response. In case there was any doubt, I was certain he was drunk now. Even worse, he seemed to be getting angry. Suddenly the meeting didn't just feel awkward and weird—it felt dangerous. I watched him lean forward slightly and was confused—for a second. Then I felt it—his coarse fingertips sliding up my leg under the table. Gently at first, then faster—past the hem of my skirt. I intercepted him after less than a second—swatting his hand away, hard. But the damage was done. I felt a disgust and anger build inside me. His hand was still hovering near my leg—I grabbed his fingers, tightening my grip around them, my nails digging in until he yanked himself back. I looked up at his face to see a shitty, slimy smile on his worn-out features.

I stood up again and yanked my purse off the chair.

"Fuck you."

I was trying not to shake, or seem like Spinoza had gotten to me—but, goddammit, he had. I felt my entire body tense up, my fingers clenching and unclenching, as if still trying to hurt him. I wanted to scream.

I saw a sleazy smile spread across the director's face. I felt a sharp, simmering distaste for not only this shell of a man, but for the entire affair. I felt the dark murkiness of Triumph Entertainment spreading, inching closer to the thing I loved—the Lynx—and threatening to poison the last pure thing I connected with comics and the books I read as a kid.

"You're disgusting," I said. The words seemed to get lost upon contact, bouncing off this slovenly, drunken man who probably wouldn't even remember any of this happened.

He mumbled something.

"What are you saying?" I asked.

That smile again. Then he cleared his throat.

"Look, I'm sorry . . . I got carried away . . . I'm drunk. . . ."

"I can tell," I said, shaking my head. "I'm going to leave now. I hope you find your way home."

I actually didn't give a fuck.

I had nothing else to say. I was sick of Spinoza's shtick. Especially now. He'd revealed himself and I didn't want to see more.

I turned around and walked out of the bar without looking back.

The sounds and smells of the city hit me immediately—honking car horns, dirt and spices, blaring music from a block away. I felt like I'd burst through a bubble of some kind, transporting myself back to the real world. I felt free of Spinoza. Of the Cheshire Cat–like taunting, the simmering lewdness. I never wanted to speak to him again. As I turned left on Houston toward the E train, I thought for a second Spinoza was behind me— the footsteps hurried and timed to mine. But when I turned around, I didn't see him. I didn't see anyone, really. Even though I was in the heart of Manhattan, it felt oddly desolate. I shrugged and kept going. It was late. I should probably just take a Lyft home. Then I thought about my bank account. Holding firm, but for how long? If this Lynx stuff became a legal problem—which, I mean, it kind of had to at this point—how long could I cruise on savings? Suing a corporation wouldn't exactly endear me to the studios. That, coupled with the shelving of *Miss Midnight*, felt like a recipe for a moribund career. I sighed and took the steps underground to the subway. I made my way toward the Queens-bound track in a daze, mulling over what had just happened with Spinoza—first in his office, and now face-to-face with the director.

"What a fucking mess," I said to myself as I stepped closer to the platform edge.

That's when I felt something in my lower back. Metal, cylindrical, and small. It didn't take long for me to figure out what it was.

"This is your final warning," a voice said from behind—low and gravelly, clearly a put-on, but terrifying nonetheless. I couldn't breathe. "Leave everything alone, and you will be fine. Go back to L.A. Make your stupid movies. Forget about everything."

A shove. I stumbled forward, leaning over the platform. I heard the horn of an oncoming train. I tried to balance myself. I felt a hand yank me backward—then that metal barrel, stabbing into the middle of my spine. I let out a high-pitched yelping sound. I felt the tears streaming across my face as I leaned back, desperate to not feel gravity pulling me down onto the tracks again.

I felt a face move closer to me, hot breath on my cheek—the smell of tobacco and something tangy invading my senses. I didn't dare turn to look.

"You wouldn't want to make your daughter an orphan, would you?"

The barrel jabbed deeper into my back, and I bit my lip, refusing to make another sound.

The barrel pulled back. I felt another rough pat. Then nothing. I waited a second before turning around. I heard the soft echo of footsteps—casual, slow-moving—in the distance.

I could hear my breathing—jagged, desperate panting. Could feel the tears stinging my eyes. But I felt something else.

A seething, white-hot rage. A spark as my fingernails dug into my palms. A laser focus I had thought I'd lost—but one I'd never forget again.

CHAPTER TWENTY-NINE

It felt like I'd held my breath until I got home.

I could still hear that voice—low and menacing, but oddly familiar—as if it were right next to me, the barrel of the gun still wedged behind me. The car ride home had seemed endless, my mind reliving each second of the encounter like some detailed forensic report, allowing for a myriad of alternatives—paths I could've taken to avoid what had happened. The message was clear. My snooping wasn't something I was doing off to the side—someone had noticed, and they were not afraid to hurt me if it continued.

I knew Margot was already asleep by the time I stepped into the dark apartment, fumbling with the entryway light switch. I exchanged hurried pleasantries with the babysitter and then zombie-walked to my small dining room table. I shook my head. No, it was too late now—too late to give up and hope for the best. I was in it. Tangled in a web that just grew stronger with every pull and struggle.

I saw it then, resting in the middle of the table—perhaps the key to it all.

I sat down in front of it and took a deep breath, my hand resting on the cold surface. What was in here? I asked myself. Did I even want to know?

I did. Especially after what had just happened.

Whoever threatened me on that platform didn't want me doing this. Which was just the incentive I needed. It meant I was getting close. I was on to something.

I cracked open Spinoza's MacBook and entered the password he'd given me—half expecting to get an error message, just a joke on Spinoza's part to fuck with me. *That creep,* I thought, my mind flashing back to the feeling of his dry fingers touching my leg. I closed my eyes tightly for a second. By the time I opened them, I realized the password had worked.

I scanned the laptop's list of files. Aside from a few documents on the desktop—a W-9, some plot breakdowns based on conversations I'd had with Spinoza, digital files of my comic page layouts and character designs, and a hodgepodge of task reminders—the computer was basically blank.

Was Spinoza this cruel? Or far gone? Probably a little of both.

I gave the list of files another glance. On a lark, I clicked on "Recent Items." That's when it popped up. Except I had no idea what "it" was, or what it meant.

It was an untitled notes file—the kind of thing I would've ignored on my own computer, but something that felt more frantic now. I clicked on the file, which was blank, except for a few lines of text.

CV—WFH contract, Berger sole signatory (according to Stu A.)

Part of CC exhibit

Call Marion P to confirm/get copy—IF SHE HAS IT!!

I reread the text over and over, for what felt like an hour but was probably closer to five minutes. This was it? I thought. Spinoza's smoking gun?

"CV" was obviously Carmen Valdez. "WFH contract" meant "work-for-hire," a contract that defined the work being done by a freelancer for the company, with no ownership stake. Berger had to be Rich Berger, the former editor at Triumph that I'd met so many years before. If there was a work-for-hire contract for Carmen that featured only Berger as a signatory, that meant someone at the company knew she was doing the work—but hadn't yet gotten her to sign the paperwork. It wasn't a rock-solid claim on the Lynx, but it was certainly better than nothing. But who was "Stu A."? The name—or part of a name—sounded familiar, and I strained to think of where I'd heard it. But it was late, and I was still on edge from Spinoza and what happened on the subway platform. I looked at the rest of the text.

Part of CC exhibit

My best guess was that "CC" meant a comic con of some kind—a museum exhibit. But that only helped so much. There were conventions all over the world, every month. Sure, not all of them had museum elements, but it could either be a well-known museum like the San Diego Comic-Con, or a lesser one off my radar. But it was a start. The next line gave me more hope.

Call Marion P to confirm/get copy—IF SHE HAS IT!!

"Marion P" had to be Marion Price. And if my guess was right, I needed to text APPARITION right now.

We need to talk. ASAP. In person.

Then I texted Yasmin Morris, Laura Gustines's former editor, using the number Pete had given me.

It's Annie Bustamante. Are you free tomorrow?

I fell asleep on the couch, waiting for responses.

I dreamt of powerful hands—sharpened claws. I dreamt of leaping across rooftops and thirsting for vengeance.

CHAPTER THIRTY

Sleep came in fits and starts. I gave up the ghost around six, the first few beams of sunlight creeping past my blinds. For a split second I felt almost normal—like it was any other day. But the mirage disappeared almost instantaneously, my mind whirring back to the night before. To the barrage of events that seemed more nightmarish than my actual dreams. Images cut through my mind, little snapshots—the sight of Triumph's perverse AI Lynx, Spinoza's coarse fingers on my leg, the pain of a gun in my back, and the gravel-laced threats that accompanied it.

I got up in one swift motion, trying to will the visions away through action, and an aching need to make sure Margot was fine. I snatched my phone from the nightstand and walked out. The messages I'd sent last night remained unanswered. By the time I got into the living room, I could see Margot was already milling around. She was an early riser by nature—her eyes just popped open at six or six thirty, unable to close after that. I was very much not like that, usually.

I caught a glimpse of her in my office, looking over something on my desk. I came up from behind and leaned my head on her shoulder. Margot gave me a kiss on the head and went back to staring at something on my desk. I followed her eyes—she was admiring some penciled pages for *The Lynx Returns!* It was a fight scene—Lynx vs. Mr. Void, her archenemy. It was part of Lynx's realization that she'd been manipulated by the Mindbender into believing she was someone else, effectively burying the Lynx persona. I liked the page—the layout felt creative, especially how the two figures seemed to be in motion with each other, plus the creative use of negative space. It moved your eye, simulating action. That was always the goal, you just didn't hit it each time.

"Good morning, sweetie," I said. "Waking up with some of my art?"

"These are pretty great, Mami," Margot said, not looking up. "I've never seen you draw like this. The pages seem really, I dunno—alive. Like you really spilled yourself onto the page."

I nodded to myself. She was right. The page was special. It also felt like it, too, was struggling with a void—the risk that it might disappear forever, lost to corporate dealings and malfeasance. It reminded me of the article I'd read on my way to the bar the night before. I felt my stomach turn at the idea of my art being used to create some kind of monstrous zombie version of this character—guided by bad people who didn't care about the Lynx the way I did. It felt like the worst kind of ending for the character.

Unless I could save her.

"Too bad the character isn't mine," I said, as much to myself as to Margot.

Margot turned to me, an innocent and confused look in her eyes.

"So what?" she asked. "Can't you change her name? Make it your own thing?"

"Just file the serial numbers off?" I asked, sarcasm coating my words.

"You say that like it's impossible," Margot said, her brow furrowing. "You can totally do that. Your dad drew the first few issues, right?"

I nodded. "He did," I said. "He died a little while after he worked on the book."

Margot's eyes widened. "Did you know he was your dad? When, like, you were small?"

I cleared my throat. "No, sweetie, I didn't," I said softly. "Abuela told me later—when I was older. An adult. When I—well, when I found out on my own."

Margot looked down at the art again, her jaw clenched. I knew that look, and I braced for what was next. Margot was kind, thoughtful, and patient—but when she wanted to say something, she said it. She turned to face me and I could see her eyes had gotten watery.

"I'm glad you told me," Margot said, her voice catching mid-sentence. I knew how much this took for Margot to say—how hard it was for her to talk about this strange, nebulous idea that was her father, this man she'd never met and barely knew about. "Told me who he was. I wish I'd gotten to, I dunno—like, see him. Or hear his voice. I don't know that much about this person, my father. It feels weird."

"It's not weird at all, Margot," I said, wrapping an arm around her, both of us looking at the page of Lynx art, eyes filling with tears, unable to look at each other. "He was a good man. He would have been a great dad. I'm sad every day that he's not here to see you grow up and become this special person he would have loved so, so much. But we also have each other, you know? We built this nice life. I know it's complicated."

Margot finally turned to look at me.

"Did you love him?"

"Of course I did," I said without hesitation—because there was no hesitation. I had loved Danny since I first met him, and that love morphed and changed and evolved.

We seemed to sit in the moment—each of us savoring a topic we rarely touched on. A no-man's-land we'd built to protect each other. But perhaps one that needed to be torn down.

"I feel like, this must sound crazy, but like a piece of me is floating out there," Margot said, looking away. I saw her jaw clenching. It's what she did when she was fighting back tears. It broke my heart. "And I may never get it, because . . . how can I?"

I pulled her in tight and whispered into her ear.

"You will get it, Margot," I said. "I won't let you feel alone. I won't allow it. Not like what happened to me."

"It must have been so hard for you," Margot said, wiping at her eyes and stepping back from my embrace.

"It was," I said, thinking back to that stretch of two weeks, over a decade before. "But I also felt like I was becoming something else. I was . . . becoming myself again."

Margot looked back down at the page, at our heroine, the Lynx, battling her archenemy, desperate to reclaim who she once was.

There was this saying in the rooms of AA, that when you stopped drinking, you became the age of the person who started drinking—and if you worked hard enough, you might be able to reconnect with the innocence and purity of that person. You might, in effect, become yourself again.

"Huh," I said under my breath.

"What?"

"Just . . . thinking about how much my life has changed," I said, my words rushed—trying to outpace the tears welling in my eyes. "How the journey's been all about—about getting back to that kid who loved to draw, you know?"

"That feels like something to keep in mind," Margot said, tapping the Lynx page. "When you decide what to do next."

I nodded, absorbing Margot's words as they hit—hard. I didn't hear my phone vibrating on the table until Margot grabbed it. I picked up once I saw the display.

PETE FERNANDEZ.

"Hello?"

"Hey, Annie, sorry to bother you," Pete said. "But . . . have you checked the news this morning?"

I felt my skin tingling.

"What's happening?"

"It's the director—the guy you were working with—Arturo Spinoza," Pete said. "He's dead."

CHAPTER THIRTY-ONE

APRIL 14, 2009

The sense of dread seemed to drape over me like a thick blanket as I woke up that morning.

I felt a sheen of sweat over my body. My eyes widened, trying to catch any flicker of light to pull in and figure out where I was.

A crack of sunlight entered my room, and I realized I was home. I'd overslept, but I was home.

Unlike times past—when I'd awoken in strange places, next to strange men—this time it was clear. I was home and I remembered everything.

I could still see Danny walking away from me at the hospital. His face gaunt. The dark bags under his eyes deeper than I'd ever known. His voice hollow and dry.

I'd tried to speak to his doctors but got nowhere. I wasn't his wife or relative, and if Danny wanted to leave and was able to, there was little they could do. There was even less I could do to find out more about his condition, if he didn't want to tell me. All I could muster was a text to Kellye, asking her to let me know how he was doing when they met up. She promised me she would.

I placed my hand on my belly. I couldn't feel anything yet, of course. It'd only been a few months since I even realized I was pregnant. But there was something in there, and eventually it'd be a person. I wanted to talk to Danny about it. To talk it all through with him. Did he want the same?

I got out of bed and slid into my clothes. I tried to push away the thoughts careening toward me—the fears, the anxieties, the failures. All the things that had collected and combined while I slept. I wanted to feel optimistic about the conversation with Danny. Wanted to feel like we were on a path toward repairing our friendship, even if it probably meant we'd never be involved as a couple. But it wasn't about just us anymore, either. I had someone else to think about, and I had to make sure I was able to take care of them—with or without Danny's help.

Let me check on him, I thought.

I texted, waited, texted again, called. Nothing.

It wasn't particularly early. If he was here in New York for work, he was probably in a meeting. It could be anything.

Then why did I feel so scared?

The problem with getting sober and not having a job was that I found myself with a lot of time to think. The time I once spent numbing my brain or toiling away at my art table was gone. I didn't have any work and I couldn't drink myself into oblivion. So I tried to fill the time with things that would help me stay sane. I talked to Sara, my sponsor. I hit a meeting in midtown.

But I couldn't dislodge the sense that something was wrong—and all through my day's activities, I still felt that dark feeling. I kept texting. Calling every few hours. Surely he was just busy, right?

It brought up old feelings. The sharp sense of abandonment—the idea that we could get close again, only to have him pulled away without warning.

My phone buzzed as I was walking up Central Park West, past the Dakota building. It was Kellye. They were supposed to get coffee right about now, I remembered.

I picked up fast.

"Hey," I said, already feeling out of breath. "What's up? Are you—is Danny—"

"You need to get down here, Annie," Kellye said, her voice strangely somber and different. Higher. Cracking slightly. I could hear yelling behind her.

"Get down where?" I asked. "What's happening?"

All I heard was "hospital" and "Danny" before I hung up and tried to hail a cab.

Kellye texted me the particulars as I got into the car. It took me into downtown Manhattan, back to St. Vincent's. I felt outside of my own body, like I was watching a reenactment of some tragic moment in history, but not fully accepting it was mine—like a slow-motion montage with no hope of escape. A barrage of texts from Kellye hit, each one sending me reeling.

> Danny collapsed as we were leaving coffeeshop—scary
> He looked really bad before that
> Doctor is saying it's Non-Hodgkins Lymphoma.
> Annie did you know he was sick???
> He kept asking for you
> You close?
> Please hurry.

I couldn't understand what was happening. It felt so alien and disconnected from reality. What the fuck was happening? As the cab passed Twenty-Third Street, I texted back.

> How is he?

No response.

A bad sign, I thought, as I tried to regulate my breathing—to think about something else. How Sara had praised my AA program. How nice the plants I'd bought looked in my apartment. About baby names and my first doctor's visit. But none of it worked. Nothing stuck. I couldn't stop thinking about now. Danny—lying in a hospital bed, maybe dying, of a disease I'd had no idea he was even struggling with. My mind seemed to sink deeper and deeper, crashing through layer upon layer, finally reaching an endless darkness.

I pictured us sitting across from each other in my room, poring over issues of *The Legendary Lynx*. I thought about Danny passing me a note in the cafeteria in middle school. Sitting next to me in high school chemistry, scanning my mixtape. I remembered sitting in Bea's car, pulling away from the parking lot at school—watching him get smaller and smaller. Weaving my arm through his on that Coral Gables night, walking into the distance. Kissing him in the park. His sad eyes. How he'd laugh with his whole body. I could see his sunken, frail body walking away—down the beige hospital hall, heading to a place where I couldn't follow, his shoes squeaking on the cheap linoleum.

Until he was gone.

Kellye was in the lobby when I burst in, wild-eyed and desperate for any kind of information. But her expression told me everything I needed to know.

"How is he?" I asked anyway, forcing her to confirm it for me.

She didn't say anything. She just pulled me in tight. I buried myself in her shoulder and just collapsed. My tears coated her sweater, which muffled the pained screams I was sending out into the world—desperate to pull Danny back, somehow.

I'd soon learn that Danny had gotten his diagnosis years ago. His mother explained as much as she was able, as we sat together during the viewing, both of us unable and unwilling to look at his body in the elegant casket. He'd felt panicked when he quit his job, she told me. He didn't want to live in California, but he needed health insurance. So he'd left. Gotten on a plane and decided to disappear. Not because he totally wanted to, but because he had to. Because anything else—any tiny opening between us—would force him to share this truth. This damning reality that I was staring down now. That he was dying.

I would process and absorb all of that later, if not fully accept it. But now all I felt, standing in the hospital lobby in front of Kellye—as I screamed and cried and tried with every part of me to get back to the Annie I'd been just a few hours before—was a deep, gaping sense of despair—of a long-held opportunity missed, of a limb torn away, and a best friend lost well before he should've been.

CHAPTER THIRTY-TWO

stared at Pete's tired eyes through my phone. Once he'd mentioned Spinoza being dead, I switched the conversation to FaceTime. I'm sure my expression was much more animated—and surprised.

"Okay, say that again," I said. I could feel Margot hovering behind me.

"Is that Margot?" Pete asked, moving his head, feigning to look around me. "She's huge. What happened to the little baby?"

"Hi, Pete," Margot said, smiling.

"Guys, I love this for you both, but I need details," I said, impatient. "I saw Spinoza less than twelve hours ago."

Pete took in a long breath.

"I have a contact with the NYPD, old friend of a friend—he knows you and I go back and had been following all the news with Spinoza, especially his latest meltdown," Pete said. I could see he was flipping through the pages of a reporter's notebook. Old habits die hard. "Once he heard they'd wheeled Spinoza in to the coroner, he tipped me off."

I struggled to feel anything, scrounging around my mind and heart for any strands or shreds of sympathy. Spinoza had been a sad, broken man—a talented artist who'd self-destructed. Despite everything, I tried to hold on to that understanding. That we're all just broken people float-ing downstream. Some of us are luckier than others.

"They can't rule anything out, but it looks like he took his own life," Pete said. "Does that track for you?"

I rubbed my eyes with my free hand.

"I mean, yeah, he was in real bad shape when I saw him," I said.

"The detectives working the case will probably want to speak with you," Pete said. "I'm happy to come up and help with that, if you need—but you're important, as one of the last people to see him alive."

"How did he die?" I asked.

"Gunshot to the head," he said. "That's all I got."

"It's impossible," I said. "No way."

Pete looked up at me.

"What do you mean? I don't need to explain to you that we have a firearm problem in this country, right?" Pete said, letting a dry laugh escape his mouth. "It's also, sadly, a fairly common way to off yourself."

"No, I get it, but not for him," I continued, wincing at the memory. "He told me—before. He hated guns. Was deathly afraid of them. There's no way he would've killed himself like that. Pills? Sure. Poison? Maybe. Something smooth and easy. But a gunshot? No fucking way."

Another pause from Pete. I could see him trying to put the pieces together.

"Did anything happen with Spinoza—when you saw him?"

"Yes, actually—he gave me the password to his laptop."

"His laptop? Which you had for . . . reasons?"

I explained how Spinoza had left me a cryptic message, how I'd taken his laptop, and the note I'd found. I skipped the part about me being threatened and chased because I didn't want to alarm Margot any more than I needed to.

There was a brief silence between us; the only sound I could pick up was Margot's slow breathing as she sat next to me. Honestly, I should've spared her this conversation in total, I thought, but it was too late now.

"Can you get out of town?" Pete said flatly, looking at Margot more than at me.

I felt my mouth go dry. Pete wasn't the type to mince words. And if he was saying this not even knowing what happened in Spinoza's office or the subway platform last night, I was worried. But his message was clear. If Arturo Spinoza was murdered, that meant I was in trouble. Spinoza had been completely off the rails the night before. Had I missed something? Could he have taken his own life? I didn't think it was possible.

"Annie? You there?" Pete asked. "You okay?"

"I'm fine, I guess," I said, shaking my head. "Do you think I'm really in trouble, Pete?"

"If, like you say, Arturo Spinoza was so averse to guns, then the only other logical solution is that he was murdered," Pete said, as if reading from a grocery list. "And the next logical question is: Who would want Spinoza dead? What did he have? Then you tell me he passed along his laptop to you, while acting really sketchy—where did you meet him? At his house?"

"No, in public, a bar," I said.

I could see Pete's eyes twitch. He was in recovery, too. We'd gone to meetings together in Miami.

"I wasn't drinking," I said.

"Not worried about it," Pete said. "I'm more worried that you met him in a public place and could have been followed. Shit."

Pete tapped his chin. I knew where his head was going. Someone saw me there. And he would be right. Someone saw me there and threatened to kill me—and Margot.

"Is there anywhere Margot can stay? Or can you guys, I dunno—go on a trip? You're a freelancer, right?"

I felt something snap in me—a feeling of anger and fear changed into something else. Resolve.

"I'm not going to run away," I said. "If anything, I'm going to run toward this."

"Annie, it's not running away—you're keeping your family safe."

I nodded but continued.

"I'm going to solve this myself," I said, turning to Margot. "Pack a bag, we're not gonna be back for a bit. Do it fast. Can you pack mine, too?"

Margot nodded and moved away from the phone. I looked back at Pete.

"Tell your friend at the NYPD I'm happy to chat with them by phone if they need me," I said. "I'm gonna see if Yasmin Morris is free for lunch before we head north."

"Any place in particular?"

I smiled.

"I've always wanted to see Cape Cod in the wintertime."

PART IV

THE GREAT
DARKNESS SAGA

Excerpt from *The Lynx Returns!* #5, published by New Wave Comics, October 2024.

SOMETHING PROPELS ME. A PRIMAL FEELING. *INSTINCT*.

Huh.

KLIK

A DOOR, HIDDEN IN THE WALL.

IN. MY. HOUSE.

THE SMELL-- MUSTY, OLD. NO ONE HAS BEEN HERE IN A LONG, LONG TIME.

I FIND IT IMMEDIATELY.

I FIND *MYSELF*.

CHAPTER THIRTY-THREE

I took a long sip of my seltzer and scanned the sprawling space, a distracted waiter weaving through a sea of empty chairs and tables.

Agra Palace was a half-decent Indian restaurant on Queens Boulevard on the border of Forest Hills and Kew Gardens. "Nondescript" was an understatement. The food was fine, as far as I was concerned—but it wasn't the cuisine that made it the perfect meeting spot. The restaurant was huge—probably raking in the money off weddings and events more than day-to-day restaurant fare. No one would guess I would be here, meeting with Yasmin Morris, and no one could overhear us, either. Even feeling secure in that, I'd taken every precaution. Margot was at my friend Brooke's house a few blocks away. I parked my car near 112th Street in a lot and hoofed it back to get to the restaurant, wearing my biggest pair of sunglasses and a faded Miami Marlins cap pulled down low. The perfect disguise? Probably not. But hopefully it was enough.

I motioned to Yasmin as she entered the sprawling restaurant, looking skittish and anxious right off the bat.

She took a seat across from me with little fanfare and placed a small envelope between us. I reached for it, but Yasmin interrupted.

She looked around—scanning the mostly empty restaurant.

"That's a key to a safe-deposit box at an Apple Bank in Astoria. Inside, you'll find Laura's manuscript. It has all her research materials, too, plus notes that she sent along with it after her interview."

"Her interview?" I asked.

"Her meeting with Carmen Valdez," Yasmin said. She tapped the envelope again. "That printout—it's the only existing version of Laura's book. After she died, my publisher was faced with legal threats from every direction, pushing for the book to never come out."

"Legal threats from who?" I asked.

"A bunch of places—different companies that our lawyers seemed to think were tied together, but they couldn't nail it down," she said, shaking her head in frustration. "It was a nightmare, and that wasn't the worst part of it."

"What else happened?"

"I was followed. Calls at every hour," Yasmin said. "I took the easy way out. I told them Laura never turned in a full draft. So that seemed to calm everything down. Until very recently."

"What changed?" I asked, leaning forward. I couldn't help myself.

"I changed," Yasmin said, looking down at the table. "I'm not stupid. Laura wasn't killed by some random carjacker. That's the easy answer. But it's not a coincidence that after she dies, after the only thing stolen from her is her phone, suddenly all these people want her book to die, too. They want to know where her manuscript is. Where her notes were. My lie about there being no manuscript only saved me a little time. I'm not proud of myself—I should have been more vocal, defended her memory. But something drove me to do something, too—to print her manuscript, with her stuff, and lock it away. I just felt like it needed to exist somewhere, in case . . . well, in case something happened to me. I know a printout and a transcript aren't the same as the audio from the interview, but they might be enough."

"Those legal threats—to your publisher, the cease-and-desist stuff," I began. "Do you remember any names? Any people or companies?"

Yasmin let out a sound—similar to a cough. It took me a minute to realize it was a laugh. But one with no joy, no humor, in it.

"I don't mean to laugh, I just—back then, we didn't know how much of a thing this was going to be," Yasmin said. "So we laughed when we saw the name of the person who'd hired the firm, because it sounded so funny—like a bug."

I swallowed hard.

"But, yeah, most of the firms that got sent after us, they were hired by this Russian lady," Yasmin continued. "Marina Pestova."

CHAPTER THIRTY-FOUR

I t was all where Yasmin had said it would be.

The trip to the bank had been painless and perfunctory. But I couldn't shake the nagging feeling I wasn't alone. And after the last few days, I couldn't afford to shrug my shoulders. Everything was a potential threat. Was that black sedan following me? The tall guy with shades who seemed to be in the bank just as I entered—what was his deal? My anxiety was spiking, and I wasn't sure if I should ignore it.

"This one's been here awhile," the stocky bank employee said jokingly as he unlocked the safe-deposit box in the bank's vault. Inside was a box about the size of a book manuscript. I didn't bother opening it—just grabbed the hefty cardboard and left. It was as if I were carrying the Cosmic Cube itself—a tiny device with the power over all things. And in some ways, it was. If there were answers anywhere, they were here.

I found a table in a tiny coffee shop adjacent to the Kew Gardens Long Island Rail Road stop. I always forgot the place's name, but it was rarely full, and the coffee was good and strong. I sat by the window so I'd be able to see anyone coming in—and carefully opened the medium-sized box. Inside was a manuscript—the pages well worn and uneven—

clearly a working document. At first glance, I could see Post-it notes on interior pages, red ink scribbled in the margins. This was Yasmin's editorial draft—in progress and not final, missing one last piece. An element Laura would never be able to add.

Next to the printout was a USB drive. Scribbled on the plastic were two letters: *CV*. Carmen Valdez.

Yasmin hadn't mentioned the audio. Was she being cagey because she thought we were being followed? Had she forgotten? Only one way to find out.

I pulled out my laptop from my bag and plugged in the USB drive. I waited a second for it to load on my desktop and dragged the contents onto my own computer. It was a single audio file, about 2GB, labeled "CV Chat_10/10/2018." I double-clicked on it and the audio started. I heard some jostling at first, then Laura's familiar, energetic voice. I felt my throat tighten. Though Laura and I were never close, it felt strange to be sitting here—years in the future—listening to her final recorded conversation. Then another, older voice—confident and clear.

"Can you say your name for me for the recording?" Laura asked.

"My name is Carmen Valdez."

I tensed up. Finally, here I was, on the precipice of something that could unlock whatever it was inside me that had felt so indecisive and lost.

GUSTINES: Okay, thanks for letting me record his.

VALDEZ: It's fine.

GUSTINES: So, I know we just had a meaningful moment and I want to record it for, well, posterity. Can you just recap what we discussed? About the Legendary Lynx?

VALDEZ: She's mine. That's what I said. The story that Triumph has crafted—that Jeffrey Carlyle had some kind of epiphany, then tasked Harvey Stern with creating a street-level hero, and that Harvey cobbled together six scripts over a weekend for Doug Detmer to draw—it's just a lie. The Lynx, or at least the basic idea for her, was an idea I'd had for years. I had stacks of notebooks—loaded with ideas, sketches, you name it. When Harvey asked me to work with him, to collaborate with him anonymously, I did the heavy lifting. Like you said— his past work, for tiny companies like Bulwark, don't sync up with his "work" on the Lynx. The style and, frankly, the quality don't match up. The truth was, Jeffrey Carlyle forbade me from pitching any more stories. I was his secretary. He didn't want me leapfrogging his friends and freelancers. So doing it in se- cret was my only option. Harvey promised me that, down the line, he'd reveal to Carlyle that I was involved. But he was the only person that knew my part in it. So, when Dan Stephenson killed him—resentful about Harvey stealing an idea from him, ironically—no one knew I was involved. I was watching the clock tick down on my baby, basically. I knew that once Doug drew the sixth script, Carlyle would have to find someone else to write it.

GUSTINES: Mark Jensen?

VALDEZ: Yes, but I didn't know that then. I just knew that at some point, the character would cease to be mine.

GUSTINES: Not to be too contrarian here, but it merits a mention—it was work-for-hire. Meaning, you were creating it with the knowledge that Triumph would own it.

VALDEZ: Well, that's the rub, isn't it? I have my notebooks. I have Doug Detmer's sketches. I never gave her away. I wrote her stories and Triumph published them. But there was no contract. I never signed a work-for-hire agreement.

GUSTINES: Okay, again, not trying to deny your story, but—isn't it understood that it was work-for-hire, especially since you worked at the company?

VALDEZ: (scoffing) You're presuming one thing—that Triumph even knew I was writing the scripts. Harvey turned them all in with only his name, that was his ruse—to get our foot in the door.

Then he was going to tell Carlyle. But then he was killed, so that went out the window. But the truth is, Triumph didn't know I was writing those stories, so how could they enforce any kind of contract? How could they give me paperwork to sign? And without that paperwork, what right does Triumph have to the IP? In fact—and I've never told anyone this—Jeffrey Carlyle knew. I confronted him, after Doug killed himself. I told him, point-blank that I wrote those stories.

GUSTINES: How did he react?

VALDEZ: (long pause) It was a hard time. I'd just been injured—I was in the hospital. I'd confronted Dan Stephenson at the Triumph offices and he pulled a gun on me.

GUSTINES: Oh my God.

VALDEZ: Yeah. He died in prison a short time later. He'd killed Harvey and attacked a friend of mine, Marion Price—she was an editor at Warren. We still keep in touch. But my point is— there was a lot going on. Carlyle, to his credit, gave me a soft landing. He knew I had something on him. His bad dealings with Stephenson. Things that could've destroyed the company. Knowing that, he just let me leave—paid me for six months and I went on my way. But he knew. He knew, before he died, that Harvey's role in creating the Lynx was minimal. And that there was no paper trail tying me to the Lynx. But I had actual evidence.

GUSTINES: There was no work-for-hire contract?

VALDEZ: There was one—Rich Berger, the editor on the book, was smart. He filled one out with my name on it, but by the time he knew I should sign it, I was gone. Ironically, that helps me more than Triumph. But I guess it's pointless—since the company doesn't exist, and—

GUSTINES: Sorry—do you have any idea where I could find that?

VALDEZ: Well, that's what I was going to say. I have no idea where it is. I'd check with Marion. She's become a bit of a historian in her old age. (laughs) She was putting together some kind of exhibit for the Comic-Con Museum about Triumph and other small companies that disappeared.

(scribbling sound)

GUSTINES: Why now?

VALDEZ: Why am I talking now? Well, you asked. (dry laugh)

GUSTINES: Right, but—you could have said something years ago.

VALDEZ: I was torn, honestly. The Lynx was mine. In the way a piece of your body is yours. When I lost her the first time, I did things I never expected to do—put myself at risk to find the truth. But after that I felt like I needed to just get away. And by the time I started thinking about her again, it was too late. Triumph was gone. Jeffrey Carlyle was dead. Who would I defy or challenge? But now—it feels like comics are everywhere. Movies. TV. Video games. It's only a matter of time before someone tries to reboot her. And I want to get this story out there before they try. (long pause) Before they take her from me again.

I stopped the audio and leaned back in my chair. After a few moments, I realized my mouth was open.

There it was, I thought. Laura Gustines had uncovered the truth—had driven home with the audio burning a hole into her phone. Had been smart enough to upload it somewhere her editor could find it. And then been murdered.

I turned my attention to the manuscript, flipping through the pages. I came upon a set of photocopied images—hasty handwriting scrawled across lined pages. It was a diary, I realized. And before I could begin to fully read the words, I felt a sharp jab in my midsection as I saw the name signed at the bottom of each page.

Doug Detmer.

This was my father's diary. I checked the date. Just days before his death. Had Laura dug up a copy of Doug Detmer's diary in her research, leading up to her conversation with Carmen? I wondered. I felt light-headed. I wanted to dive into these pages. Immerse myself in every line, quirk, or clue that might bring me even a centimeter closer to the man that could have been my father, this man I'd never get to know. I tried to focus in on one passage, in the middle of the small stack, a few months before Detmer died.

No way Stern had much to do with Lynx. Just not possible. A passable writer on his own, but this stuff has verve and style. Feels hungry and confident. Like someone desperate for a chance with the chops to make it count. I'm drawing this book because the story is great. And I know the story isn't Harvey's. Carmen is the creator here. I hope she finds a way to let Carlyle know it, too. But that's not my problem anymore.

I tried to imagine his staccato voice filling out the hasty cursive I saw on the page. I'd only heard snippets of Detmer's voice—usually old, grainy audio interviews or the random YouTube clip. I swallowed hard.

The note from Spinoza's computer reappeared in my brain, as if projected on a billboard above the Van Wyck.

CV—WFH contract, Berger sole signatory (according to Stu A.)

Part of CC exhibit

Call Marion P to confirm/get copy—IF SHE HAS IT!!

I went over the message, line by line.

Carmen Valdez. There was a work-for-hire contract somewhere with Rich Berger as the sole signatory—proof that Carmen had never signed away her rights. That paperwork might exist as part of some kind of exhibit for the Comic-Con Museum, curated by Marion Price. The same Marion Price I'd read about before—who'd been working on another exhibit trying to dig up the same information.

I pivoted back to my laptop. I found the site for the Comic-Con Museum. Scrolled to the bottom of the page and discovered a contact email. There, listed among a number of other names I could not recognize, was what I was looking for.

Marion Price—Curator, Lost Comic Book Companies Exhibit:
mprice@comicon.org

I clicked on the link and sent a brief, vague email.

Hi Marion,
You don't know me at all, but I have some information on Triumph Comics that might prove useful to your exhibit. And you might have something that could help an old friend of yours. Can we chat?
—Annie Bustamante

I didn't believe in coincidences. Laura being carjacked in Queens—her phone the only thing missing—felt too tidy. I thought of Arturo Spinoza, the disgraced director—struggling for redemption. Now he was dead, too, felled by a weapon he would never use.

I reached into my purse and pulled out my phone, dialing Pete.

"Pete," I said without any kind of greeting. "I need a favor."

"Your tab is open, Annie," he said.

"Well, this might sound weird, but—can you find out who was investigating the murder of Laura Gustines?"

There was a long pause on the other line. Then a throat-clearing.

"Annie, what are you getting into?" Pete asked. "You need to leave New York. It's not safe for you to be at home, or close to home—okay? I can ask around, but promise me you'll get out of town, like, yesterday."

Before I could respond, I felt my phone vibrating in my hand. I looked at the display.

APPARITION: Have you figured it out yet?

Vibrating again.

I got back on the line with Pete.

"I need to call you back," I said.

"You called me, remember," Pete said with a chuckle. "I'll hit you back with the intel. In the meantime, Annie—please don't do anything I wouldn't do."

"That's giving me a lot of wiggle room, Pete," I said before hanging up. I switched over to Signal.

Guess you got my email, Marion?

I didn't get a response as I packed my bag and speed-walked to my apartment. It was time to go.

CHAPTER THIRTY-FIVE

I made a beeline for my apartment, the box containing Laura's manuscript, Doug Detmer's diary, and the Carmen interview feeling so much heavier than it actually was. I needed to pick up my overnight bag, head back to the car, grab Margot, and hit the road. It felt like time was moving faster than it should. Like I was being pulled by an unseen force—as if I were being shunted into a large, star-spanning adventure I couldn't fathom.

The first inkling that something was wrong—seriously wrong—came when I slid the key into the lobby doors of our apartment building. I'd been texting with one hand—sending a message to my friend Brooke, asking her to please get Margot ready to be picked up in twenty minutes. But I froze when I noticed it.

The main door was ajar, propped open. That never happened. The super hated it when residents did that—"Security risk," he'd complain. My building had the usual problems—packages going missing, random people waltzing in. But nothing out of the ordinary for New York. This felt weird. Whoever had set it had done it recently.

Pete's words blared in my skull.

"You need to leave New York."

The voice in my head repeated Pete's warning. Over and over as I turned left at the main door. Louder as I took the short flight up to our second-floor apartment. The sentences kept repeating in my mind, smashing into each other until all that remained was a long, painful drone. As I reached our door, I realized it, too, was ajar. The light in the long hallway that led into the living room was lit. I knew I'd turned it off before leaving. I swallowed hard as I stepped in.

I saw the shelf—the bookshelf that greeted visitors, that held all of Margot's favorite graphic novels and the few that I had worked on, splayed out on the floor. It took me a second to register that the shelf had been toppled, that the books strewn around the floor were mine.

"I called the police," I said, raising my voice—just in case someone was still around. But I didn't hear anything—or see any movement.

I was speed-walking now, scanning the entire apartment. Our lovely apartment, which was now a wreck—TV screen shattered on the floor, tables turned over, couch cushions sliced open, my iPad tossed in a corner, the dining nook table and chairs splayed out around the room. Margot's bedroom was equally destroyed—bookshelves broken, clothes everywhere, bed flipped over.

Someone had come in here—into my home—and taken it apart, destroying and attacking pieces of my life. Margot's life. My fists clenched.

I pulled out my phone, my breathing heavy and ragged. I dialed Pete.

"Yeah, hey . . . Annie—are you okay? Two calls in one day—"

"I'm fine . . . I think," I said, panting, looking around at the destruction. "They were here. In my apartment."

"Okay, listen to me clearly—you need to leave," Pete said. "Right now."

"I was attacked, Pete—before this," I said, the words spilling out. "At Spinoza's office. Then after I saw him . . . on the train. I just couldn't—"

"Right, right—Margot was on the call. Annie, listen to me," Pete said, his voice growing louder. "You have to get out of there. Please."

I walked through the wreckage again, with Pete on the line, his voice sounding distant and panicked. Then I remembered something and ran to my office. I reached my art table and crouched down, pulling out a long black folder from beneath. It was my Lynx folder. Where I stored all the art and notes for *The Lynx Returns!* I opened the folder hastily, rummaging through the pages. It all seemed to be there. Had it been so well hidden? Did whoever trashed the place just not want them? What had they been after?

"...Annie?"

Pete. Pete was on the line.

"I have to go," I said, still wandering around, my folder of Lynx pages clutched in my free hand. "I'm going to get Margot and leave, okay? Don't worry."

I hung up.

I walked back into the living room and looked at my destroyed iPad. Remembered my own computer was in my purse. But there was something missing.

The laptop. Spinoza's. It was gone.

Had someone seen me take it? Was that what they were after?

It had to be. I couldn't find it anywhere. Which meant they knew what I was looking for—and what I might already have.

I pulled out my phone and opened the Signal app.

> We need to meet. All of us. Now.

APPARITION: What do you mean?

> Look, cut the shit, Marion. They're on to me.
> My life is in danger. But I have it.

APPARITION: You have what?

> Enough evidence to take them down.
> But I need the rest.

PART V

BORN AGAIN

Excerpt from *The Lynx Returns!* #5, published by New Wave Comics, October 2024.

CHAPTER THIRTY-SIX

I pulled the rental car onto the gravel driveway. I turned off the engine and sighed, letting my back fall into the seat after what felt like hours hunched over the steering wheel, eyes on the road, the sounds of the other cars around me the only noise entering my mind. I'd turned my phone off. It'd been just us—me and Margot, off the grid, heading toward some kind of salvation.

"You okay, kiddo?" I asked, turning to her.

She looked up from her tablet.

"My legs are gonna feel sore when I stand up, so I can only imagine how your old bones will feel," she said, trying to stifle a laugh.

I gave her a playful shove.

After discovering our apartment in shambles, I'd sped over to my friend's house and collected Margot—heading straight for our car. It was late in the day, so we knew we'd face some serious traffic getting out of the city, but I didn't care. I wanted to leave. I wanted to be as far from New York as possible. And I wanted to think about what was going to happen next.

Someone was after me—and they knew exactly what I had and what I might be looking for.

I thought of contents of the safe-deposit box that were in the back-seat, everything I'd collected—the file, documents, screen captures, the audio, and Detmer's diary. I'd itemized everything to Apparition, who I knew had to be Marion, via Signal at a Connecticut rest stop, as Annie bit into a Dunkin' Donuts chocolate frosted and I tried to stretch my legs.

APPARITION: You're just driving to Cape Cod?

Yes. Send me her address and it'll
make it easier for everyone.

APPARITION: Will do. See you soon.

Marion Price—a forgotten piece of comic book history, helping out her friend Carmen, who'd also been consumed by the endless churn that was comics. Two women who refused to be forgotten.

CHAPTER THIRTY-SEVEN

I took a deep breath. I felt Margot's hand in mine, clutching tightly.

"You can do this," she said with a nod before stepping out of the car.

I opened my car door and walked around the silver Prius. Margot handed me a large bag, long and wide and thin—the perfect way to carry original art. We both looked up at the door to the tiny, cute little house. Like something out of a catalog or nursery rhyme. I moved to the backseat and reached for the contents of the safe-deposit box.

I wasn't a detective—I was an artist, a mom, a filmmaker. But I also knew a terrible wrong had occurred, a deep-seated theft of something so primal and important that no matter what magnificent work I injected into the Lynx—even on my own, going rogue—it would not redress it. It was also going to be perverted—all the work Carmen, my father, and I did to create and reinvigorate this character was going to be ground into something robotic and false, something that should never exist.

Carmen Valdez created this character. Had borne her out of her own mind and experiences and pain. Had poured herself into this comic book superhero and then watched as it was swept away. First by the mundane machinery of comic books—then by corporate greed and a desperate desire for "IP" to "maximize" and pervert. I wanted nothing to do with that part. But I did love the character. And the Lynx belonged with Carmen Valdez.

We walked up to the red door and I rapped on it with my free hand. I heard shuffling and a muffled, "Coming!" from inside. The voice was familiar. I'd heard it just the day before, sitting in a tiny Kew Gardens coffee shop.

The door swung open and the woman on the other side—petite, with sharp features and a stylish, close-cropped haircut that accentuated her almost-white hair and deep dark eyes. She looked us over, recognition flickering on her face. She gave me a slight smile.

"Hello," Carmen Valdez said. "I think you have something of mine."

I smiled.

"I'm Annie Bustamante," I said, then nodded to Margot. "And this is my daughter, Margot."

"I've been expecting you," Carmen said, before stepping back and motioning for us to enter.

I walked into the house slowly—my eyes scanning the living room, which felt crowded but in some kind of order. I caught sight of copies of *The Things That Saved Me*, Valdez's illustrated memoir. I remembered rushing to the bookstore and buying it on release day—loving it—but also feeling like it was incomplete. Not because Valdez had been barely over fifty when it was released, but because there seemed to be a sense of fast-forwarding. Through her time at Triumph, the Lynx, and comics in general—all the stuff that had happened before she became an acclaimed if not bestselling science fiction author. I understood that better now, and could even relate. I'd done the same. Carmen Valdez had skimmed over the parts that hurt too much to think about. Then she'd gone off the grid.

"Marion Price sent me," I said, my voice sheepish. "At least, she told me to say that."

Carmen smiled, not just with her mouth, but her eyes, too. A genuine smile.

"Oh, Marion, she's always stirring the pot," Carmen said with a laugh as she walked farther into her house. "She's a dear friend. The kind of dear friend you never talk to, because what you went through was so painful. She's always up to something. She told me you were coming, too. Knew I'd be pissed if some random person showed up at my door. I've had my fill of that. I've chosen to disappear from publishing. It's done wonders for me."

"Your house is cozy," Margot said, looking around, her arms wrapped around the contents of the safe-deposit box. "It feels like a home."

Carmen turned to Margot and placed a hand on her shoulder.

"That is very nice—and very true," Carmen said. "I've worked hard to build a safe place for myself here. Away from anything bad or hurtful."

I felt the comment dangle there—between the three of us, a sentence unfinished. I suddenly felt tired—as if all the momentum and pain and emotion that had pushed me here had suddenly dissipated into nothing. I thought of Danny, sitting in my room and looking at me with those wide, hungry eyes, as I explained the importance of Carmen Valdez. I pictured my father, the father I'd never met—Doug Detmer—sitting at a rickety art table, drawing Carmen's words, bottles circling around him as he spiraled further and further away from the world.

"I feel like I've been here before—so many times," I said, surprised by my own words.

Carmen spun around and looked at me, as if sizing me up. Then she nodded, understanding the feeling of what I'd said, if not the words.

"The last person I had here, to talk about what I think you want to discuss—she died," Carmen said. "A lot has changed since then."

I motioned to my bag, and the stuff Margot was carrying.

"I just want to say—I mean, this is a big deal to me. To my life. Even with everything going on. Now that I know what I know, I can't, well, I don't think I can thank you for everything," I said, stammering, but pushing myself forward, knowing that this moment—this chance—would not come again. "I want to do right by you, and I think I got a little clouded on how. I thought I could write a story to honor your work—to evoke what you did when you created the Lynx—but there's no way to do that, to be fair about it, even if I do it alone, apart from the company that stole this character from you."

Carmen looked down at the floor, to her feet, then back up at me.

"Why don't we sit down in my office?" she said. She looked at Margot. "Do you want something to eat? Some books to read?"

She could've offered my kid bricks of gold and she wouldn't have agreed faster.

Carmen set her up with some cookies and a stack of graphic novels—a book called *Euthanauts* and another I'd never heard of, *Wynd*. I gave Margot a strong kiss on the top of her head and turned to follow Carmen.

Carmen spoke as we walked down a long hallway, the walls covered with different mementos from Carmen's life. The original cover to *The Legendary Lynx* #11 ("A gift from Doug," she said), a photo of a younger Carmen and another woman on a tropical vacation ("That's my wife, Molly—she's visiting family. We were on our honeymoon," Carmen noted, pride in her voice), and another picture—this one clearly from decades ago, perhaps the mid-seventies. Of an even younger Carmen, seated behind a desk in front of a large glass-enclosed office, her head tilted as she took notes while on the phone. Behind her, through the glass of the larger office, I could make out copies of classic Triumph comics like *Avatar*, *The Freedom Alliance*, *The Black Ghost*, *The Dusk*, and more.

"Unhappier times," Carmen said as she opened the door to another room.

Carmen motioned for me to sit on a small sofa positioned across from a tiny desk, the bulk of the room taken up by a series of massive bookshelves behind her chair. It was a who's who of science fiction, with a meaty, meaningful comics section, too. I recognized many of the names. Colleen Doran. Kieron Gillen. Neil Gaiman. Jeff Lemire. Brian Michael Bendis. Kelly Sue DeConnick. MariNaomi. Ed Brubaker. James Tynion IV. Julia Wertz. Grant Morrison. Jaime and Gilbert Hernandez. Maia Kobabe. Kelly Thompson. Adrian Tomine. Kate Beaton. Mark Waid. Scott Snyder. Tini Howard. Alan Moore. It was a veritable hall of fame. But the names also stood out because they were creators who were fearless. Who tried new things and weren't boxed into one kind of narrative or style. They were versatile. They were gifted. I understood, without even asking, why someone like Carmen Valdez might be drawn to their work.

I was yanked from my reverie by the sound of Carmen's hands slapping her desk.

"I was intrigued when Marion told me you wanted to meet," she said, the words coming out slowly, chosen carefully. "I was also a little bit surprised. I spoke to your friend—Gustines—years ago. I felt like that would finally blow the lid off everything. Put to rest these stories about Jeffrey Carlyle creating the Lynx and at least, I dunno, bring me back into the conversation. Then she gets killed and I'm back to zero. I was distracted, too. Life happens. Molly is a musician, so she travels a lot. I was with her—bouncing around. I was also trying hard to just . . . I can't describe it. I was trying to just live. To not be part of the conversation. But then, a few weeks later—I'm sitting here, and I'm wondering . . . how will people remember me? Sure, I wrote some books people loved. Yes, there's some dispute over the Lynx, but no one knows, you see? My lawsuit is buried in legal briefs and motions. And the evidence I have is . . . just my word. Why would I lie? Why would I say I created something if I hadn't? But that and a few bucks might get you a latte, I guess. Then Marion calls and tells me to meet with you—with the artist cashing checks from this new, zombie Triumph—and I'm just . . . intrigued by what this conversation might mean. Because honestly, how can I expect you to know me? Or my life? Or what I've done?"

"I do know you, though," I said, my voice dry, sounding like someone else's. "I read Laura's book. I heard your interview."

Carmen's eyebrows popped up. "How is that possible?"

I straightened up in my chair. "Laura, I guess, was so excited she . . .

she uploaded it and it got to her editor," I said. "And the interview confirmed a lot of speculation she'd already dropped into her manuscript—about you, about the Lynx, about Triumph and where their money came from."

Carmen nodded, mouth agape. "Can you . . ." she began, her eyes squinting as if searching for the right words. "Can I see the book? Those tapes?"

I leaned over and opened up my bag. I pulled out Yasmin Morris's photocopied version of Laura's last draft and placed the small USB drive containing Laura's interview with Carmen atop it.

"That's a lot of ammo," I said, motioning toward the stack with my chin. "But Marion said it might not be enough."

Carmen sighed. "Yes, she told me the same thing. It was all circumstantial, he-said, she-said," Carmen said, shaking her head.

"But you mentioned a contract—a work-for-hire document you never signed," I said. "I'm trying to figure out where that might be."

I leaned forward, my eyes on Carmen's.

"You said Rich Berger signed it, right?" I said. "To show that he knew you wrote it? That he knew you and Doug created the character with Harvey?"

I watched as Carmen's eyes began to well up. She wiped the tears back roughly.

"Rich, Rich, Rich . . . yes, he was a sneaky, wonderful man," Carmen said, her voice hoarse now. "He did it on purpose. He did it to fuck with Carlyle. This proves the company knew I wrote those scripts. There's no other way to look at it. But how do we find that?"

"I think I know," I said. "The movie director—Spinoza, the guy attached to the Lynx TV series—he knew about this, had the details on his laptop. But it felt like some kind of Morse code. Eventually I was able to figure out what it meant."

My mind drifted back to that fateful New York Comic Con, so long ago—standing in the Javits Center, looking at my BlackBerry. Reading an email about a comic book archive theft, belonging to a man named

Stuart Alford. The item about Marion's exhibit. I mentioned what I knew.

I watched as Carmen's face contorted.

"Stuart Alford? Well, that's a name I haven't heard in . . . almost fifty years," she said with some disdain. "He was a comic book journalist, probably one of the first—maybe before Don and Maggie Thompson. Like Heidi MacDonald or Graeme McMillan now, if you know them. He covered comics back before comics even knew they needed to be covered. When I was trying to figure out who killed Harvey . . . Harvey Stern . . . his files helped me. It's just so . . . trippy, I guess, that they're helping me again. How did he get his hands on this, though?"

"According to Marion, Alford bought all the Triumph paperwork when the company went under. Then it was stolen, after Alford's death, years ago."

"So where are the files now?" Carmen asked.

"Marion tracked them down to this abandoned warehouse in Astoria," I said. "Someone didn't want this stuff to be found. They just weren't sure what they had. I'm going to get them."

"Why are you doing this?"

Carmen's question boomed across the room—an announcement. Our eyes met. Two women who'd given their lives to comics. Given their best years to comics. Two women who shared a passion not only for the medium, but for this particular character. This street-level hero, scarred by her past, who chooses to help those less fortunate—to sacrifice herself to protect the innocent, in a way she had never been protected. But the Lynx was Carmen. And the Lynx was me, too.

I didn't answer right away. I went back to the bag and pulled out a thick stack of pages—comic art pages. I saw the glimmer of recognition in Carmen's eyes as I spread out the pages on the small stretch of floor between me and Carmen's desk.

"When I got the gig, or thought I had it," I began, "I felt like my mission was to make sure that this company, or whatever it is, didn't screw it up. Didn't mess up this character that had meant so much to me—as a kid, as an adult, as a person. I didn't realize that, in the process, I'd almost become complicit to some greater mistake and injustice. These people took her from you, and I was, in a way, helping them. But even before they reached out to me I'd been working on this, because I wanted to tell a story—a story that felt as strong or as good as what you and—"

"Doug," Carmen said. "Doug Detmer."

"My father," I said, not looking up. I heard Carmen's gasp before I saw the surprise on her face.

"How is that even possible?" Carmen asked, tilting her head. "Annie Bustamante, where on earth have you been all my life?"

I raised a hand, as if to say, *There's more.*

CHAPTER THIRTY-EIGHT

Adiary?"

I watched as Carmen slowly flipped through the worn, faded pages of Doug Detmer's diary and smiled, nodded knowingly, and frowned at least once every few turns of the page.

"I never met him," I said, eyes still on Carmen. "I never got to know him."

Carmen looked up, tenderness in her expression.

"He was a demanding man," she said. "And he was an amazing artist. His name, honestly, should be up there with people like Jack Kirby, Alex Toth, Steve Ditko, or Jack Cole. He was a genius. But he was complicated. He was passionate about the work, but only if he was passionate about the work—if that makes sense. He couldn't hack it out. And if something was bad, if he thought you weren't pulling your weight, he would tell you. He figured out I was writing the scripts before I had the guts to mention it to anyone. He liked my work. That meant more than I could imagine then . . . and now."

Carmen gently closed the diary.

"He confirms you created the character in there," I said. "If we get that contract—do you think that'd be enough?"

Carmen let out a humorless laugh.

"Oh, how I wish it were that easy," she said. "All it gives us is a little ammo. But that's a lot more than we had this morning, I'll tell you."

Carmen stood up and walked around her desk, positioning herself by my shoulder. I looked up to see the writer staring down at the pages of inked artwork featuring my version of the Lynx.

"That's a good one," Carmen said, pointing at the sequence of Claudia Calla waking alone, then seeing her own reflection in the Lynx's costume. "I like it. You really do draw like your dad. How wild is that? You didn't even know him, and you draw just like him."

I started to speak, but the words wouldn't come. Carmen was right. I had never met the man. But in some way, perhaps my entire life, we'd been talking to each other in a different way. Through the panels and pages of these comics. Both the stories I pored over as a child and the art I created—first influenced by Doug Detmer's dynamic artwork, and then later trying, perhaps in vain, to improve upon it.

"These are all good, honestly," Carmen said, crouching down, with a slight popping sound and a wince. "But you said you're not working on the book anymore? They let you go? Did they even look at these? What a bad decision."

"I think I was a little too demanding for them," I said with a laugh. "I didn't want to water down my story to fit what they thought they were looking for. They just wanted to sell the idea. Get rich with a movie or a show. They're using all the art they have—Doug's, mine—to create some, I dunno, artificial version of the Lynx. They didn't care about comics. Or the character. It felt like a golden cage."

I almost jumped as I felt Carmen's hand on my shoulder.

"Sounds about right," she said, pulling herself up to her feet.

Our eyes met.

"Do you have a script?"

"A script?" I asked, confused. "For the comic? I mean—yes and no.

I wrote out a plot and started laying out the pages, but I hadn't gotten to the dialogue, not yet. I just wanted to tell the Lynx story I wanted to read, well, after your stuff ended."

There was a long silence between us.

"Let me help you."

Carmen's words landed like a bomb. I felt dumbfounded—my entire body tingling. I'd never anticipated this as a possibility, not over the hours it took to drive here from Queens, or over the years I'd spent working on my own Lynx story. It was not on the table. Like Spider-Man showing up in Metropolis to team up with Superman, or the supernatural avenger Spawn crossing paths with Batman, some team-ups just felt impossible until you witnessed them.

Carmen Valdez, the actual creator of the character, wanted to write a Lynx story for the first time in decades. With me.

How could we do it? It would be a lost legend—the kind of story that fans would clamor over but never see. *Big Numbers* in overdrive.

Then it hit me.

I remembered Gary's words, about a newsletter platform willing to pay me to create content for their site. *Could this work?* I wondered.

I blurted the thought out.

"Let's just . . . post it," I said. "Post our story online. I can scan the art. I can get a friend to letter it. I can color it myself. Let's just do it. What's the worst they can do? Sue us?"

We shared a long, relaxed laugh—the kind old friends share.

Carmen moved toward the door to the office.

"Let's get some coffee," she said. "You're going to be here for a while."

CHAPTER THIRTY-NINE

I wanted to honor what came before, but also—please don't be offended by this—modernize it a bit," I said, rubbing my hands together. "I wanted to play with the idea that someone had messed with Claudia's mind, and made her forget she'd ever been the Lynx. But somehow, some way, she pulls herself back to it—and she overcomes this villain."

"Mindbender," Carmen said, flipping through the pages again. "That's a deep cut. She warps people's memories—I had so many big plans for her."

"Oh, well, I don't mean to step—"

Carmen raised a hand. "Please, don't do that. This is your story now. I'm just helping a little bit, if I can," she said, scoffing. "But I'm coming in late. This is fun, though. I feel energized. So, don't worry. Tell me more."

"Right, so Mindbender has basically taken Claudia off the board—no one remembers the Lynx," I said, the words coming out fast. "Not even Claudia. And, well, we don't explain it—but we're in the modern day. So, it's a soft reboot, but we don't lose anything. Every story counts. But we're pushing the Lynx forward."

"What's it called?" Carmen asks.

"*The Lynx Returns!*" I said with a smile.

"I like that," Carmen said, looking over another page—this one of Claudia Calla meditating, then discovering a hidden compartment with a spare Lynx costume. "This is powerful. This speaks to me. A woman who's kept her own history buried—by choice and trauma, but also because the world doesn't want her story out there. Am I wrong?"

I felt my body pulsing with power—a kinetic feeling. Like two powerful frequencies coming together to create something louder and stronger.

"No, that's exactly what I wanted to say," I said.

"Let's say it together."

Excerpt from *The Lynx Returns!* #5, published by New Wave Comics, October 2024.

I BET YOU'RE WONDERING HOW I GOT HERE--
ON A FRIGID TRIUMPH CITY ROOFTOP, BRAWLING WITH A TWISTED, EXTREME VERSION OF MYSELF.
I WISH I COULD TELL YOU-- BUT HONESTLY, I'M JUST FOCUSED ON SURVIVING.
ONCE YOU'RE GONE, NOTHING CAN STOP ME! THE REAL LYNX!
HATE TO BREAK IT TO YOU, LADY, BUT--
The LYNX in
DOUBLE INDEMNITY!
ANNIE BUSTAMANTE PLOT & ART
CARMEN VALDEZ SCRIPT

CHAPTER FORTY

W hat the hell are you doing?"

Gary's voice—a muted bellow—shook the sleep away. I rubbed my eyes and looked at my phone display. Twenty missed calls. Twice as many text messages. Most from Gary. Some from unknown numbers. A few very terse ones from Bert Carlyle. None very happy.

"Hi, Gary, good morning to you," I said, rolling off the couch and looking at my weary reflection in the living room mirror. I'd stayed up late the night before, doing proofing corrections on the first black-and-white installment of *The Lynx Returns!*, making sure that my lettering work, done in a frenzy as Carmen crafted a pass on the script, was ready for prime time. By three that morning, I had uploaded the pages with an introductory newsletter note and collapsed on Carmen's couch, Margot safely ensconced in Carmen's guest room upstairs.

The book had come together fast—and I'd soon dispensed with the idea of bringing other people in, or prolonging the process. I'd been so amped by the wave of collaboration—by the energy between me and Carmen—that I hadn't stopped to consider the potential consequences of just posting our story.

But I didn't regret it.

I wanted this story out there—damn the consequences.

I could almost feel the sparks of anger coming from the other side.

"What's wrong, Gary?"

He let out a long, annoyed sigh before speaking.

"Did you think, at any point while putting together this project, to alert me—your agent and representative to the outside world?" Gary said, his voice rising in pitch and volume with each word. "This thing is everywhere—it's trending on Twitter or X or whatever it's called, you seem to have close to ten thousand subscribers to your newsletter, and the trades are all over it. *Newsarama* and *Popverse* sent breaking news alerts, for God's sake. And now I'm getting questions from *Deadline* and *Variety* about the film rights. Not to mention the long cease-and-desist letter your old bosses at Triumph just had delivered . . . in person. Have you lost your mind?"

I smiled. I wanted to laugh, but I didn't think Gary would appreciate that.

"They're really pissed, Annie, and I can't argue with them," he continued. "You used the work they paid you for and published it on your own platform, with a character they own—and you did it in tandem with the woman suing them for ownership. Again—are you insane? You can't be serious, can you?"

I was dead serious. And I'd never wanted anything more.

"Don't talk down to me, Gary," I said, finally recognizing the voice—clear, fearless. It was an Annie I'd been waiting for. "This is a dream project. To get to draw and co-write a new Lynx comic, with the woman that created the character. It's a true sequel—not the AI abomination they were doing. Triumph Entertainment can go fuck itself."

I could've heard Gary stammering a mile away.

"Look—it's my job, as your agent, to advise you to stop . . . this, well, whatever the fuck you're doing, Annie. I mean, for Christ's sake, you have zero—"

I hung up. I clicked on my browser and went to my saved newsletter drafts. I scrolled through the most recent file titled "Documents!" It was almost ready.

Then I scanned my contacts and pushed a button.

Pete answered on the first ring.

"You've certainly been keeping busy," he said. "Seems like you've riled up all the right people today."

"I have something I need to show you," I said. "Check your email in a few minutes. I need you to post that if you don't hear from me in less than twenty-four hours."

CHAPTER FORTY-ONE

The building seemed to hover in the distance—like some faraway structure, solitary and impenetrable. But this wasn't some secretive villain's lair. This was something else. The place that held the answers I—we—needed to win.

The warehouse was on 37th Street in South Astoria, right next to Long Island City. I parked my car on the street and walked up to a tiny terminal set up next to a drop-down railing, like a highway toll. The man seated inside looked like he'd rather be careening toward the sun than at work this early in the morning.

"Help you?" he said, not looking up from his phone, which seemed to be streaming some kind of network comedy.

"I need access to one of the storage facilities," I said. "It's under the name Stuart Alford, or was."

The man put his phone down and swiveled his seat to a computer that appeared to be running BASIC or some kind of stone-age DOS-like operating system.

He tapped a few keys, then responded without looking at me.

"Got nothing for Alford, sorry, ma'am," he said.

Damn. I figured we'd hit a wall eventually. Nothing like this was ever easy. Marion had said as much when I called her on the drive down from the Cape. Margot had been having such a good time reading through Carmen's entire graphic novel library, I didn't have the heart to bring her with me, and Carmen graciously offered to keep an eye on her. But here I was, at the crack of dawn, standing outside a desolate warehouse in Astoria, trying to get in. It felt like waiting in line for a Comic Con badge, minus the cosplay, crowds, and hot dog smell.

"I'm with the Comic-Con Museum," I said. "They believe the items in one of your storage facilities has stolen materials."

The man shrugged. "You can call the cops," he said flatly. "If they show up with a warrant or a key, then I'll happily open the door. But, lady, you don't even have a name."

I bit my lip. I had maybe one more shot.

"It might be under Decibel," I said.

More keys tapping. Then the man, Connor according to his name tag, wheeled around.

"Now we're talking," he said, pointing toward the center aisle that seemed to divide the large storage facility in half. "The Decibel stuff is in unit 1G, so go straight and make a right, then it'll be on your left. Just keep an eye out. Use your key and you'll be all set."

"My key," I said to myself.

Connor scoffed. "You did bring your key, right?"

I cleared my throat.

"You know, this is my first week on the job," I said, grimacing. "Bert was yelling at me late last night to come down and get some documents and, well, shit—I totally forgot the key, and I live in the Bronx, so it took me forever to get here . . . I could get fired, dude."

I thought I was sunk. Connor's expression was flat. A few moments passed, then he shook his head and stood up. He opened the door to his little security station and closed it behind himself.

"You talk a good game," he said, shaking his head. "Follow me."

* * *

Connor had led me to the nondescript unit, a large storage container at the far end of the right building, just as he'd described. He nonchalantly used his master key and motioned for me to enter, waving as the door closed behind me. The loud thud seemed to signal my teleportation to another dimension—like leaping through one of Kirby's Boom Tubes into the Fourth World.

I was surrounded by Triumph.

It was a mess, first and foremost—but what a glorious mess. Stacks of comics everywhere—any Triumph issue imaginable, from an entire run of *The Legendary Lynx* to every single Len Maynard–written issue of *Avatar*. Posters seemed to be hung over every inch of the space— sometimes on top of each other, showcasing almost every character in the Triumph Comics library—the visor-wearing avenger known as the Dusk, the all-star superhero team the Freedom Alliance, the teen fire- blasting hero Carly Candela, the street-level vigilante the Black Ghost, and—finally—her. The Lynx.

The poster was a blowup of Detmer's first cover—iconic and perfect to me. It hung loosely on the wall, at the far end of the storage unit, a series of file cabinets resting under it.

I knew a sign when I saw one.

I looked at my phone. It was six in the morning. I had to work fast. They knew I wanted this—but I hoped they didn't know I'd figured out where it was supposed to be. I had that going for me. But if I'd learned anything over the last few months, it was that any advantage was mar- ginal in these kind of trench battles, where corporations and creators struggle for some kind of control.

I dove in.

I saw it all. Over a few hours of scouring documents and reading memos, I felt like I'd lived through Triumph Comics' entire publication history. The money laundered to Bulwark. Jeffrey Carlyle's lucrative pulp business. Invoices and contracts with names I'd seen on comics—Mark Jensen, Howard Mortkin, Steve Tinsler, Len Maynard, Rich Berger, Harvey Stern. Editorial notes from people like Trunick, Mullin, Hahn,

Purdin, Wood, Lehmann, Aitchison, Sainz, and Conroy. It was a blur, all of it. By ten o'clock, I'd gone through most of the file cabinets, just a few drawers left. Then I saw it. Folded and tucked behind a stack of manila folders, a solitary contract—signed in blue ink by Rich Berger. At the top, in the field listed as CONTRACTOR, was a hastily scrawled name: *CARMEN VALDEZ.* Below it, in the TITLE field, was the kicker—in the same shaky cursive was *THE LEGENDARY LYNX #1—??* But Carmen's signature was nowhere to be found. Jotted down in the margins of the contract, ostensibly by Berger, were the words: *has not signed—or been asked . . .*

Rich Berger, man. Not only did he make sure to leave a paper trail, he spelled it out. Someone knew Carmen was working on *The Legendary Lynx,* and this confirmed she hadn't signed a formal deal with Triumph.

I thought back to Carmen's hesitation in Truro. It rang true. There was no smoking gun here. But we'd just gotten a lot more bullets.

I grabbed the contract and gently placed it in my coat pocket. That was when I heard the loud thump of the storage space's front door closing. Except it had already been closed. *Maybe it was Connor,* I thought. But I knew it wasn't.

I spun around, but didn't see anything. I heard enough, though—footsteps, and a heavy, desperate intake of breath. I saw the outline of the figure—the moonlight sneaking through a distant window showing me that someone was standing near the entrance, facing my direction. That was all I could make out.

That and the gun.

I scurried to my feet and took a hesitant step toward the exit. The shadowy figure didn't move.

"You really went too far." The voice was deep—distorted. Someone was making an effort to hide who they were. Never a good sign, but the whole gun part of this moment made it much worse. "You should've just let it be. But you couldn't, could you?"

I tried to stand totally still, tried to figure out if this person could even see me yet. I wasn't sure.

"The Lynx . . . was never yours, Annie, was never Carmen's," the put-on voice said as the figure took a tentative step forward, moving the gun around like a flashlight—looking for a target. "You think you can just post your story and there won't be any consequences? Any repercussions? We knew you were coming here. So predictable."

They didn't see me, whoever they were—that was my guess. The storage space was big enough that I might be able to sneak past—and then hope I could outrun them.

I took a few slow, cautious steps toward the far wall, but immediately ran into something, which was followed by a loud clang and rattling as a stack of metal poster containers fell to the floor and rolled into the center of the storage space. I froze—watched as the figure swung around—gun pointed in my direction. Shit.

Then the moonlight seemed to spread over the obscured figure to give me a better look.

I'd never considered Bert Carlyle the gun-toting type.

"Have you lost your mind?" I said, stepping into the slim shaft of moonlight—revealing myself to Bert. "You're coming at me with a gun?"

"You don't know me very well," Bert said, a strange, knowing smile on his weary face. He didn't look well. The dark bags under his eyes were more pronounced, a thick stubble had collected on his once-clean-shaven baby face. Even his clothes looked like he'd pulled them from the laundry hamper as he rushed out the door. But there was something else—a manic, cunning energy I'd never seen in him—a man I'd mostly written off as a putz from the drop. My confidence turned to smoke. "And you've caused me a great deal of trouble."

He took a step toward me, gun still trained in my direction.

"Let's talk, Bert, you don't need a gun," I said, raising my hands. "You know me."

"That's the problem, isn't it, Annie? I do know you. I knew you'd be a problem from the beginning. I was happy to let you go," Bert said, clutching the gun with two hands now. "But you kept buzzing around—

poking and prodding when you should've just moved on. You didn't need us. You're a successful filmmaker. But you couldn't leave us be. And now you're here—rifling through things that don't belong to you, to help some woman take something away from me—from my family."

He took another step toward me, the gun unmoving.

"Now give it to me," Carlyle said, motioning with his hand. "Give me the contract. The files. Everything. I'm assuming you have it, no?"

"I don't know what you're talking about," I lied.

Carlyle laughed—a terrifying, throaty laugh, unlike anything I'd ever heard from him. This was a very different man from the Bert Carlyle I'd met and clowned on before. Had he been putting me on the whole time?

"You think you're so smart," he said, shaking his head. "But I know everything you have. I've been a half step behind you the whole time. I'll admit, I didn't realize there was a manuscript, or that the audio survived. But we can fix all that."

He paused, and I could feel his eyes on me—as if seeing me for the first time.

"I'm not worried about that at all."

I felt dizzy, like I was high above a crowd—trying to balance my way across some kind of wire, without a net below to catch me.

I thought about Doug Detmer, and Danny, and Carmen . . . and the Lynx. What would they do here? How would they get out of this?

And I had my answer.

I doubled down.

"The files are gone," I said. "We had the contract already. We had the manuscript. We had the interview. The contract Carmen never signed—but that Triumph did. Concrete proof that Triumph knew Carmen was working on the Lynx, even when it was a secret. They knew and let her keep doing it."

Carlyle started to speak, but I ignored him.

"How do you think that's going to play in court? That someone—a

high-ranking editor at Triumph knew Carmen Valdez created this character," I said. "They were so sure, they prepped a contract for her to sign.
A contract she never saw or signed. What do you think that says about
it all?"

I heard a hissing sound. It took me a second to realize it was coming
from Carlyle.

"Those documents belong to me," Carlyle spat, moving even closer.
We were a few yards apart now. An easy shot, even for someone who
didn't play with guns often. I looked at the floor—littered with poster
tubes. "I don't really want to have to hurt you, Annie. There's still a way
out of this. For all of us. A way to fix it."

My instinct was to run. To dash past Bert Carlyle, close the door
behind me, and rush away. But I couldn't do that. I needed to know
more. And I needed to get this document out of this desolate warehouse
and into the light—for people to see the truth about the Lynx, Carmen
Valdez, and . . . me.

"You killed her, didn't you? Laura?" I asked. "Or Arturo Spinoza?"

Carlyle shook his head in disappointment. "Where are the files,
Annie?"

"You don't get it, do you?" I asked. "They're gone. They're not just
somewhere else—I posted them. They're online. Anyone can read them.
Right now."

Carlyle seemed to spasm briefly, as if shocked by an exposed electrical
wire.

"What?" he said, stepping closer to me, inches from the poster tubes.

"I posted it all this morning, I scheduled it last night—now the world
can decide what's true. If Carmen Valdez is really one of the creators of
the character, and if she deserves to own it," I said, taking a hesitant, half
step back. "It's over, Bert."

"Well, aren't we the little Nancy Drew, huh?"

"I'm nosy by nature—and when this project went south, I realized
why," I said. "It all just seemed too precarious. Everyone was so desperate

to get to step twelve, they didn't care about the initial ones: the comic itself. It made me wonder: How did someone like you, the son of a washed-up comics publisher, dig up the finances to launch this company? Where did you get the money? And what would happen if you didn't pay it off the right way? If the Hollywood play took too long? Who would get upset?"

Carlyle's eyes locked on me.

"I followed the money. From Triumph to Decibel to Pestova to Spinoza and back again—but I still wondered, who else did you find yourself indebted to?" I said. "Who would be mad if your promises—of fame, fortune, the silver screen—went up in smoke? Did Jessica Doyle make it all sound easy and breezy?"

Another low, humorless laugh from Carlyle.

"Oh, Annie, Annie, Annie—you speak with such confidence, such ego. It's admirable, really, as if you figured it all out," Bert said, shaking his head. "But life is rarely that simple, or linear. Jessica Doyle doesn't know what she has. She just brings in the money. She taps into her network—and yes, that network includes some bad, unsavory people. People who invested millions in Triumph and Decibel and beyond. We owed them everything. But Jessica had no idea what we had—what my father built, with his bare hands, before you were even born. We live in an age where we're seeing movies about Ant-Man or Peacemaker, and we're here, sitting on a huge library of characters, not just the Lynx. Characters people might recognize, might want to see. I knew the potential. I knew what we could do. But we needed money, resources. I knew I could make something of it. I knew if I tapped the right people, we could all be rich."

"So that's when Doyle brought Pestova in?"

Carlyle was shaking now, hovering in place.

"There is no Jessica Doyle, Annie. Are you daft? Marina was Jessica," he said, leaning forward, struggling to retain his composure. "Jessica Doyle is a mirage, a mask—like the supervillains you love. There's only me, Bert Carlyle, son of Jeffrey, and Marina Pestova, an investor with the kind of connections that make sure things get done, who doesn't mind pretending to be someone else—putting on a good act for people like you."

Now it was my turn to step closer. "Even if it means killing people that stand in your way?"

Carlyle scoffed, waving the gun slightly.

"Have you ever been so deeply in debt that you never knew if you'd get out? I imagine not," he spat. "Jessica had promised everything to the people backing her—and they were bad people. Sometimes she'd promise more if they helped in . . . well, extra ways. Getting their hands dirty. If the Russians couldn't do it, they'd outsource it to some other two-bit gangsters and promise them a slice of the imaginary pie, too—those magical profits that would come once the Lynx made it big, or the Freedom Alliance, or whatever. She was so desperate to make this happen, she'd sliced and diced these characters into oblivion. Every thug or mobster had a percentage, and we weren't even sure we owned these characters. The copyrights and trademarks were a mess. So the only shot we had was to fake it until we made it—act like we owned these characters—get rich, pay off our debts, and hope to clean the slate. We had to win. And Jessica understood how risky it would be to us—to our lives—if Valdez's story got out there. The second we heard about the Gustines book, saw her stupid blog post, we acted. Jessica had her friends take out the reporter. But that isn't free. It costs money. Percentages. Eventually Triumph was out of chips. There were no more people to ask to do the dirty work for us. So here I am, trying to get us back to zero."

"So you killed Spinoza?" I asked.

"This isn't a comic book, Annie, you nosy little cunt," Carlyle said. "This isn't the part where I unveil my master plan. I fucked up, and I was pretty close to fixing it, until you woke up and realized you had some kind of ethics. What was it? Sad we took your half-baked art and smoothed it over? Did you realize your father was a piece of shit? Did that make you remember—"

I ran.

I cut left, fast, and sprinted away from Carlyle. Out of the corner of my eye, I saw him swing his arm around—trying to follow me with the gun.

"Come back here, you—"

He was cut off, his foot slipping on a slate of poster tubes, the long, round pieces sliding under his feet and sending him backward. I heard his back slam onto the floor, hard, followed by a series of surprised curses. I was almost at the door.

I felt my heart pounding in my chest, underneath the contract—the paperwork I'd told Carlyle was public but wasn't. The last piece of evidence that could hopefully free the Lynx, forever.

A gunshot. I felt a whizzing wind by my face. I reached the door and spun around. Carlyle was back on his feet, a little worse for wear, taking a wobbly step toward me. Closer now. The gun still in his hand.

"I guess this is fitting for you, Annie," he said, out of breath. "You always wanted to be remembered, right? Now you can join your father in hell—two footnotes forever tied to a forgotten character."

A sound seemed to crash into the storage area—red and blue lights visible through the windows. Sirens. They were close by. Right outside.

"It's over, Bert," I said, my back against the wall, my hand on the door. "Don't do anything stupid."

Carlyle tilted his head, that sick, insidious smile still on his face, like a cat noticing a new toy. If there was a time for him to do something stupid, this would be it.

"It's over," I said again.

A voice over a bullhorn.

"This is NYPD—we need you to vacate this space immediately. Please come out with your hands up. If that damn door doesn't open up in thirty seconds, we will be in there with guns drawn."

I watched Carlyle's face—saw him calculating his options. I'd always considered Bert Carlyle to be a doofus and a clown. In this moment, I hoped he was much smarter than that.

"Just put the gun down, Bert," I said, my voice cracking. "It's over."

The gun clattered to the floor. Carlyle stood there, mumbling to himself, looking down at the weapon—looking down as everything melted away. I half expected him to start sobbing, but he didn't. He just stood there.

I almost felt bad for him.

EPILOGUE

MARCH 31, 2024

I took the stairs up to Midtown Comics two at a time, Margot a few steps behind me. We were late. But that was okay. When it was your event, it couldn't start without you. At least that's what Margot reiterated as we walked into the comic shop—the wide, sprawling wall of new issues and collections looming over us. I saw the line forming then—long and winding, leading to another room where it was all happening. I started to make my way there, but stopped.

"I wanna look around for a second," I told Margot. "Can you tell Carmen I'll be there soon?"

Margot nodded and slipped past the line of fans.

I let myself walk by the rows and rows of long boxes loaded with older back issues—some dating to before I was born. My fingers slid over a section of *Animal Man*, the surreal and meta take on the minor DC character by Grant Morrison and Chaz Truog. The grungy sci-fi of John Byrne's *Next Men*. A healthy run of the Australia-era issues of *Uncanny X-Men* by Chris Claremont and Marc Silvestri. A smattering of *X-Factor* issues by writer Louise Simonson and artist Walt Simonson. The teen superhero soap opera of Marv Wolfman and George Pérez's *The New Teen Titans*. Ann Nocenti's politically charged and left-leaning run on *Daredevil*. The classical, timeless beauty of Steve Rude's *Nexus*. Kelly Sue DeConnick and Val De Landro's sci-fi uppercut, *Bitch Planet*. Rachel Pollack's progressive and engrossing work on *Doom Patrol*. Alan Moore and Kevin O'Neill's mesmerizing pastiche, *League of Extraordinary Gentlemen*. The list went on. *ElfQuest, American Flagg!, Hellboy, Love & Rockets, Astro City. Sandman Mystery Theatre*. Each book seemed to beckon to me, like the store was talking to me—for different reasons. Reminders of why I loved comics and why I still wanted to work in comics—despite the people, angst, and death.

The last few months had given me a sharp sense of whiplash—as pieces fell into place after what seemed like years of hovering out of reach. Jessica Doyle née Marina Pestova and Bert Carlyle were indicted on charges of conspiracy to commit murder. What remained of Triumph Entertainment folded, coming to a settlement with Carmen for the rights to the Lynx—confirming in a press release that Carmen Valdez and the estate of Doug Detmer, which consisted of me, and of Harvey Stern, which consisted of no one, were controlling owners of the intellectual property and all stories published by Triumph, dating back to her first appearance in 1975 and including all characters that appeared in those stories—including Apparition. I was still unsure how to proceed. I'd enlisted some archival editors to repackage the comics online and in print, but I hadn't thought about it further. I still couldn't really believe it.

I walked a few more paces and, then, as if on cue—I found it. *The Legendary Lynx* #1. The cover seemed like a mirage—a dream brought to life. I looked at the price tag. Five dollars. So much story and importance packed into these twenty-odd pages, and I could get it all again for a few bucks. I held on to the book, even though I owned it a few times over. It'd become a ritual of sorts. If I saw one, I bought it, as if I could somehow collect all that remained—and channel their power into my very being. These were the books that shaped me. These were the stars I chased in my own work. These were the gods I worshipped.

I looked across the shop and caught sight of Margot, standing by a long table immersed in a book, Carmen Valdez seated behind it—a stack of comics and Sharpie pens next to her, that line forming in front of her. Margot had a copy of Kate Beaton's latest—*Ducks*—open, her eyes scanning each page carefully.

Then I glanced down at the Lynx, cornered on the cover. Looked at her pupil-less eyes.

"Your story's not over," I said to the stapled pieces of paper, as if they were alive. And they were. To me.

My work with Carmen on *The Lynx Returns!* continued apace—garnering positive reviews and some sales, critics pointing to the smooth melding of my modern art style and story pacing with Carmen's vibrant script and knack for dialogue. The collaboration itself had been almost too easy—the kind of back-and-forth that creators only dream about. We would talk by phone, hashing out ideas, then I would roughly lay out the story. Carmen would script over the layouts, and the next thing we knew, we had another installment.

Gary had gotten over his anger once the money started coming in for the new series. I thought of Pete Fernandez—nosy, paranoid Pete—who'd called his people in the NYPD and tipped them off that day at the storage facility. I wasn't sure what would've happened otherwise.

"This is my business, Annie. I knew something was wrong when you said you were going off the grid," he'd told me. "The second I saw the documents you dumped online, I knew you'd crossed a line."

I felt tears streaking down my face, slowly, but there. I was crying for myself. For Margot, my sweet girl. For Carmen Valdez and Doug Detmer and even for Harvey Stern and Arturo Spinoza, a fucked-up man who'd done wrong, who so desperately wanted to get just one more shot he didn't deserve. For Laura Gustines, who would never get to write that book.

Margot looked up from her book and saw me from across the room. She made her way over. I wiped at my face hastily and walked toward the table. The fans were waiting. I had copies of *The Lynx Returns!* #1 to sign. We both did. Carmen and I.

Margot grabbed my arm a few feet from the table.

"Mami, are you okay?"

"I think so, sweetie," I said, trying to force a smile. The constant plight of the parent—to make your children feel safe and secure, even if such a thing is a fantasy. Like a comic book. "I just get a little emotional some-times."

"It's okay," Margot said. "Your signing is starting."

I nodded and started to move, but realized Margot hadn't let go. She was looking at the copy of *The Legendary Lynx* #1 in my hands. Our eyes met.

"You know what? Margot, after this signing I'm going to take you out," I said. "Maybe we can get some milkshakes at Black Tap? Then we can have a talk."

"Uh, okay, sure. About anything specific?"

"Yes—I want to tell you about Danny—I want to tell you about your father."

Excerpt from *The Lynx Returns!* #6, by Annie Bustamante and Carmen Valdez, published by New Wave Comics, coming December 2024.

ACKNOWLEDGMENTS

Some books simmer and stew in your mind for years. Others pop up, as if by their own will.

That, to me, will always be the core difference between *Secret Identity* and its follow-up, the book you hold in your hands—*Alter Ego*.

A lot of the responsibility rests on the shoulders of my amazing editor, Zack Wagman. From my perspective, as we put *Secret Identity* to bed, I was done with the world of comics, Carmen Valdez, and the Lynx. I'd set out to do what I thought I wanted to do—tell an entertaining murder mystery story set in the 1970s comic book world. But Zack had other ideas.

"Where's Carmen now? What if we get a tease of what's happening in the modern day?" was a version of what Zack asked me. I hadn't considered the question. I really liked the cloudy, gray ending I'd given her and wasn't sure there was more to tell. But the match had been lit. What *was* she doing?

That idea and conversation begat the epilogue some of you read at the end of *Secret Identity*. What I didn't expect, and perhaps what Zack was trying to shake out of me, was that those few pages would spawn an entire other novel—and be the inflection point of a new mystery. But once I started to consider *Alter Ego*, which Zack very smartly called "the dark side of the *Secret Identity* coin," I couldn't stop—and found myself gripped by a novel obsession unlike any other.

Though I outline and map out my books in great detail—apologies to my writers' group friends—I'm very much an instinctual writer. I need to poke and prod and dust off an idea to get to the root of what I want to write about. Only then, once the table is set, can I welcome the guests— the characters—and let them interact to create the story. I realize this sounds a little unhinged, but it works for me—which is all that matters. The loose idea for *Alter Ego* appeared first—the table setting: What if someone got the chance to write a seminal story featuring the Legendary Lynx—only to discover the dark secrets that lurked underneath? I knew that I wanted Carmen to be in the book, of course, but not as a protagonist; I wanted her to be felt from page one—but I wanted her actual appearance to feel almost mythical, like Luke Skywalker at the end of *Star Wars: The Force Awakens*, or something along those lines. Which begged an important question: Who was the protagonist of the book?

I hate to say anything comes easy in the writing game, because you're definitely grading on a curve—but Carmen appeared to me fully formed, merging seamlessly into the general idea for *Secret Identity* quickly. But Annie was a little more stubborn. It was only when I looked for her through the prism of *Alter Ego*—a book I wanted to be about grappling with the obsessions of your past while struggling with the adult responsibilities of your present, like death, parenthood, and getting older—that I found Annie. Annie was a working single mom. She'd found some success in her field, but had to leave comics behind—only to find even greater success elsewhere. Annie was nostalgic and anxious in a way Carmen wasn't. They had similarities, but they both felt apart and alive in their own ways. When these big pieces came together, and as I outlined the book, I joked with friends that if they were looking for a book about generational trauma, parenthood, and comics, boy, did I have a novel for them. But we write what we're thinking about—and for me, writing only works when I'm knee-deep in something, feeling it in every waking moment, and living in the head of my protagonist as if I were in my own.

But the obsession doesn't stave off challenges—and, in many ways, *Alter Ego* was the hardest novel I've ever written. Zack, ever patient, had to talk me down from giving up at least two times I can remember, meaning there were a few times I probably erased from my mind. Like many, I'm not a fan of sequels for the sake of sequels. I say it often—it's okay for things to end. So, from my perspective, *Alter Ego* didn't just need to be good, it needed to count and matter. A few times, after the release of *Secret Identity*, some well-meaning friends and peers suggested I write a book set in comics every decade—like, Carmen in the eighties, reading *Watchmen*, or Carmen reacting to the Image Revolution of the nineties. I understood the conceit, but I couldn't think of anything less interesting to do to her—to make her a talisman of comics just wandering through the decades, serving as some kind of fictional recap of comic book history. *Secret Identity* was a story about Carmen set during the only time it would work—when the industry was dying and no one knew if it'd survive. In the same way, *Alter Ego* is indelibly tied to the modern world—a time when comic book movies, TV, video games, and awareness are at an all-time high. Where the struggle to collect IP to flip into other media and get rich is commonplace and predictable. So, I wondered, where did this leave art for art's sake? Must everything we do work on a multi-platform level just to survive? Sometimes it felt that way. Once I hit upon that—blending Annie's personal journey with the bigger "art vs. commerce" questions I dwelled on endlessly in my own life as a writer—the engine started to purr and the book got moving.

But no matter how much people talk about writing as a solitary journey, writing a book is actually a team effort—and *Alter Ego* was a book I couldn't complete without the assistance of some sharp-eyed beta, authenticity, and early readers—including my wonderful writers' group (Kellye Garrett, Amina Akhtar, and Liz Little), Kelly J. Ford, Kurt Busiek, John Cunningham, Ivy Pochoda, Ellen Clair Lamb, Alexis Soloski, Brian Cronin, Rob Hart, Amanda di Bartolomeo, Isabel Stein, Robert

Greenberger, and a few people I'm sure I'm forgetting. Their notes and insight made the book better, and that's all you can ask for from an early reader. Many creative friends also graced me with their time and inspiration, like cartoonist Hilary Fitzgerald Campbell, writer Tini Howard, editor/artist Heather Antos, friend and writer Henry Barajas, writer/artist and collaborator Monica Gallagher, editor/writer and dear pal Greg Lockard, and more.

This book wouldn't exist without the work of Sandy Jarrell, who once again proved to me why he's one of the unsung heroes of modern comics. Deftly changing his style to better reflect "Annie Bustamante" instead of "Doug Detmer," Sandy, with his art, added a depth and nuance to the story that I could never evoke on my own. I'm so lucky to work with him and even luckier to have him as a friend. Letterer Jack Morelli is also deserving of huge thanks—giving the Lynx pages a powerful readability that only confirms his place as one of the best letterers ever, and one of the best guys in comics.

Huge thanks to old friend and superstar art director Steve Blackwell for his design work on the *Merlin Magazine* Lynx excerpt, and to Rich Douek for his design help on the Lynx house ad. Both added to the verisimilitude I was always striving for. Though not as research-intensive as *Secret Identity*, *Alter Ego* did require its fair share of homework—and led me to a solid dose of inspiration. Here's a quick overview of some of the books I pored over while crafting the novel:

Joanna Robinson, Dave Gonzales, and Gavin Edwards's deep dive into the history of the Marvel Cinematic Universe, *MCU: The Reign of Marvel Studios*, was a good crash course in the Hollywood part of comic books. Patty Lin's *End Credits: How I Broke Up with Hollywood* made for a painful peek into the machinery of television and writers' room culture. Mark Seal's *Leave the Gun, Take the Cannoli: The Epic Story of the Making of* The Godfather was an often-funny and surprising look at the birth of one of the most beloved films ever, and how it almost didn't get made. *Monsters,* by Claire Dederer, gave me some much-needed insight into how the culture grapples with talented people who do bad things—and how we, as consumers, might want to engage with their art. In the same vein, Josie Riesman's book on ex-WWE boss Vince McMahon, *Ringmaster*, was meticulously researched and damning in its findings, making for a cultural analysis you can't look away from. *Tell Me Everything: The Story of a Private Investigation*, by my friend Erika Krouse, was a mesmerizing and personal story of investigation and coming to terms with your own past, and found its way into Annie's own story, too. *Poisoned Chalice: The Extremely Long and Incredibly Complex Story of Marvelman (and Miracleman)* by Pádraig Ó Mealóid, a deep dive into the fraught and complicated business history of the beloved UK superhero, was eye-opening and gave some much-needed context on the Lynx's fictional journey. Stephen J. C. Andes's similar look at the pop culture saga of Zorro, *Zorro's Shadow: How a Mexican Legend Became America's First Superhero*, was equally insightful. I read two books about the beginning and ultimate demise/absorption of TSR, the company that launched Dungeons & Dragons—Ben Riggs's *Slaying the Dragon: A Secret History of Dungeons & Dragons* and Jon Peterson's *Game Wizards: The Epic Battle for Dungeons & Dragons*. Both shed light on a story that felt very relevant to comics and was hugely useful while writing this book. In the same vein, Jason Schreier's two books on the video game industry, *Blood, Sweat, and Pixels: The Triumphant, Turbulent Stories Behind How Video Games Are Made* and *Press Reset: Ruin and Recovery in the Video Game Industry*, gave meaningful, warts-and-all looks at an industry that has more than a passing resemblance to comic books in terms of how people are treated and how the work is created. Though barely touching on the topics of superheroes and corporate comics, Brian Doherty's *Dirty Pictures: How an Underground Network of Nerds, Feminists, Misfits, Geniuses, Bikers, Potheads, Printers, Intellectuals, and Art School Rebels Revolutionized Art and Invented Comix* shed light on a lost era of comics in a way that I found riveting. My friend Jeremy Dauber's comprehensive *American Comics: A History* was also an invaluable resource in contextualizing and finding a way to spot larger trends from thirty thousand feet.

In terms of fiction, there was a stack of comics and novels that I felt were in conversation with *Alter Ego* at various stages of its development—including Kurt Busiek's two metatextual superhero origins, *Superman: Secret Identity* (with artist Stuart Immonen) and *Batman: Creature of the Night*, which inverted many a trope of the genre to create something that felt wholly new and inspiring. I found myself revisiting some other beloved comics during my work on *Alter Ego*, which I'm sure reflected back to me in the work—including probably my favorite comic book work ever, Jaime Hernandez's hilarious, heartfelt, and unforgettable "Locas" stories from *Love and Rockets*; the public domain metatextual adventure of Alan Moore, Peter Hogan, and Yanick Paquette's *Terra Obscura*; Jeff Lemire and his various artistic collaborators' grand superhero opus *Black Hammer*; and Tom King, Mitch Gerads, and Evan "Doc" Shaner's powerful examination of pulp hero Adam Strange in *Strange Adventures*. In terms of novels, Emma Cline's hypnotic *The Guest*, Marie Rutkoski's sublime *Real Easy*, Silvia Moreno-Garcia's metafictional Latinx horror thriller *Silver Nitrate*, Rebecca Makkai's nuanced *I Have Some Questions for You*, and Gabrielle Zevin's unforgettable *Tomorrow, and Tomorrow, and Tomorrow* all provided doses of equal parts hope, inspiration, and jealousy during my writing.

I'm grateful to have many friends in life, comics, fiction writing, and beyond. I can't endeavor to list them all, but I'm forever grateful for their support and special places in my life—especially Andrea Vigil, Phoebe Flowers, Shawn Cosby, Wanda Morris, Rachel Howzell Hall, Megan Abbott, Christian Font, Michael Moreci, Chantelle Aimée Osman, Sara Century, Jesse Thompson, Ryan Penagos, Rickey Purdin, Connor Goldsmith, Austin Trunick, Yasmin Angoe, Eli Cranor, Brad Meltzer, George Gustines (thank you for letting me use your name!), Preeti Chhibber, Paul Kaminski, Julio Anta, Laura Lippman, Sarah Weinman, Alison Gaylin, Rachel Pinnelas, Michael Siglain, Alafair Burke, Fabian Nicieza, Jim McLauchlin, Geraldo Borges, Nickolej Villiger, Enid Balám, Javier Fernandez, Steph Cha, Alfred Soto, Alan Gomez, Benjamin Percy, Elizabeth Keenan, Todd Casey, John Morgan, Lauren Amaro, Nick

Lowe, Mark Paniccia, Zoraida Córdova, Charles Soule, Lori Rader-Day, Mark Waid, Heidi MacDonald (thanks for the *Beat* cameos!), Jeremy Atkins, Tyler Jennes, Pamela Mullin-Horvath, Michael Connelly, Lauren Beukes, David Baldacci, Victor LaValle, Ben Percy, Gerry Duggan, Zoraida Cordova, Charles Soule, Chuck Wendig, Andrea Bartz, Gail Simone, Tom Brevoort, Brian Michael Bendis, Brian Cunningham, Brian Cronin, Allison O'Toole, Grey Allison, Jack Morelli, Geoff Johns, Brad Meltzer, Chas! Pangburn, Mike Marts, Chris Fernandez, Mark London, Erica Schultz, Liana Kangas, Sara Harding, Mia P. Manansala, Sandra Wong, and many more. I'm blessed to know each of these people and so many more.

As noted at the top of this lengthy thank-you section, *Alter Ego* would not exist without my editor, Zack Wagman. His patience, support, and unflinching belief in the novel propped me up during frequent moments of doubt. He knew how to bring the best out of my work, and I will always be grateful for his peerless abilities as an editor and loyal friend. Excited for whatever is next in this very special partnership. To the entire team at Flatiron, especially Maxine Charles, Marlena Bittner, Christopher Smith, Bria Strothers, Dave Cole, and Erin Kibby—your tireless support means the world to me. No one does it like Flatiron.

Huge thanks are in order to my agent Josh Getzler, his superstar #2, Jon Cobb, and the whole crew at HG Literary for not batting an eye at every new project and for helping me stay focused on what matters most. Thank you for advocating for me and my work, always. Also, hearty thanks to Hailey Dezort and Thomas Flynn at Paratext PR—your help was priceless.

To the readers—who have followed my work for more than a decade, who shared their stories of reading *Secret Identity* over the last year and a half, who send notes, buy books, post on social media, or come to my events: Thank you from the bottom of my heart. I still find it novel to interact with someone who's read my work that I don't know personally. I hope I never lose that wonder. To the indie bookstores, librarians, event organizers, reviewers, and tastemakers who have used their platforms to amplify my work—thank you. I'm humbled and grateful, always.

People often ask me how I'm able to juggle so many projects at a given time, and the answer is deceptively simple: I'm supported by an understanding and grounding force: my family. My wife, Eva, is the pillar I lean on frequently—a constant inspiration and forever the voice of reason in my head or in my living room. Without her love and support, I doubt I'd be anywhere today. The same goes for our two lovely children, Guillermo and Lucia, who bring light into my days and keep me focused on what counts. My most important job in life is being a good dad to them, and everything else is a distant second.

Thank you for reading.

Warmly,
Alex Segura
Queens, New York
April 2024

ABOUT THE AUTHOR

Alex Segura is the bestselling and award-winning author of *Secret Identity*, winner of the Los Angeles Times Book Prize for mystery/thriller, a *New York Times Book Review* Editors' Choice, and an NPR Best Mystery of the Year. He's also the author of the Pete Fernandez series, as well as the *Star Wars* novel *Poe Dameron: Free Fall* and a Spider-Verse adventure called *Araña and Spider-Man 2099: Dark Tomorrow*. He lives in New York City with his family.